The Trumpet of Harmony

The cool, crisp, snap of autumn his smoky shop. Absently, he wiped his dirty hands on the stout, leather apron hanging from his waist. He was glad for an early start. It had allowed him to finish up the minor mending in the coolness of the morning. The sun would grow hot as the day progressed, he thought, starring into the crystal blue sky.

Feeling vibrant and alive the Smith turned and walked back into the darkened smithy. He scanned his shop in smug satisfaction. The fire in the furnace still glowed cherry red though the billows lay quiet, unattended for the moment. The spillway which brought water into the smithy gurgled softly as it ran through the building and then back out into the stream. His tools hung neatly from their racks and his finished work lay, proudly displayed, on a small table near the door.

With a stride that fit his tall muscular frame, the Smith covered the short distance to the back of the smithy. There concealed in the half shadows was an old cupboard. In a series of well practiced motions, he opened its doors and removed from a shelf, a thickly bundled object. Carefully he laid it down on his work bench. With an exaggerated gentleness, he unwrapped the layers of skin, pausing only when the half light revealed the treasure within.

Treasure it was, if only to himself. What lay so lovingly preserved in the skins was not an object of beauty, nor one of historical significance. Yet, to him, it was greatly prized. It was an unadorned chalice, made from a type of heavy, silver metal that he had never seen in any of his other work. Polished, it had a soft luster that drew the eye.

His father had given it to him, as had his father's father before him. So, it had been for many generations. The purpose of the cup had long since vanished into the depths of time. The giving of the cup from father to son had gained its own tradition. So it was, that on the eve of his departure from the farm hold, ten years ago, the cup had come to him.

The Trumpet of Harmony

Ten years was a long time, mused the Smith. When he had first apprenticed to Galen, the village smith, he had been but eight years old. Thin and scrawny, he had learned his craft at his master's side. The physical labor and the excellent table kept by Galen, soon put knotted muscles on a frame that just seemed to keep growing. Today, he stood strong and tall. Still the boy's face, peered back at him from his reflection in the chalice.

It was early in his training when he had first manifested a talent for working with metals that was magical in nature. According to the traditions of the land, by displaying true magic, he lost the Use Name by which he been called all of his short life and became simply the village smith, or Smith.

Time passed. His master died of a coughing sickness and his father of a fever. He was truly alone. Still he had not wanted for company and his work had kept him satisfied.

Shaking himself out of his reverie, the Smith examined the polished surface of the cup once more. He had longed to fashion some worthy design with which to adorn its surface. Like so many times before he could not picture such an image in his mind. So, he carefully rewrapped the chalice in its coat of skins and returned it to its place of honor in his cupboard.

He had barely closed the cupboard door, when a dull noise reached his ears. Looking around his shop, he noted that everything was as it should be. The sights and sounds within the smithy as familiar to him, as his own two hands. Yet the noise grew persistently louder.

Now the sound could be heard coming from outside of his shop. He ran to his door and from the outskirts of his small village, the Smith heard quite distinctly, the excited voices of children, yelling and shouting to each other. Mingled with these were the playful barks of dogs on the chase. Almost covered by the ruckus, were the sweet chime of cymbals and the steady roll of a drum.

The Trumpet of Harmony

Curious, the Smith peered from his doorway, out over the small village square which fronted his shop. The cobblestones remained empty but he could feel a vibration in the soles of his boots. Just then a vanguard of young villagers burst into the square. They were followed by three of the most colorful and ornate wagons that the Smith had ever seen.

The wagons were each pulled by four huge horses. The mighty beasts vied to out do the wagons for garish, brightly colored decorations. The music came from a collection of people who smiled and danced alongside of the wagons. Their clothes were fashioned of bright, multi-colored cloth. The shiny metallic sequins which adorned them were blinding in the late, morning light.

The small caravan soon filled the square. The lead wagon had pulled to a stop in front of the Smith's shop and the driver jumped to the ground. He easily outstripped his troupe in appearance. Stretching his body mightily, the man straightened himself to his full height. He stood at least half a head smaller then the Smith. What he lacked in height though, he made up in broad shoulders and bulky muscles. With a flashing smile, he swaggered up to the on looking Smith.

"Good day to you stranger," said the Smith, as the man approached. "It is not often that we get visitors to our little hamlet." The Smith pointed to the knot of youngsters who looked on from one corner of the square, quiet for the moment in an attempt to overhear the words of their elders. "You've made quite a stir."

The man's eyes flashed in amusement, as he drank in the sight of the village square. "We enjoy bringing excitement into peoples' lives. It does us no greater honor then to see smiling, laughing faces all about us. The world is a gloomy place and needs people like us to brighten it up a bit."

He turned back to the Smith and bowed formally as if to a Liege Lord. "We are Gypsies, good Smith. We travel from village to village in this God forsaken land in an attempt to amuse, entertain and to profit from and by those that we meet."

The Trumpet of Harmony

"We stay on the outskirts of towns that we visit and play our music in the night air. Each evening we offer dance, song and other worldly amusements, to those whose lives are held by the close confines of a small village, life."

"Unfortunately, before we move on, we have need of your services, Sir Smith. That is if the price is right!" At the mention of money a sly, calculating look came into the man's eyes.

The Smith smiled. He had spent many long nights sitting by the fire in the common room of the village meeting house. There he would listen in rapt fascination, to tales of the outside world. Occasionally, travelers would appear in the village, having come up one of the almost forgotten roads that ran between the inhabited areas of the land. Often they would stay in the common room and regale the villagers with stories of their travels.

He did not normally credit much truth to the tales that were spun for the villagers. Their owners were nothing but the rag tag vagabonds of the world. However, mixed in with their tales were stories of the Gypsy Tribes. So he chose to frame his reply to the man standing in front of him, with some care, just in case of their authenticity.

"Sir, I am but a humble servant of my village. Tell me what you need done and I will accept what payment you would offer in return."

For a moment the brightly clad man's eyes were alight with joy at finding such easy prey and then his shoulders slumped and he sighed heavily. "Ah, sir. You do not play the game fairly. I can now understand that rumor of our tribe has reached your ears. For it is true what is said, that should a man enter into a bargaining with a Gypsy Master, then surely he would lose all that he owns!"

The Smith smiled and replied, "I have no doubt of your skill, oh Master of the Gypsies, but truly that is my price to all people. I have no desire to accumulate wealth or material goods. I want for nothing, nor do I fear losing anything, for I have nothing that anyone would want."

The Trumpet of Harmony

The Gypsy Leader grinned ruefully, as he said, "I wonder, Sir Smith, which of us is the freer man." He shook his head and continued, "No matter. Please accept the hospitality of my camp for a meal, some drink and the finest music that you have ever heard. I would also give you my name in thanks, for it is pleasant to meet an honest man in these troubled times."

The Gypsy then signaled to the members of his band to bring forth the mending that needed to be done. When they had all assembled, their leader turned back to the Smith. Slapping a muscular hand on the Smith's large shoulder he said, "Let it be known to all my tribe that this man is our friend and calls me by my Use Name." With a warm grin he said, "Smith, I am Yoseph, leader of these brave people."

The band of gypsies cheered. As each pressed forward with dented pots, broken saddle fittings, gouged pans or some other item needed in their day to day existence, they gave him their Use Names. For his part, the Smith tried to remember all of the colorful names but was soon at a loss to put name to face.

The giving of names was strictly ceremonial, for they lived in a world of magic and the true Soul Name of an individual was a direct pathway to the very essence of that person. As such, it was guarded perhaps more carefully then even the owner's life. So Use Names were given, colorful, sometimes funny but always fictitious.

The last of the tribe to approach the Smith was a young woman, whose figure was not yet full and whose face, though comely was pinched with care. Midnight hair formed a cloud around her face. Her features were sculpted and were framed by a pair of dark liquid eyes. Those eyes flashed and danced like the flame in his hearth. Her name was Rosita.

As they exchanged glances and the Smith looked into her eyes, a strange feeling came over him. For a moment, he seemed to sense the pulsating energy of a wild beast, running free through the forest. Then she broke eye contact.

He shook his head slowly, murmured a greeting and then the girl was gone. Was it only his imagination or had there been a frown on her face? It did not matter. Barely did he listen to Yoseph tell of their camping area, a few miles down the path, to the south. Scarcely did he even remember the band's departure.

All that day, as he mended pots and pans, his mind was filled with excited thoughts. What was it like to travel the lonely roads and see the sun come up each day on a new place? The Smith's imagination pictured many sights and sounds. Creating new adventures in which he would triumph, the hero of the day!

Still every hero needed a damsel in distress. As he worked he pictured the dark haired Rosita. Embellishing her beauty in his mind's eye, placing her in the many dangers that the world outside might contain and rescuing her in heroic fashion.

Why he picked Rosita to play his lady fair, he could not say. Many of the local girls had tried to attract his attention. Some of them had been prettier then Rosita. Still he had always put them off, thinking them a waste of his time. He was young and had needed only his work to make him happy. Now as he hammered, the image of Rosita and her liquid eyes flashed into his mind.

Perhaps, it was just because she was someone new and thus exciting. After all, she was a Gypsy girl! Pleased for the moment, the Smith went back to his work with a vengeance. None of the repairs were difficult and there was magic in his hands. As pieces melted together to form whole pots, he grunted and nodded to himself in satisfaction. There was not even a dip to show where the deep gouge had been in the last of the pans.

Finishing with the work the Smith gathered up an assortment of small tools and bits of scrap metal. He packed them into his travel kit along with some of the things that he would normally take with him to the outlying farmsteads. He also removed the treasured chalice from its cupboard. Wrapping it carefully against damage, he placed it in the sack. He could not say why he did this. Perhaps he would see a design worthy of the chalice while he was on the road?

Quickly, for it would be dark soon, he borrowed the cart and a donkey from his friend the barrel wright. He loaded up the gear and the repairs. The smith climbed onto the driver's seat and with a gentle flick of the reins, started the cart through the village and down the path at its southern edge. Anxious now to see the Gypsy camp.

CHAPTER TWO

It was full dark as the Smith drove the donkey cart down the overgrown path south toward the Gypsy camp. His mood was light and gay. He was on the road, heading into the unknown. His mind populated each tree or darkened night shadow with fiends, devils and monsters of all sorts. Each was banished by a wave of his imagined sword.

It wasn't long before the glow of firelight appeared from the darkness ahead. The sounds of merry voices, lifting high in song, came to his ears. The melody reached out to wrap him in its warmth. He guided the donkey quickly along the path, happy to be approaching his goal but sad at the loss of his highway adventures.

Rounding a turn in the path, he came out upon the Gypsy camp. There, were the three wagons drawn up to form a rough circle. The horses were penned in the gaps between the wagons, making for a fairly large space at the center of the grouping. In the clearing, a brightly burning campfire lent light to the scene. It reflected, spectacularly off of the gay colored wagons and the bright Gypsy clothes of the people that moved around it.

The men and women whirled in a fast paced dance. Music from violins sang in the air and the small cymbals on the fingers of the dancing women chimed sweetly in counterpoint.

At the sight of the Smith, Yoseph walked, smiling, towards him. In a loud voice he hailed his people. "Look everyone, it is our young Smith, come to join us in merriment." Reaching up, he took the reins of the cart from the Smith and tossed them to a waiting companion. "Peter will take care of the animal and unload the cart for you, friend Smith. Now you must join us around our fire and share in our supper."

Willingly the Smith followed, looking from face to face smiling, trying to remember their names. The group wasn't a large one, perhaps twenty souls in all. At the moment that did not mean much to him for the one that he hoped to see was not there.

The Trumpet of Harmony

Yoseph saw the puzzled expression on the Smith's face and watched the man's searching eyes. "Friend Smith, who is it that you seek in our humble camp?" There was a spark of mischief and a knowing smile for the Smith.

The Smith, startled from his inspection of the gypsy people replied. "I seek the girl, Rosita. The image of her face plies my imagination and I would see her again."

The smile on the Gypsy Leader's face shifted and was now a deep frown. As the silence filled the air, he replied with a heavy growl deep in his throat. Misunderstanding the Smith's intentions, he said "What you ask for is forbidden. Our women have been known to dally with men of the villages that we visit but Rosita is not for any man." The Gypsy Master eyed the Smith, "Had I known of your feelings, you would have been waylaid on the road here."

Pausing, he looked into the Smith's distraught face and said in a thoughtful voice. "Still we invited you to share our camp and we would lose honor if we treated you as less then a welcomed guest. Come Smith, eat by the fire, while I talk your problem over with the elders of our band."

As the Smith was escorted toward the warm welcome of the fire's glow, he tried to tell Yoseph, that all that Rosita meant to him, was the addition of spice and romance to an active imagination. The Gypsy Leader was having none of it, gruffly he led the Smith to the fire ring.

There an ancient woman, dressed in the gay clothes of the tribe, stood boldly in his way. The Smith looked up questionably at Yoseph. The leader shrugged and turned away to a small knot of older men standing by his wagon.

The Smith looked down into the dim eyes of the old woman and smiled. "How may I be of service to you my Lady?" he said.

The crone returned his smile with a crooked tooth grin and reached out for the Smith's strong hands. Holding them in her grasp, she looked at his palms, following the seams with a knowing eye. With a gasp and a tremble that rocked her whole body, she released his hands as though she had been holding a deadly snake.

Raising her eyes to his, she looked long and searchingly for something. Without saying a word, she turned and hobbled quickly away from the fire and over to the elders.

"Don't mind them, Sir Smith," said a young voice by his elbow. Turning, once more he beheld a young girl of thirteen or fourteen, bearing a platter full of meats and carrying a flagon of dark wine. "My name is Kathia. I am Rosita's half sister. I heard what my father said to you. Please do not take offense. We mean you no ill will. It is just that Rosita is necessary to the well being of our people and my father is afraid that you will take her from us."

The Smith frowned, trying to understand the meaning of what she was not saying. "Tell me, what is it that you are afraid of? I will not hurt you nor any member of the camp. Why is it hard to grant my wish? I would like to see Rosita again. To tell her of the visions she has made in my mind." The Smith's shoulders slumped in defeat and the girl looked at him sadly.

"I can tell that you are a good man, and honest. Yet there is much about you that is unfinished." She paused and looked thoughtful. "Have you never felt this way toward a woman before? You look to be strong enough and old enough to have known how it is between a man and a woman. Why does your tongue betray you? For know this Smith. Had you asked any other girl in camp to love you this night you might have found your pick. Yet you come to us, your heart in hand. Desiring the one woman that no man can touch."

The misery that gripped his soul made his words weak, "Up to this morning I had only found joy in my work, never did I feel the need to seek out companionship. It would have only distracted me." Looking up slowly, he tried to make her feel his confusion. "I dreamed many times of the distant horizons and the world beyond my village. I only sought

Rosita, because she became a part of the adventures in my mind, and I wanted to thank her for the pleasure that her company had given me."

Yoseph and the elders had come up behind the Smith while he had been speaking and had listened quietly. "It would seem, friend Smith, that we misjudged you. We had thought that payment of music and food were not enough for your work but that you had sought a lustier coin." The gypsy smiled. "My daughter is away on business for the people of this camp and will not return before the dawn. When she does you may speak to her."

The Smith looked no happier but nodded. "To the Leader of this camp, my thanks. I will await the dawn." He turned to leave the fire lit circle but found his way blocked by the smiling Gypsy Leader.

"Come now Smith, would you not have our hospitality this night? Eat, drink and enjoy gypsy music, for the morrow comes soon enough." So saying, he sat the Smith next to him while strange exotic foods were served and strong drink was poured into the Smith's flagon. Soon the strains of music filled the air. It was an oddly haunting and beautiful melody that reminded the Smith very much of Rosita.

The absence of Rosita bothered him. What could be so urgent as to send the gypsy woman out into the night? What had made the young woman so special to these people? The Smith wished that he had never ventured forth on the road, yet he knew that he could not have done otherwise.

Yoseph filled the Smith's cup once more, the heavy liqueur smelling of honey. "Drink a toast with me, Sir Smith, to love and to despair, for aren't they one in the same for all men?"

The drink was heady and the Smith, unused to drink of any kind, soon found the light from the fire growing dim. Sleep fell over him like a warm blanket, heavy and comfortable. The voices of the gypsies faded in and out, soon to be lost altogether.

The Trumpet of Harmony

Dreams he had then, of faraway places with forgotten names. Faces of people he had never known appeared before him. Each paused to consider him, weighing his soul and smiling in smug satisfaction. Some spoke in voices, rusty and shrill. Others looked sadly at him and turned away.

At last his vision cleared and he perceived himself to be sitting in a room with a small fire at its center. On the other side of the flames sat the old gypsy crone. She seemed to be speaking but the words were in a tongue that the Smith had never heard before. Her attention was focused on a small crystal globe held reverently in her lap. Suddenly, she looked up, catching and holding the Smith's eyes. In a clear voice she said, "Who are you man, who enters our world as if it were his right? There is that about you that I can not see, it lays hidden, as if in ambush."

Her eyes probed deeply into his. "Answer me Smith and do not lie, for the magic that is upon you now would strike you down if you did. Why did you come to disturb our peace? We have no quarrel with the forces of the outer gate. We are a small band and go our own way causing trouble for none. Why do you seek our destruction? "

The Smith's mind was clear but the magic held him in silence, yet there was an answer. "Old one." Came a deep voice resonant with power. "You are not to meddle in the affairs of those greater than your dreams could ever paint them. You and your people are safe from this man and that which he must do. But beware, there are forces stirring from whom you have thought yourself safe. There is that which troubles their sleep and they waken."

The old crone crouched down, bent unmercifully over her globe. Fear and awe were written in every line of her body, but with the spirit that had made her wise woman of her band, she struggled to form a name. Her lips would not move and in her eyes there was a tear.

Once more the voice spoke from the Smith. "You are a valiant creature and have served your people well. Serve them this last time. Tell them to leave this man unharmed and aid him in any way they can. There is that which he must do, in which great sorrow and pain he must endure. Yet great will be his reward. Great also will be the name of Yoseph's people, for the fate of the young woman, Rosita lays with the Smith."

The voice was gone and the vision vanished, leaving new voices filling the air. Soft excited voices that carried a note of fear. Quickly, these faded as the potion finally overcame the Smith and he lapsed into a deep, dreamless slumber.

CHAPTER THREE

Rosita's senses were alert. The damp smells of the forest were an open book to her knowing mind. It was the dregs of the evening, the shadows thick as pitch around her. Still the darkness was no hindrance to her progress as she moved in her nightly patrol.

There were many dangers that could be hidden by the cloak of night and here in the wild any unwary traveler would be easy prey. It was in this wilderness between the scattered villages that her people lived. They survived by being cautious, wary of anything unusual and by the use of her keen animal senses.

There was nothing out of place in the forest tonight. The life forces that were within reach of her keen nose were all native to the area. Nothing to cause alarm. It was going to be a quiet night. She found shelter under a low laying tree and curled up into a tight ball of grey fur, to rest in a bed of last year's leaves.

It had been a strange day, she reflected. Towns always made her nervous. They were unsavory places, with the smell of unwashed bodies and old corruption. The odors and the strange people made her lose confidence in her abilities, but her father always insisted on her company when ever they entered a town. He had come to rely heavily on her natural instincts.

Today the village was small, of little consequence, except for the fame of the local Smith. There were always odd repairs that needed to be done around the camp which required a true Smith. The old ones were beginning to complain loudly about the sorry state of their cooking utensils. So Yoseph decided to take advantage of their position so near to the village, to quiet the noise.

She had been on edge, noting the sour smells that came from living to close together and listening to the din of shouting youths as they drew the usual gawking crowds. The smell of clean heat on metal and the sound of a rushing stream reached her senses even as they passed the first cottage at the village edge. Somehow the astringent smell and the cheerful noise eased her tension.

They had found the smithy at the edge of the village square. Their wagons pulled up and her father jumped down and walked over to the waiting Smith. Rosita eyed the man with mild contempt. The tall, strapping frame fit the mold of smith well enough, but it belonged to a gangling youth. The Smith's face appeared to be untouched by a man's beard and his eyes showed an open, friendly spirit. This would be easy pickings for her people.

Losing interest, she started to catalogue what her senses could tell her. The village was quiet as these things went. The shouting youngsters who had followed them in stood in one corner of the square, quiet for the moment. There was a certain harmony which seemed to spread throughout the cottages. The people she had seen all had smiles and a goodly number had greeted them pleasantly.

There were no voices raised in anger and no clash of arms. In fact, they had seen no officials or town bullies. By this time, they would have haggled with three or four of them. There had been no one to question their presence here, holding out their hands for the customary bribe, allowing them passage. It made her uneasy. Through long years she had learned that anything that was out of the ordinary, was to be questioned and certainly not to be trusted.

Her attention came back to the smithy. She was just in time to catch her father's voice, "Yoseph is my name", he was saying. She knew then that the bargaining, such as it was, had ended. It seemed that the poor young Smith was to do the work needed in exchange for a meal at the camp that night.

"Come meet my people," Yoseph said loudly. One by one, the members of her small band stepped forward, smiled and gave the Smith their Use Names. Rosita hung back, for some reason reluctant to face the man she had summarily dismissed. At last her turn came, she walked up to meet the

Smith and to look into his eyes. What she saw there frightened her. Tenuous as smoke, she felt a shadow fall across her spirit, binding her gently. Her eyes hardened perceptibly and her smile turned into a frown of displeasure. She turned away as hastily as she could, while under her father's watchful eye.

As Yoseph made his farewell to the Smith, Rosita stayed out of sight behind one of their wagons. When at last they had begun to move out of the small village toward the site of their camp for that night, she allowed her muscles to relax and breathed easier once more.

As she had been trained, she detached herself from her reaction and started to seek the meaning behind the feelings. For as long as she could remember, she had roamed free. Even though she was the daughter of her peoples' leader, she had escaped the normal traditions. Customs and duties that tied the other Gypsy girls did not bind her. There had been no marriage price set for her, so that she might go to one of the other bands to make a strong alliance for her father.

The pain of that slight, sprang sharp into her heart and had not dimmed with time. Still, it had given her freedoms and responsibilities, unknown to any other lass. She realized that it was this freedom that she feared for and that the Smith represented a threat to it in a way that she did not understand.

When was it that her Tribe set her apart? She could remember playing, as any young babe should, with the others of her clan. Those were indeed golden moments and well treasured. Then unerringly her mind turned back to the day when she had been picking berries alone, at a distance from the camp.

She had known that no one was allowed to wander without another for company. Still none of the other children would go and the adults had all busied themselves with chores for the camp. She had not been gathering berries long when a shadow fell across her. Afraid she looked up. There standing on the other side of the clearing where she labored, stood a large wolf with bright yellow eyes.

She was very frightened and yet was compelled to walk closer to those knowing eyes. In her mind a soft cool voice told her not to fear, but to listen. It told her, that her Tribe was in great danger. She must carry word back to her father, to remove the clan from these woods and head away north, speedily.

Within a day's march, a band of outlaws had layered. These were waylaying any they came across. Swift death for the men and a lingering death for the woman and children awaited if the warning went unheeded. Then the voice bade her run and she ran, not from fear but with an overriding need to carry the message back to Yoseph. She had only been five.

Three times did such a visit occur, saving the lives of her people. After each, she found that the people, especially the other children had begun to shy away from her company. As time passed she found the other lasses would whisper and laugh when she was near.

Once, when Rosita had been but the shadow of a woman she had run with tears in her eyes, to the old crone who served as wise woman to her father. She had poured her heart out, demanding to know why Bride Price had not been set for her, the eldest daughter.

Even her younger half-sister had already been given in Axe Marriage to the band that was led by Sevan. In fact it was Sevan's own son that she was to go to on her sixteenth birthday.

The wise woman had listened to Rosita with the patience of her profession. When the girl had finished, collapsing in a bundle of cloth and tears, the seer bade Rosita to sit in front of her brazier.

The old woman pulled a handful of scented herbs from the pouch that she wore on her belt. Tossing these onto the hot coals she commanded Rosita to breathe in the vapors.

Rosita did as she had been instructed and inhaled deeply of the fumes from the brazier. They were of a sharp and pungent nature, pleasing and heady. Soon she found her body relaxing and her mind dipped into a light, dreamless slumber. In her sleep she seemed to hear the voices of the wise woman and her father in heated conversation.

"Yoseph", the old crone was saying, "you knew the portents cast at her birth. The sign of the Were rose dominant in her house. She can no more escape her fate then her mother could. May the Gods rest her soul!

"Yes! I knew it. Yet when it did not outwardly manifest itself these past years, I had hoped that you were wrong." He continued sadly. "When my beloved Malinda died giving Rosita birth I had hoped that my family had suffered enough."

"Yes , I know Yoseph", said the voice of the crone, taking up the stillness, "but the time has come to put your tragedy aside and to think only of the good of your people. The girl must know and in that knowledge come to control her powers. For a time yet, she must serve as protector and after that well, her future is clouded."

Yoseph's voice came back with much more energy. "I have done what custom has demanded and have kept from Rosita the natural rights belonging to any lass. I did not arrange marriage for her even though she is my eldest, but instead remarried quickly to a woman of unquestioned heritage. From her I have given birth to another daughter, who goes to marriage, making the Tribe's future more secure."

"I have allowed Rosita to wander freely, restricting her not to customs or duties, but allowing her room to find her own destiny. I will not have the powers which nature has given her, hidden from her any longer. If Malinda had lived she would have taken her daughter into the wilds and shown her the things that Rosita must know to serve this camp as our Protector." His voice hesitated once more and then continued. "How can we guide her along the path that she now must follow?"

The Trumpet of Harmony

"There is a way, Yoseph. Leave us now and I will think upon our problem. Rosita will remain here with me tonight. Please tell all the others to stay away from us until morning's light and tell them not to be alarmed at any sounds that they might hear. No one, including you, must interfere with me in this matter. Now go and trust me to care for the girl."

Even as the voices faded from Rosita's drug clouded mind, the gypsy leader grudgingly left to do the old one's bidding. Turning the old crone opened her bag of simples. Rummaging in it she finally found a smallish vial wrapped in old, yellowed parchment. Carefully she added more herbs, from her waist bag, to the brightly burning coals in her brazier. As the smoke reached Rosita, she stirred moaning in a low voice. Her eyes opened wide and she fell into a deep trance.

"Rosita, can you hear me?" asked the Wise Woman. Slowly the girl nodded her head. Satisfied, the old woman removed the colorful clothing that she wore pulling on instead, only an old white shawl stitched in intricate deigns. Taking some paints from her stores she drew a diagram on her breast, so that it rested just over her heart. With a branch from a nearby overhanging tree, she drew a larger diagram which encircled the brazier, the girl's prone form and herself.

With some effort, she broke the seal on the small vial. Reciting some sacred words of ceremony, she dribbled a few drops into the girl's relaxed lips. She watched carefully to be sure that she swallowed them. Taking the parchment, in which the vial had been wrapped, she cautiously unfolded it to its full length and placed it gently under the girl's head.

Once more the Wise Woman pulled a handful of herbs from her bag and threw them onto the coals. She waited until a pillar of smoke had risen up ten feet and spread out to cover the entire area of her symbol. Then taking the vial, she drank the last few drops and sat down cross legged by the Rosita's feet. With deep breaths, she too was deeply entranced.

The evening twilight turned into night's dusky hues as the Wise Woman waited in silence. Her mind was free of everything but the need to contact the spirit of Malinda. In her heart, she knew that trafficking with the dead bordered on the dark side of Magic and as such could turn against the one who so summoned. What precautions she could take, she had, so in the dark she waited for what the fates would offer.

The night crawled slowly by. It was well past the midnight hour, when even the hunter's moon had disappeared below the horizon, holding everything in the deepest shadows of night. In the uncanny stillness, a soft glow formed over the sleeping girl's body. Gathering substance it drew itself to a small man's height and solidified into the specter of the departed Malinda.

Sadly, the ghost looked down on her daughter's face. The light of her glow gentled with her smile. Glancing up at the Wise Woman, softness was replaced by grim disapproval. The cool voice that entered the woman's mind was sharp as the winter's wind. "You risk much old one. Much that isn't yours."

The powerful mind of the Wise Woman responded. "Speak softly, my lady shade, you have no power in the here and now. I did not approve of your presence here whilst yet you lived. You placed a stain on the name of Yoseph's band. Do you think that I would summon you now, if it were not for your dear husband's command? Your daughter has been banned by the tribe from being given a proper lass's due. Thus, Yoseph is determined to give her the birth right that you had bequeathed her."

The apparition glowed brightly, then dulled. "Alas, Seeress, I can no longer run in my physical form, to show her the ways that she must learn. The transformation is dangerous. At first it will disorient and frighten her. Unless someone is there by her side who is able to make her understand, she may go mad!"

"Nonsense, Malinda. I have prepared against this day. Long I have searched the ancient lairs and at last I have solved the problem. With the spell written on the parchment beneath the child's head, you will be able to enter her mind. She will feel as you would feel. She will see as you would see, but be warned there is a time set against which you must work. At the end of the third day you will be banished once more to the nether world. Do you understand?"

Mutely the shade nodded and then glided to a spot just above her daughter's head. "I am ready old one. I have longed to be near the daughter of my body and for that I thank you. I only hope that she is the daughter of my spirit as well."

Silently the Wise Woman agreed with her. Still entranced she began to recite the ancient formula taken from one of the oldest tomes that she had found. As she struggled to form the words of power, her mind felt the fabric of reality begin to tear. Time lost its place in the stream of natural order and she beheld scenes of terror unremembered in this world. She could not stop the incantation or all would be lost, so summoning what courage she could she watched the destruction of an alien world.

In her vision, there were mighty towers of crystal and metal. Some were twisted, melted beyond recognition. Amid the carnage the image of a man appeared, his face was handsome in demeanor but as he turned to face her, she beheld his eyes. Those eyes glowed with powers beyond belief and from them she felt a wave of overpowering, evil trying to engulf her. She could not be sure but she thought she could detect recognition and then cynical mirth in those burning ovals.

Struggling with the last mystic words, she quickly added the word of command and suddenly she was back in her own reality. The image she had seen had burned itself into her mind.

The sound of the cock's crow drew her out of the stupor. She glanced to the place where Rosita had lain only to see her gone. She hoped that it had worked and that Rosita would at last find the freedom of the forest. If not, the sacrifice would have been in vain. Quickly she gathered up her herbs and erased the symbols of protection, shaking her head at their unexpected failure.

The Trumpet of Harmony

CHAPTER FOUR

It was the cock's crow that stirred Rosita from her comfortable bed beneath the tree. Stretching mightily, she raised her muzzle to scent the morning air. The memories of her night dreams brought a sense of purpose and satisfaction back to her, along with a fond remembrance for a mother that she had come to know most intimately.

Her peace was short lived however, for the scents that came to her were all scents born of the forest. There was no smell of smoke from the camp's cooking fires and no trace on the air of the people nor their animals. Something was terribly wrong. With an agility and speed that matched her form, she sprang from the brake and sped off toward the camp.

The distance was not great, for she had been casting only a few miles from camp during the night. She cursed herself for allowing a seemingly peaceful patrol to lure her into a memory filled slumber. Still, if anything unusual had occurred she was sure that her senses would have alerted her.

As she approached the final line of trees, she slowed to a cautious trot. It would do no good to run blindly into danger. She tasted the wind once more but the smell of the cooking fire was old and bitter. It had been some time since it had gone out.

There was a scent on the air though, one that she could not remember but one she knew that she had tasted before. Peering around the trunk of a thick tree that stood by the edge of the clearing she took in the sight of the Gypsy camp.

There in the early morning light she beheld an empty meadow. The trampled grass betrayed where the wagons and horses had rested. That alarmed her. The people had always been sure to disguise their campsite so that no one would be aware of their passing. To find such signs spoke of a hurried and undisciplined departure.

The Trumpet of Harmony

Sweeping her gaze across the grasses once more she spied a still form by the dead fire ring. He stirred sluggishly and forced himself into a sitting position. Even though the slumped figure hid his face in his hands she recognized the Smith, and at once the scent that had eluded her became clear.

She ducked back behind the bole of the tree. What, if anything, had the cursed Smith to do with her people's disappearance? There was no blood on the air, murder had not been done. That would not explain the missing wagons either. She knew that something was terribly wrong but she would have to bide her time and wait for the reasons to be made clear to her. With a last glance at the now moaning form of the Smith she set off to circle the meadow in the hope of picking up her people's trail.

It had not been more then a few minutes before she came upon the unmistakable sign of wagon tracks. It was strange, for they were headed out away from the meadow in a direction that the people had not taken before. If they were to continue on to the north they would soon leave their territory and venture into that of Seven's.

Still bothered by this odd turn of events she trotted off to follow the trace. She hadn't run for more then a quarter of a mile when she was brought up short. There in the center of the wagon rutted turf was a token from which emanated a powerful, pungent smell. Wolf's Bane! Her own people had placed a barrier against her. In her present shape, she could not pass that amulet. If she were to cross it in her human form it would be two full days before her powers would return. She would be as helpless as that dullard Smith.

At the thought of the Smith, a deep growl escaped from her throat. He must be the key to this mystery. She would force him to tell her what had happened even if she had to rip him apart to convince him.

A sudden chill fell over her. Such a thought ran against every Code that she had sworn to uphold. Her mother's words came to her down through the years. "We have been given a special gift, my child. It is to be used only for the preservation of life and the protection of our kin. That is why we exist. To go beyond that, to yield yourself to the animal half of your nature is to venture into the world of madness and despair." Rosita cooled at once. Well, all good and fine, but she must find out the meaning of this mystery and the Smith was the only piece of the puzzle that she had to work with.

Her decision to confront the Smith, now caused another problem. Usually when she returned from nightly patrol it was in the comfort and modesty of her family's wagon that she performed her transformation. She was young and blushed despite her anger, the thought of approaching a strange man without the proper clothing made her hesitate. Glancing around helplessly, she spied a bundle laid carefully off to one side of the trail.

She hurried to the spot and tears sprang into her eyes. It was her own travel bag that laid there, along with a bag of provisions, if her nose had the right of it. Propped up next to the bag was a short but deadly looking dagger.

With a quick glance to be sure that she was not being observed, she allowed the ritual of transformation to run through her mind. As the images in her mind's eye melted from wolf to woman, so to did her physical form transform. The discomfort of her body was deadened by the Code of the Were, as it repeated itself over and over again in her mind. The transformation took only seconds to preform, but it was a time of great peril. During those brief moments, she was totally unprotected and in danger from those who would do her harm. Drawing a deeper breath, she released herself from the spell. The air was somehow duller and the sounds around her were muted, but she knew that even in her human form, her senses were still many times sharper then that of a normal person.

Rosita opened the bag and drew out some tough traveling clothes that she found within. It was not her usual garb and she wondered at this, as she dressed. It was as if her family had packed for her the needs for a long and rugged journey in the wilds. Shouldering the pack, she slid the dagger carefully into the sheath that she found in the bundle. She smiled grimly at this irony, even in her human form she had formidable teeth. Turning her back on the forbidden trail she squared her shoulders and started toward the clearing and the Smith.

CHAPTER FIVE

A roaring sound pierced the silence that had fallen, like a shroud, over the Smith. It might have been a death cloth that covered him. Not a glimmer of light nor a stray fragment of memory disturbed the emptiness in which he floated. Yet the roaring sound grew persistent.

Someone was groaning in pain. In a moment of decision, the Smith opened his eyes and was immediately blinded by the brilliant morning light. Blinking back tears he turned his head looking around. In doing so, he closed his own mouth. The moaning stopped. Puzzled and groggy, he realized that he was the source of the very sound which had pulled him from his dreamless slumber.

The sour smell of half burned wood reached his nostrils, gagging him. Choking the Smith rolled over and pulled himself into a sitting position. The pain which laced through him was excruciating. He cradled his aching head in his hands to ease the throbbing. Slowly the pain passed and he looked around. At once he realized, that he was alone. Running his hands through the ashes in the fire ring he could tell that it had been at least six hours since it had died.

Gingerly the Smith got to his feet. Looking about him, he saw a bundle laying on the other side of the fire ring. There was a short sword, sheathed in a battered leather casing, propped up beside the bundle. Without much hope, he stumbled over to it and pulled it open. There were the tools that he had packed away yesterday afternoon. Hurriedly now, he pulled out a pouch made of a rich velvet material, opening the draw string he exposed the silver chalice to the morning sun. "Why would the Gypsies leave such a valuable piece behind and why wrap it up in such a royal covering?"

Laying the chalice carefully aside, the Smith dug deeper into the pack. He found provisions enough for many days rough journeying and travel clothes, tough and strong, yet light and supple. He wondered at the meaning of these items, then he remembered the evening's fire and the strange dreams that came over him. There had been many excited voices as he had succumbed to sleep. Yoseph must have taken the crone's word and this was his way of aiding the Smith.

The import of his thoughts flashed sharply into the Smith's mind. He had been the center of a very strange dream and he could not shake the feeling that, someone or some thing was trying to take hold of his destiny. Sinking down to his knees he realized that he should seek the advice of someone who dealt with this kind of Magic.

It was then that the Smith remembered the Conjurer. The people of his village thought the man to be deranged, but they never hesitated to seek him out for portents and minor spells. If anyone would help him, the Conjurer could.

In the meantime, he had a more pressing problem. The donkey and cart that he borrowed from the village barrel wright, had vanished along with the Gypsy band. The law of his village was lenient in most matters, but theft of a work animal was still punishable by indenture until the value of the beast was paid off. He would have to persue his host and reclaim the donkey and cart.

Taking a deep breath the Smith squared his shoulders and got back on his feet. The pain in his head had subsided to a dull throb and he could think more clearly. He now began to look through his limited resources closely, keeping a journey of some days in mind. By dividing the food into equal proportions, he decided that he could go for a week or two without having to find a new supply. Water would not be a problem, at least for a time. The rainy season had just ended and the streams were full, riding high in their banks. With any luck at all he would find the Gypsy band quickly and recover the cart and donkey before any one missed him in the village.

When he had set things to right and had a small kettle on the fire that he had rekindled, he examined the short sword that the gypsies had left. With a shudder, the Smith buckled the belt which held it, firmly around his waist. He certainly hoped that he would not need to use it. Fantasizing was one thing, taking the life of another creature, even in self defense, was another.

Feeling more or less secure, the Smith picked up one of the yellowish looking journey biscuits, which was to be the main part of his larder for many days. He sniffed at it cautiously, before he bit into its rough textured substance. The taste and smell of honey were strong. The frown with which he had approached this trial soon turned into a gratified smile as he gobbled down the remaining crumbs.

"Go easy there, sir Smith." came a voice from behind him. "You have just eaten enough for a long day's march."

Turning in surprise, the Smith found himself looking at the shiny blade of a wicked looking dagger. The hand that held it's point close to his face belonged to the object of his previous day's fantasy.

"Now Smith, you will tell me what happened here last night and why my people would risk their lives without my guidance." Rosita's dark eyes flashed brightly in her irritation.

The irony of this turn of events was not lost on the Smith. As he looked into the steely eyes of the young woman before him, he realized that she was quite capable of slitting his throat if she thought that he had, in some way, harmed her kin.

Then irritation of his own poor usage worked up to the surface of his emotions. "Girl, I have no real memory of last night's occurrences, past my arrival here and some haunting dreams. If anyone should be angry, it should be me."

"I did not take advantage of your people. I did their mending with my utmost skill. Every pot and pan was perfect. I traveled out to your camp to receive your people's hospitality in fair exchange. This morning I awake with a head that wants to split open and a missing donkey and wagon. What do you say to that?" The Smith carefully folded his arms and stared back at the slight girl.

"I do not pretend to know what you are talking about, Smith. Just be grateful that there is no sign of deception about you nor any trace of foul play about this camp, for know this Smith, my blade would drink gladly of your blood if it were so."

Pausing in thought, Rosita continued. "I do not know what transpired here. My Tribe would not move away from this place and into the night's dangers without good reason. I have followed their trail for as long as I was able but there is a barrier in my way that I cannot, safely cross."

Suddenly, she was overwhelmed by a sense of loss. She had never been without the security of her family and now she did not know if she would ever see them again. Worst of all, she did not even know why. Sheathing her knife and moving away from the Smith, Rosita lowered herself down next to the fire. She fought desperately to regain her confidence and to quiet her nerves.

The Smith freed from the threat of her dagger point, tried to understand why the girl had simply not followed the Gypsies after she had picked up their trail. She was in fine shape and did not seem to be afraid to face the trail alone. She had mentioned a barrier but there could be no blockade long enough that she could not get around it. Still she sounded defeated and lost.

"Listen Rosita, I don't know what happened or why you can't follow your people, but I will gladly help you get back to them. Besides, I want to ask them a few questions of my own." He smiled briefly.

The dark-haired girl's shoulders slumped forward as he spoke, then suddenly she sprang out of her crouch, chin defiantly in the air as she peered up into the Smith's eyes. "You don't realize, do you Smith, what all this means? No of course you don't. How could a man who is not of the blood, understand the meaning of the Gypsy's ways?"

The Smith stood by and listened intently, trying to follow the girl's meaning.

"Don't you see? I've been left behind. It was ever the way to part from one of my Tribe." She sighed heavily. "They have left a portent on the trail as plain as day to one of my nature. It means do not follow. You are not welcome!"

The Smith was at a loss, words of comfort rose up in his throat and died on his lips as he caught the forbidding in her eyes. He felt pity for the young woman, until he remembered the look of cold steel in her hand.

Uncomfortable and thinking upon the road ahead, he turned his back to Rosita. Clearing his throat, he began to speak about his idea of visiting the Conjurer. He made it plain that until he recovered the donkey and cart, that the door to the village had been closed to him. He said that the Conjurer might be able to help her understand why her family left, abandoning her to her fate.

He made no mention of the dreams from the night before. Turning with the argument that Rosita should go with him to the Conjurer, he was surprised to find her digging through his pack and dividing up it's contents into even smaller packets.

"You had too much for each meal." She said by way of explanation to his unasked question. "If I am to travel with you, I must be sure that you do not squander our resources."

"Travel with me girl!" The Smith sputtered. "I was going to send you back to the village for safety until I could return."

The Smith looked so ludicrous standing there with his brow furrowed and his hands on his hips that Rosita actually laughed. "Safety, Smith? You, who have never strayed more then a few miles from the village where you were born. You, who barely have the fuzz of manhood upon your chin, want to send me back to your village. To do what? Serve as a scullery maid until you should return from your desperate venture?"

Pausing she caught her breath, another taunt upon her lips and then as if in thought, she composed herself. "You are an uncommonly brave man, Smith, throwing away the only chance that you have to survive more then the next sun rise. Allowing me to go to your village to relax and think sweet thoughts while the vultures feed on your liver."

Her sarcasm was more then he could bare. In one quick stride he had reached the packs and with a sharp tug freed the one that she had indicated would be his. Slinging it over his shoulder, he walked quickly away from the campsite and on into the forest at its southern edge.

It wasn't until he had covered a few miles that he began to wonder at his actions. Never had anyone so angered him. His pride had been hurt by her taunting words, but now his temper had boiled away and he felt confused.

After all the girl was now alone in the wild and despite her apparent ease at the prospect, he could not see how she was capable of surviving by herself. With an inward shrug, he turned and started along his back trail. He was uncertain what to say to Rosita or what to do with her once he returned.

The Smith had only been walking for a few minutes when he became aware that he was being watched. He could feel unseen eyes, burning a hole into his back. But no matter how quickly he turned, nor how stealthily he watched the trail behind him, he never caught a glimpse of movement. After an hour or so, he drew nearer to the deserted Gypsy camp and the feeling left him.

The morning was getting fine and hot as the Smith once more entered the clearing. The girl was where he left her, still tending the small cooking fire that he had started earlier that day. He hesitated, now unsure how to explain his sudden disappearance and his return only a few hours later.

It was Rosita that broke the silence. Without looking up she said, "So you have come back, Smith. I thought that I would have to go and find you come the night. There are those within a day's march of here that would freeze your blood. Which by the way, is what they feed on, Sir Smith."

Pointing to a nearby rock she said, "Lunch is ready. Come sit by me and we will eat and talk. If you do not agree to my suggestions then you will be off and I will not feel responsible for your safety."

She had taken control of the situation and her confidence galled him. Yet, he was pleased to find her receptive. Feeling a little more in control of his own emotions, he sat down next to her. The smells rising from her cooking pot made him forget his problems for the moment.

She filled his camp plate and shook her head in mild dismay. "This is but poor fare, I could not find the necessary herbs with which to turn this trail food into something fit to eat. Of course, if our travels take us a little further south, we will be able to pick up some fine seasonings. They will come in handy when the trail food runs out and we will have to forage for our meals."

Her tone and manner were so casual that for a few minutes the Smith did not react to her words. The food that she had cooked up was a feast to him. He had grown so accustomed to heating up odds and ends over his hearth at the smithy, that he had forgotten what a well tended meal could taste like. He looked at her over the rim of his mug and said, "If I am such a babe in the woods, a threat only to myself, why is it that you would travel with me? It seems that you would fare better on your own."

Her eyes filled with laughter but her words were cool. "You are right Sir Smith, yet wither else would I go?" She shook her head, her hair gently flowing with the movement. "No, our paths will stay together for a time yet but worry not if one day you turn and find me gone. I am my own person and I will choose the hour of our parting, although fate may choose the manner."

She glanced up into the sky and sniffed the wind as if it held tastes that she alone could savor. "The sun sets later these days but we must make use of the time. We would be well away from this place by nightfall. For even though I found nothing amiss during the night, the passage of intruders runs swift through the land and this camp will be marked for all to find."

For once the Smith could agree. With one bad night here already, he was not anxious for another. It seemed that he had no choice but to accept Rosita on her own terms. For many reasons, he was glad for her company. "I do not know how much faith we can put into the wisdom of the Conjurer, but he has existed for many generations of men, giving advice for payment."

Rosita replied. "Do not discount the wisdom of an ancient. The Tribe has the services of a venerable woman, who at times has been of great aid to them. Let us go visit your Conjurer and perhaps he will know why my people have left me!"

They broke camp. The fire was smothered, their packs straightened and sealed. Shouldering their burdens and with a weak grin for each other they headed back up the path toward the village.

The path leading to the conjurer's home soon broke off from the main trail that had led south from the village to the Gypsy camp. As they walked the Smith told Rosita about the strange being they were going to see. "The man lives in the trunk of an enormous and ancient oak tree. How long the Conjurer has lived there is a matter for conjecture. He was old and ornery when I was born. My father could remember him from his youth and even then he looked the same as he does today."

The Smith shrugged his powerful shoulders. "Each to their own Magic," he said, as they came at last into the pale thin shadow of the towering oak. Craning their necks, they tried to follow the long graceful lines of the trunk, losing it at last in the wide spread canopy of golden yellows, rusts, oranges, and green of the oak's early autumn coat.

They walked toward the trunk of the oak and soon found themselves in a wide valley formed by the giant roots of the tree. At the base of the trunk, the boles, shadowed and partially hid a round, bright green door with a brass knob at its center. It stood less then the height of the Smith. Beside it, dressed in a shimmering blue robe was the one that they had come to find.

The Conjurer sat at his ease on the top of a giant toad stool, smoking a long stemmed pipe. He pointedly ignored Rosita and the Smith. Patiently they waited until the early afternoon sun road high into the bright, blue autumn sky. At last, with exaggerated surprise, the old man exclaimed, "Good day to you, Master Smith. I didn't see you come up." Turning his piercing eyes on Rosita he said, "And who might this lovely creature be?"

Rosita said nothing but looked closely at the Conjurer. The creature was only half the height of the Smith and his wrinkled face looked be carved out of the tough bark of the tree in which he made his home. The man's hair was just a fringe around his shining pate and had the color of pale wheat. It was the eyes that told Rosita that this man had power and confidence. For those eyes sparked and snapped with a light all of their own.

The Conjurer's rough manners did not put the Smith off. He smiled at the old man and said, "We have been here for some time, good Conjurer, admiring the peace of your woods and enjoying its silence."

This of course, was the right thing to say. First, because it would have done no good at all to become irate with the little man for making them wait and secondly, the Conjurer loved his trees. After all, he lived in the king of that region's forests.

"By the Moons of Calgus, it's good to hear kind words from one of your race. Usually they show up asking all sorts of bothersome questions about their pointless lives." He paused to refill his pipe, impolitely forgetting to offer the Smith or Rosita a fill. "Well I make them pay, I do. Every question has its price and I live well enough because of it."

Suddenly, the old man's pipe flared brightly, illuminating the shadows. Some of the light remained caught up amongst the convolutions of the bark and glowed brighter still. Once the space at the base of the tree was free of shadows, the light steadied.

The Trumpet of Harmony

The Conjurer's eyes fastened onto the Smith. "And what price are you willing to pay? You think to question the mysteries of the Gypsy Wise Woman, but that is not your true question is it, Smith? Little will you like your answer and often you will chafe at the cost."

Pausing, the Conjurer looked over to Rosita. She had stood listening to the by play between these two strangers and had not spoken at all. "My lovely Gypsy, you wonder why your family has packed up in the middle of the night and left you alone to fend for yourself?"

Rosita gasped, for she had not told the Conjurer why she was there, the man just knew. She could feel a shudder pass through her body, for she realized that the little man saw with true sight. She replied, with the courtesy that she would give the Wise Woman of her Tribe. "Your Wisdom. I had not known that any of the true sight lived in this part of the Land." She paused as the old man guffawed at the title of respect.

She hurried on. "I have been the protector of my people for almost six years now. They rely on my senses to warn them of danger. They would no more go off into the wild woods without me then they would walk, unarmed into an enemy camp. If you know what caused them to make this reckless move, then I am willing to pay the price you would ask for that knowledge."

The Conjurer looked over the slim, attractive Gypsy woman and replied. "I will not ask you to pay a price, young lady. You will undergo many tests of courage and sacrifice before you fulfill your destiny."

Rosita started to interrupt but the Conjurer spoke over her protests. "I will tell you two things. First, your family is quite safe for the moment. The Gods themselves have given them protection. Secondly, you will not be allowed to return to them. That door is closed. But you have become part of a greater history, one which dates back to when this world was young and stretches into the far future. What you do now is closely tied to the destiny of this young Smith."

The Trumpet of Harmony

Rosita stood for a moment, her mouth open in protest and then she turned on her heels and walked back down the Conjurer's lane toward the southern path. The Smith started to go after her, calling her name, but the Conjurer stopped him with a word. "Stay, Smith. The girl has much to think about and needs time to be alone."

"Now then," the Conjurer said in business like tones. "You already have part of your answer. You now know that Rosita's fate is tied with yours, but that does not help you, does it Smith?"

"Sir," the Smith replied. "I will not bandy words with you. The day is passing and I, at least must try to catch the Gypsy band. They have taken a donkey and cart that does not belong to me. If I ever want to go home to my smithy, I must bring them back."

"Ah yes," interrupted the Conjurer, rudely. "Do you think that the Gypsy's are without honor? The donkey and cart have already been returned to the barrel wright." The Conjurer fixed the Smith with a knowing eye. "Hurry and ask your true question, Smith. Ask! Or I will forget about my manners and you!"

Now that it came to it, the Smith couldn't just simply say what he was on his mind and heart. He needed to gather his thoughts and emotions together. Half thinking out loud and half talking to himself he began. "All my life I have labored for my fellow villagers. Helping where I could, taking only what was given. I was happy and content that it remained so." Closing his eyes, the image of Rosita's face came to his mind.

There came a tightness in his stomach. "It was just yesterday morning, when the Gypsies rolled their wagons into the village square, that I came to realize how alone and empty I truly was. Suddenly, I felt the need to leave the village. To go and see the world out beyond its borders. But more then that to share the adventure with someone who could understand my desires."

The Trumpet of Harmony

Again, the old one spoke. "When was it, Smith, that you first noticed this "need," as you call it?"

In his mind's eye, the Smith floated above the dark limpid pools of Rosita's eyes. Under their surface, he could feel the fire that warmed her heart and much to his surprise, he hungered for that warmth. He was not aware that he had spoken his thoughts aloud, until he heard the sound of Rosita's name filling his ears. Blushing a bright red and wishing for some concealing shadows, he said, "I am sorry Conjurer. What was I saying?"

"Never mind, whelp," laughed the Conjurer. "I have an answer to the question that you have asked, so delicately. Now you must tell me if you are willing to pay my price."

Shaken out of his night dreams the Smith answered. "Old one, you know that I have no wealth and only the services of my hands and mind, with which to pay my debts. If these will suffice, then they are yours."

The hunger that filled the face of the Smith, was such that the old Conjurer, felt a passing remorse at the excesses of a long-forgotten youth. The Smith continued, "I must know the answer to this yearning in my soul. I know now that I will not be content to remain working at my smithy. There must be something or someone more for me."

The Conjurer sat in silence for a time, letting the ages roll through his mind like cool water down a swift stream. He peered at the honest youth from under his thick eyebrows. He knew that he held the boy's heart and his future balanced in his hands. He was saddened by the burden he must lay upon the lad. Yet he was hopeful, for there was a chance, a slim one at least, that this boy's future might be more then anyone in these back waters could imagine.

The Conjurer had waited here, in this huge tree for twenty generations of men. He had waited for the Smith. It was the beginning, and no matter what laid along the path it was time to give this youth his answer.

The Trumpet of Harmony

"First I will tell you what I require from you. If you search your heart and find the strength to agree, then I will tell you what you would know." The Smith nodded mutely, suddenly unsure of himself.

"What do you know of the world outside of your village?" Asked the Conjurer, as his bright eyes once more fastened on the Smith.

Startled the Smith answered. "There is little to tell. We are isolated here from the nearest village by miles of trackless forest. The only news that we do get is from such traveling bands as the Gypsies or the vagabonds who occasionally wander into our village half starved and more then a little crazed. There is no way of knowing the truth of what is said." A far away look came into the Smith's eyes. "Even so, I love to listen. To try and imagine those places." Sighing, his eyes came back to the here and now, to focus on the face of the Conjurer. "Still such things are not important to our people. We live our own lives without the influence of the outside world and are happy in doing so."

Patience was never one of the Conjurer's strong points and it had grown less so over the years. Angrily, he said, "Have you nothing behind your eyes but rocks, boy? Do not the stories you hear, tell of wars that ravaged the lands and of awesome Magic that shook the world? Do you not wonder boy, why no one has sought out your puny little village and laid it to ruins, like so many others?"

The Conjurer was now so worked up that flames jumped two inches from the barrel of his pipe. "Have you not heard the legends of the Old Ones and how they came to pass from this mortal plane, leaving chaos to rule the land? It has been many years granted, since the Great Wars, of which our world was only one small part. Many of the scars on our land have healed, but underneath there lies, festering like an open wound, the darkness of evil. An evil so strong that the knowledge of it would wither your bones. It sleeps for the moment but soon it will wake again to rule the lands. When it does, then I think, Smith that you and your village will be no more."

The Trumpet of Harmony

A flash of colored light leapt from the Conjurer's pipe and formed a beautiful smoke ring that floated away on the soft evening breeze. "Still, these histories may have little to do with you and your present desires. What I need from you is difficult enough. Although with courage and a stout arm you may succeed."

"There are within this forest and the lands surrounding it, four very special plants. Each, is the only one of its kind and has grown for generations uncounted. Drawing nourishment from the very soul of our land, they have stored up incredible amounts of power." The old one's eyes glittered. "There is a time, once in every thousand years, in which they bloom. The blossom is the focal point for all of the power that each has held and built during those years."

"Beware! Heed me well, Smith. It is important to gather all the powers together, for only when each of the four stand assembled may the power they possess be used only for good. Without the other three, each becomes a symbol that could be turned to terrible evil. Together they have the power to change the course of our world's destiny."

The Conjurer glanced at the Smith and wondered if so young a man could succeed in so vital a quest. Yet destiny had pushed this young, stripling into this course of action and only the fates could say if he would triumph. "You Smith, must quest for these blossoms and return them to me. Each in perfect detail, not a petal out of place, mind you. Your road will be difficult and you will find much danger along the way. Yet you may find happiness also. At any rate, you will get to see the many places that you have tried to envision and some that you'll wish that you could forget!"

The Conjurer paused and took a pensive puff of his pipe. "The flowers are different in nature," he continued. "The first is in the shape of a trumpet. Its cloak is royal purple. The trumpet has a voice that is clear and clean as the morning air after a spring rain. The second is a sunflower." He smiled wryly. "But with a difference. The third is a flower of crystal, whose form is so delicate that it is impossible to touch, lest it crumble."

The Trumpet of Harmony

At this the Smith started to protest, but the Conjurer hurried on. "Last of all, but perhaps the most spectacular of all, is the flower of knowledge, from which all things magical and mundane flow."

"These you must bring to me in payment for your answer. Search your heart carefully my son, it is a heavy burden that will be laid upon you and it is one that you might not live through." If the note of warning surprised the Smith, he did not show it. "In any event, your life will never be the same again," intoned the Conjurer, solemnly.

The minutes dragged by as the Smith wandered in thought. Two days ago the things that the Conjurer asked would have made him laugh. All the more sure that the old man, was insane. That was before Rosita, before he had experienced that strange half waking vision in the Gypsy camp.

The Smith thought about his life in the village. He had become a part of the backdrop against which the people in the village had played out their lives. He could see himself many years from now behind the bellows of his smithy doing the same sort of work that he had already been doing for a decade. The vision frightened him. Yet here was the Conjurer offering him an outlet for his adventurous spirit and perhaps a chance at something more.

The Smith thought about various legends of gallantry performed by brave men for their ladies' fair. He laughed, surely finding a few rare flowers and returning them to the Conjurer, was less dangerous then fighting giant trolls or dueling with an evil wizard. He knew, of course, that all such things were just a matter of legends and that this quest was going to be real. Yet the spell of adventure and romance were strong. He knew that he would accept the Conjurer's terms.

Throwing caution away, he straightened his back, squared his shoulders and looked the old man in the eye. "I do not know why you ask me to do these things, but I do know that I must find a key to the chain which holds my life and my heart prisoner." Taking a deep breath he plunged on in a rush of words. "I will do as you ask Conjurer. Now answer my question.

The Trumpet of Harmony

Show me the way to my heart's desire."

The Conjurer's face broke into a regretful smile and as if to himself, he said, "So it begins at last!" Then he spoke clearly, with a ring of true power in his voice. "Hear thy doom, Smith. To find your heart's desire you must learn Rosita's Soul Name and what her hidden talent might be. Further you must learn that talent and join her freely without remorse, in the practice of it. Also at a time of great peril, you must use your own talents and in doing so reveal your Soul Name to her."

The colored light flared all around the tree. Throwing the midday shadows at the base of the tree into a star like brilliance. Then the light died altogether leaving the area in deep shadow. From the dimness the Conjurer's voice came one last time.

"Now you must leave. Rosita is waiting for you. Take the road south into the forest and beyond, to search for the Flower Trumpet of Harmony. From there use your heart to guide your path and fate will point the way."

In the silence that followed there was the sound of an opening door and the sharp clank of a falling lock. The Smith was alone, stricken by the words of the Conjurer. How could he, a Nameless person, give a Soul Name, no matter how desperately he wanted to?

Turning away from the silent door of the Conjurer, the Smith walked the lane back to the path. His mind was filled with the Conjurer's words. He had accepted the quest to locate the flowers of power, but he could not be happy with the answer that the price had given him. He could not really have said what he had expected from the Conjurer. Perhaps some clever words that would have magically brought Rosita into his arms and fulfilled his every dream. Certainly, he did not expect the grim words and hinted warnings that the Conjurer had supplied.

Magic! That was the key. There was so very little of it spread through out the land. Powers tended to vary and it was an oddity that his village could boast of two workers of magic wonder. Of course, his own power was that of working metals. He could mold them into whatever shape and strength required for each task. Yet there were limits to his powers. He could not change one metal into another nor could he change their basic properties. The people of his village had come to take his work as easily as that of any common farmer. He was grateful that it remained so, for even a man of magic could be murdered if his assailant thought to gain by stealing his treasures.

The Conjurer was a different sort. He would weave small spells for the locals in exchange for food and occasional casual labor. He never seemed to change, he always appeared to be ancient. Normally he never said much, but he seemed to know the small goings on in the village. Still it was odd that a worker of small charms would be interested in four symbols of awesome power.

To the Smith's mind there was more to the Conjurer's request then met the eye. But such thoughts were wiped from his mind as he came up to the main path. There sitting with her knees drawn up tightly to her chest was Rosita. Her long dark hair concealed her face from the Smith but in the quiet of the early afternoon he could hear the racking sounds of her sobbing crys.

The Smith, stood silently in the center of the Conjurer's lane for a few moments and then quietly walked up to where Rosita was sitting. Carefully he knelt next to the Gypsy girl and gently brushed her hair from her face. He felt strange as Rosita turned, her tear streaked cheeks, blushing bright red.

Rosita, angrily pushed the Smith's hand away from her face. Coming to her feet, she wiped the tears from her eyes and looked down at the kneeling Smith. "I do not know how our destiny's have become entangled, Smith. I do know that I've lost the only family that I have ever known and now, because of a whim of the Gods I have become entangled with a clumsy village oaf."

The Trumpet of Harmony

The Smith got slowly to his feet, never taking his eyes away from those of Rosita's. After a few moments he turned away from her and looked back down the path to his village. He was at a loss, words of comfort rose to his lips but died there before he could give them voice. He felt pity for the young Gypsy woman, until he remembered the cold reflection from the edge of her knife as it flashed in front of his face.

Uncomfortable and thinking about the road ahead, he turned back to Rosita. "I am sorry that you have lost your family, Rosita. I would have never come to your camp last night, if I had known what that visit might bring."

The Smith smiled ruefully and continued. "But, I too have lost a family this day. The only family that I have ever known, my village. I have agreed to a dangerous quest from which I might not return. You see Rosita, my question had a very high price and now I must pay for the foolishness of my heart."

Rosita stood listening to the Smith. The anger that had taken hold of her heart eased as she thought over his words. She was Rosita and she was free. Freer then ever she had been during her short life. She could turn on her heels right now and dive into the forest, leaving the Smith staring at empty air. Yet she had become intrigued by the words of the Conjurer. After all one did not spit lightly into the face of the Gods.

An awkward silence filled the space between them and the early afternoon sun beat warmly on their faces. Rosita broke the stalemate by bending down and grabbing her pack from the side of the path. "It seems, Sir Smith that we must travel together for a space, but remember these words. I am my own person and only I can decide what is best for me. If you should turn and find me gone one day do not be surprised."

The Smith in turn settled his pack on his shoulders and said, "Well enough. For now we head south. I seek a symbol of power and it lays to the south." Turning back down the southern path, the Smith walked away, with Rosita by his side.

CHAPTER SIX

Quickly the Smith and Rosita covered the distance back to the glade where the Gypsy's had camped. Here they decided to take to the trees for a few miles. Walking alongside the path, just in case the recent activities around the camp had drawn any of the forest's hunters.

Shouldering their burdens and with an excited smile for each other, they headed down to the southern edge of the dell and the waiting forest. Pausing for a last sight of clear sky, Rosita said, "We will cross into the trees here and move through the thinner stands. Soon we must angle to the left and rejoin the road south."

"This forest is many days travel in width and becomes thick, almost impenetrable the further south we go. The southern track is the only one known and where it ends is only a vague memory in the knowledge of my people. Yet we must use it while we can."

As they moved swiftly through the trees, Rosita walked next to Smith keeping the pace easily and talked of her knowledge of the trail ahead. "My Tribe, only traveled a dozen leagues in this direction. Yet, I've heard stories that tell of distances far beyond that. Those tales also speak of nameless horrors and death."

She looked up sheepishly at the Smith and explained. "Late one night when the moon had set, I overheard the elders talking in hushed voices. They thought that everyone was asleep, but my hearing is sharper then most and I sleep lightly during the night. So it was, that when my father started to speak, I listened. He spoke of the wanderings of his youth and how he came to a place as still as death where not even the plants would live. In that place he found an ancient village in whose bones, horrible things stalked. He said it was a place of the old ones." As she said it her eyes grew round.

The Smith had seen a few odd pieces of metal that the old ones had shaped. Those legendary giants who had once walked the land and who had dared to touch the stars. They had been swallowed up when the world was torn, so the legends said. He grew excited, soon they might see more substantial proof that they truly had existed.

The sun was setting when at last they rejoined the road. By mutual agreement they had spent more time traveling the forest then need be, so that anyone that might pass on the road would not connect them with the gypsy camp. Scouting a few yards into the trees along the side of the road, they found a glade. It was not visible from the road and had a small stream running through one end.

Its grasses filled the late afternoon with a sweet wholesome scent and the flowers which grew amongst them sent a perfume of their own into the air. The Smith was well pleased. After the initial feeling of loss, he forgot to think of his little village and enjoyed the thrill that his sense of adventure had brought him. His smile reached out to include his unlikely traveling companion. "A pleasant place, Lady, in which to spend the night."

Rosita looked sharply up at the Smith, ready to regale him for lack of caution, when she noticed how closely he was scrutinizing their surroundings. With some respect in her voice she said, "It is pretty and I can not scent danger on the breeze, only the sweet smell of peace."

They followed the edge of the glade, not yet wishing to expose themselves to the open. When they reached the line of trees overhanging the stream, they found a grassy bank under their shadows. The rounded shoulder of the bank ran steeply down to the stream, where the water flattened out over a gravel shoal.

Behind the shallow, the stream backed up, the waters forming a deep, quiet pool. Around the rocky point of the shoal the pent-up waters found their release in a noisy swift, flowing freshet that babbled merrily into the late afternoon sun.

The long rays of sunlight caught in Rosita's dark tresses, turning her hair into sparkling obsidian. Her eyes flashed with a hidden fire and for the first time since the Smith had known her, her full lips relaxed into a warm smile.

"It may be long before I have the pleasure of being truly clean again." She pursed her lips in thought. "When first we met, Sir Smith, I thought of you as a gullible bumpkin, one who the family would use and leave behind." Pausing she looked at the Smith and tried to gauge his reaction to her words. Pleased by his attentive pose, she went on. "Now it seems, that for a short space at least, our lives are running together." She smiled briefly at his happy grin. "I would therefore ask you to give me some privacy. I entrust myself to your vigilance, the protection of my physical self as well as my honor."

A heated blush swept over the Smith's face. He nodded and hastily moved away from the stream and entered the clearing. He was delighted by Rosita's overture of companionship and angered at his boyish reaction to her simple request.

He was suspicious of Rosita's reasons for offering to continue on the road with him. He had a notion that if blows were ever struck on this quest, that it would be Rosita who would be doing the rescuing. It would be his life if not his honor that would be saved.

As a distraction, he sought kindling for their evening camp fire. While picking up the small pieces of dried wood, the Smith thought about the girl and his rather mixed feelings about her. It seemed strange to him that he could feel passion under the surface of his bantering conversation with her. The Conjurer must have known something, because he had used the Smith's feelings as a lever to make him agree to the Quest.

The Smith shrugged his shoulders, only time would tell, he thought to himself. Still they were beginning to feel comfortable with each other and there was a certain sense of companionship in their sharing this adventure. This seemed to satisfy him. Suddenly he found himself hoping that this would be a long quest indeed.

The Trumpet of Harmony

He started a cheery little fire and placed the camp pot over it, braced on two stout sticks. Looking around he spied some fair sized rocks, which he dragged over to the fire to serve as camp chairs. The late afternoon sun was quickly giving way to the evenings shadows when he began to wonder about the girl again. He let the image of her face drift into his minds eye. She could be considered beautiful, he admitted. If she would only let her mouth settle into one of her rare smiles instead of that disapproving frown she wore all too often. Yet there was that fire in her eyes which had first drawn him to her. The appeal of her independent nature which, although galling at times, was fast becoming an endearing quality to him.

His reverie was broken by the sound of singing. It was Rosita's voice coming from the stream and the words were none that the Smith had ever heard before. He could not make them out as they rose and fell, with a strange melodic rhythm, but the song soon formed visions in his mind. As he paid closer attention to them, the images became clearer.

The Smith could sense himself running through the forest. The sights, smells and sounds of the wood a euphoric to his senses. He was powerful, swift and free, daring any to challenge him and knowing that none could.

He could not say how long he wandered those paths but as the song faded out of his mind, the Smith was left with a feeling of wonder and delight. With a start, he came to his senses. Looking quickly around, he noted nothing amiss. Feeling guilt at his lack of vigilance, he threw some more wood onto the fire and braced himself against another lapse in his vigilance.

Deep shadows had gathered, the light of the fire glowed softly on his face. The strange song had ended some time ago and he was getting anxious. Wondering if he should go and see to the girl's safety. He was startled by the sound of a contented sigh. Even though he had listened for some sign of the girl, she had come up to him without any sound at all.

Rosita looked up into the evening sky and sighed once again. She felt wonderfully clean and was at peace with the world. Pulling herself back from her study of those distant points of light, she looked down and smiled at the expression on the Smith's face. "I sometimes move very quietly, Sir Smith, when I do not wish to disturb the evening's silence."

Taking some branches from the stack that lay by the fire, she quickly sharpened one end of each with her dagger and then planted them firmly in the grass, up wind of the fire. She then put the clothes that she had rinsed by the stream carefully over the branches. "There! They should dry over night and be ready for packing in the morning."

Clearing his throat, the Smith suddenly felt a little musty himself. Seeing that Rosita was comfortably seated by the fire and throwing a fresh faggot onto the blaze, he said, "If you feel safe enough by the fire, Rosita, I would also like to clean off the day's travel before I sleep tonight."

Rosita was startled for a moment and then smiled warmly at the Smith. "Certainly, Sir Smith, be sure that I am safe by the cheery glow of your fire. I will yell out and speedily, should danger threaten."

A tiny thrill ran down his spine with the warmth in her words. Smiling he grabbed a spare set of clothing from his pack and hurried off to the waiting sound of the rushing streamlet.

Reaching its banks, the Smith gazed out in wonder, the moon had risen, giving a bright glow, which illuminated the water's surface. Cool light reflected from its ripples. He would be bathing in a molten pool of pale light. He removed his soiled clothing. Slipping quietly into the deep pool he ducked his head under its surface letting his long hair flow freely in it's substance. He could wish for some sweet sand or soap leaf but made do with the clear water that nature had provided.

Having soaked for as long he dared, he gave his travel stained clothing a brief but energetic scrubbing. Satisfied that he had them as clean as possible he left the silvery pool and was drying himself briskly when he spied a pair of golden eyes.

The Trumpet of Harmony

They stared at him steadily from the opposite bank of the stream. Whatever the beast was, it must have stood waist high and watched him without moving. Slowly reaching down, the Smith gathered up his clothing and began to back away from the stream. The eyes did not follow. Just as he reached the screen of brush at the edge of the glade, the light from the eyes blinked out. Anxiously he listened for the sound of splashing water, telling him the beast had crossed the stream. The night remained still. For a few moments more he waited and then he quickly dressed.

The Smith turned back into the glade, the dim glow of the camp fire a welcoming beacon. Soon he was within it's light. Rosita had wrapped herself in her camp blanket and sat huddled in the gentle warmth. Debating with himself, the Smith was unsure if he should scare the girl with the tale of what he had seen. Yet, she had much more experience in the wilds then he. Perhaps she might be able to place a name on what he had just witnessed.

Rosita smiled at him as he had come into the light, but her smile faded at his worried look.

"Rosita, it may only have been a trick of moonlight and night shadows, but a few moments ago I thought that I saw two large golden eyes watching me from across the stream. If their height above the bank were any sign of the owner's size then it must have stood belt high, at the least. As I moved away the eyes disappeared. I listened for any noise of its crossing, but there was no sound of it's passage through the stream."

He looked down at her and wondered just how foolish he appeared. Talking of strange things in the night and holding his cleansed clothing carelessly in his arms. "Have you, in your travels seen or heard of such a beast and if so, are we in danger?"

Rosita remained silent for long minutes, the fire crackling in the stillness. When she spoke at last, the hesitation in her voice betrayed her troubled mind. "There is much in our two worlds that is different, Smith. Much of it difficult for you to understand. Yet, now I must tell you of one such difference and hope to have your belief and not scorn."

Pausing for a moment, she gazed into the fire. "I was considered special within the family, set apart and it was for this reason. Sometime in my early childhood, a great beast of the forest came upon me alone. I had been picking the berries of autumn and had wandered from the sight and sounds of the camp. I was very frightened, yet the creature made no move to harm me. Instead, I heard a voice, the words forming in my mind. It bade me to be unafraid and spoke of many things strange and wonderful."

This is what the voice said. "I will guard you and your's day and night, for you are one foreordained for greatness in our world."

"Having made such a cryptic remark the wolf, for wolf it was, sat on its haunches and watched my look of astonishment. It then melted back into the forest. Needless to say, I ran as fast as my young legs could carry me, back to the camp. I went straight to my father and spoke of what I had seen and heard. He did not laugh but looked at me with tears in his eyes."

The light of the fire had dimmed, hiding her downcast face. The Smith reached out and threw another faggot onto the embers.

Rosita turned her face away and continued. "From that point on my life changed. I was not treated as the other girls of the tribe, but was accorded the freedoms that would be given to any lad. My father began to take me with him as we entered each new village and each night's camp. He asked me how things felt to me and I was able to sense things. Several times warning him of danger."

She looked at the Smith, her eyes filled with tears. "Do not laugh Smith nor doubt my words. Until I reached early womanhood, the same beast has appeared to me three times. Each time with a warning of a trap set to snare my family that would have killed them or worse. For that I am grateful, yet it has been years since the beast has appeared and during that time I have learned to rely on my own abilities to safeguard my clan. I wonder greatly at its presence now."

The Smith, now harkened back to last night, Rosita's half-sister had said that Rosita was one set apart. Kathia had also made Rosita's importance to the family known to him, now he understood why. Looking compassionately at Rosita he said. "Then we are safe from the beast but not from what it portends?"

Rosita nodded and he continued, "I'd feel better if we took turns at standing watch tonight and when tomorrow comes, putting as many miles between us and our evening camp as may be."

After Rosita settled down to sleep as best she could, he stood guard, his thoughts filled with her.

CHAPTER SEVEN

During the days that followed, the Smith grew to respect the travel wise opinion of his companion. When at first, she took the lead in their trek, he felt ill at ease. He harbored a feeling that he, the strong man, should protect her, the weaker appearing female. He realized quickly that his fears were misplaced. Even as he gained insight into the ways of the wild, she saved him time and again from painful, if not deadly missteps.

He learned to observe his entire surroundings, not just sight but sound and smell as well. Slowly nature's patterns began to surface and like a child whose eyes light with excitement when at first they understand, the Smith took delight in the simple knowledge of the forest.

It was nearing the end of their sixth day, when the nature of the land changed. The rich greens and browns of the forest giants thinned. In place of their pillars, a pallid twisted growth appeared. Leaves of sickly yellow clad their scrawny branches. The air, which had been filled with the noisy twitter of birds and the secretive sounds of small animals, fell silent. The stillness quickly became oppressive. The Smith swore that the sound of his own beating heart could be heard quite clearly. Their breathing, was a harsh rasping in the silence.

The very ground had begun to change, from the rich dark humus of the forest floor, to a grey dust which ground under their feet. Their shoes became small mill wheels grinding with each step they took.

Rosita paused in their advance, her nose tilted into the air, nostrils flaring. A look of distaste and uncertainty flashed across her face. "I do not like this! I will not camp in such a place!"

The Smith turned back to face the way that they had come and in the late afternoon light saw the healthy green of the forest. "I too, will not willingly rest in such a place. We will backtrack into the true forest's cover and find a friendly camping site."

The Trumpet of Harmony

He paused and surveyed the way south. "I want a full day's light to travel this path." Quickly, for the light was fading, they turned away from the path ahead and marched back to the edge of the forest.

Darkness had nearly overtaken them, when Rosita led them into a small, sheltered dell. A fresh spring bubbled out of a rocky basin along its one wall. As they joyfully slid their packs off their aching shoulders the Smith reflected on the terrain ahead and their limited provisions.

"Did your family ever come this far south, Rosita?"

Rosita paused in the opening of her pack. "No Smith, it has been three days travel since we left the lands known to my family." Sitting down on the thick grass of the dell, she continued. "Do you recall that conversation I overheard? My father spoke of the road south, of the ruins of the old ones and the horror of its memory. It is for this reason, I believe, he ever guided the family away to safer parts."

She began to unpack the rations from their bags. Holding the packets, she hesitated and then slid hers back into her pack.

"I do not recall, my father speaking of the land ahead in any detail. It may well be many days before we can forage for food. Also, I feel that we should fill what empty skins we have at this spring. I do not trust the scent, blowing over that waste, but there is no moisture in it that I can sense."

The Smith nodded in agreement. Once more counting himself lucky to have such a canny companion. Yet a disturbing thought crossed his mind. "Why should we venture through the desolation at all? If we follow the forests edge surely we would come upon another way to the south?"

Rosita pursed her lips thoughtfully and said, "What you say is true and would not faze me at all. Yet consider, we have no way of knowing how many miles travel would be lost in such a search." She looked directly at the Smith. "Recall to mind the reason for our presence here, Smith. You are under the burden of searching out the blossoms of four great powers. The only direction that you've been given is that the first such flower lays to the south. How do we know, that out there in that arid waste, the Flower of Harmony doesn't wait for us? Dare we take the chance of missing it? The road south plainly goes through the wasteland. You must follow or risk the failure of your quest."

A surge of scarlet heat burned his cheeks, but he answered her coolly and with truthfulness. "What you say bears thought. I have no loyalty to the Conjurer and his plots." His face hardened, "Yet, if a man's word is not of worth, then he is unfit for living among his fellow men and none would trust him henceforth."

Softening, he said. "If I must endure the dangers of the road ahead, you do not. I have come to know you, a little over these last days. You certainly would survive in the wild." He smiled at her ruefully. "In fact, you would manage much better so without me."

She smiled back up at him from the warming fire. "As I have told you, Smith, I will pick the hour of our parting." Her face set once more with determination, she motioned him to sit by her at the fireside. "Now be quiet long enough to eat your meal. I will take the first watch. I sleep better at the turning of the night."

Slowly, with relish, they enjoyed their meager meal. The evening shadows gave way to night's dark cloak and only the cheery crackle of their camp fire broke the stillness of the night. When his eyes became too heavy to remain open, he bade Rosita a good watch and pulled his blanket up around his chin. He was soon asleep.

The early part of the night had dragged into the midnight region. Rosita had been alert, all of her senses reaching out to touch her surroundings. Everything was as still as death, even though they were not in the grey waste which lay close by. It was uncanny. Wishing that she dared change into her Were form, she sighed. It was time to wake the Smith.

The Trumpet of Harmony

Turning away from the mysterious dark, she turned back to the huddled form of the Smith. Shaking his shoulder and stepping back she waited for him to become alert.

As he came groggily awake, Rosita's voice filled his ears. "Come now Smith, the night's tide has turned and morning begins." She paused starring out into the darkness and then said in a quiet voice, "Even though it is only we two who greet her."

As he sat up stretching mightily, Rosita settled down into her camp blanket. "All is quiet, the forest is silent for miles around. Even though such is not natural, I see no need to be fearful. The birds and the beasts are wise. I know that I would not live near that grey waste, would you? Well good morrow Smith wake me at the dawning." So, saying she rolled away with her back to the fire. Her breathing slowed and its rhythmic sound told the Smith that she slept deeply.

The silence of the night had at first unnerved him. All that Rosita had taught him, calling for an awareness of the natural order of the forest was here now, in violation. It was several hours before the silence became background and he found himself nodding to sleep. Starting from one such doze his bleary eyes caught the glimmer of a faint light away south, into the waste.

Coming fully awake, he stood rubbing his eyes. The glow did not depart and after a few moments seemed to be brightening. He turned to see if Rosita stirred but all was still by the fire. Turning back to the south he saw that the light had become a brilliant luminescence. A yellowish haze had filled all the southern horizon. Even as he watched the light dimmed and then brightened again. Soon the pulsations fell into a steady pattern of light and shadow.

Watching intently, the Smith did not notice his head slightly bobbing up and down, in time with the rhythmic lights. A heaviness fell over him and just as he felt himself slide into unconsciousness, a surge of panic fought against the insistent message of the lights. It failed. He slept as he stood

The Trumpet of Harmony

and as he slept strange visions of the distant past played in his dreams.

CHAPTER EIGHT

The tension of the past weeks, eased. Muscles that had been knotted, released for the first time in days. This trip into the National Forest with his wife and son had been just the ticket. Even though the forest's edge was only a few miles from the outskirts of town, it had been enough to get away from the pressures of the lab.

They had found a sheltered dale a little way off one of the marked forest trails. There was a clear spring that bubbled merrily out of one rock wall and into a natural stone basin. The soft shadows cast by the dell's rounded shoulders eased the heat from the noonday sun.

While his wife had busied herself with the task of setting up their small camp for the night, he spent some time chasing his small son around the grassy lawn of the dale. After a few minutes, they fell into a laughing heap near the basin's edge and his wife joined them. He spent the next half of an hour lecturing them on the natural geological formation in which they found themselves. Pausing after a time, he looked only to find his wife and son had fallen deeply asleep. Laughing at himself, he shrugged and settled down to join them.

It was early evening when they awoke. They set about making an evening meal and putting the finishing touches on the camp. It had felt good to laugh and romp with his family again. He had been spending so much time in the lab, working under the pressures of impossible deadlines, that he had little time to be with them.

The evening had just turned into night when the first sign of the ensuing doomsday presented itself. There came the sound of loud sonic booms, as fast moving rocket planes broke into the upper atmosphere. The shrill whine of displaced air caused them to cover their ears.

Throwing his wife and son down onto the soft turf of the dell floor, he screamed for them to cover their eyes and to stay down no matter what happened.

The Trumpet of Harmony

They did not have long to wait. A brilliant light flared about them, blinding him through his closed eyes. A massive roar reached their ears, deafening them and a scalding wind screamed over the dell's lip. He felt, rather then heard the racking cries of his young son. Reaching out with his free hand he cradled the boy's small frame to his side. A series of secondary explosions followed but no more atomics were detonated.

The winds died along with the fission light. For a long time, they lay there shivering in reaction. Then slowly, in a daze, they got to their feet. Taking his wife in his arms he held her close. The pain of his returning senses paled in the light of the love that he felt for her.

As sanity returned to him, he wondered at the lack of fire power brought to bear by their attackers. The complex had been on alert for days. There would be whole families nestled in the safety of the deep underground shelters. The labs themselves which were also hidden in deep caverns, would surely not have been damaged in that one blast.

Holding his wife out at arms length he looked into her tear-filled eyes. Often in the past few days they had spoken of just such a disaster. He had insisted that if fortune did indeed smile and they lived, that she take their son to the safety of her parent's home. They lived in quaint little village a hundred miles to the north. There they would be as safe as anyone could be in these troubled times.

He could not go with them. The best that he would promise was to follow if he could. He had to reach his lab to destroy the work and records there. Parting was painful, tearing at his soul. Sadly, he turned away, losing sight of the ones he loved as he crossed the lip of the dell.

The journey back to the lab was one filled with horror. Parts of the small town which had grown up around the lab, were burning. Parts were unrecognizable under the steam of glassy slag. He knew that deadly radiation was being given off by those pools of liquid stone. Death already stalked his veins, yet he could not stop.

The Trumpet of Harmony

Judging by the damage done, he thought that the main blast had been targeted only for the military defense sites located a few miles to the west of the town. The area was damaged, but most of the research facilities would have survived. He felt sure that an invasion was planned as a follow up to the attack and that those would be the targets.

The work that he did was not meant as weapons research, but to improve the human condition. By genetically altering the structure of DNA in man, certain diseases could be completely eliminated. Powers of the mind, which had been locked away by nature, could be opened to expand man's horizons in directions not even dreamed of before. Even the physical form of future generations could be modified to fit any environment. The implications for space travel and colonization were mind boggling.

At the moment though, all that he could think of was the destruction of such reports and records that he could reach. The fumes of hot metal and burning wood, stripped his throat of its moisture. His eyes burned in the hot breeze, blurring his vision. He stumbled down the street that led to the lab's entrance. The smoke was now so thick it was like walking in a dense fog.

He had seen no one. The air was ominously still. He thought that there should have been someone. There should have been an effort at emergency rescue for those who may have been trapped in some of the collapsed buildings. Still nothing disturbed the morbid scene around him.

It was only a few hundred feet from the labs access door, when disaster overtook him. From out of the fog came the muffled sound of whining servomotors. He instinctively ducked behind the wall of a nearby building, but it was already too late. The infrared eyes of the robot drone had already picked up his body heat from the surrounding radiation. Sensitive audio pickups had tuned into the sounds of his breathing and rapid heartbeat.

Crouched down, he looked around the corner of the wall just in time to see the heavy, armored vehicle roll into view. He turned to run but a blast of ultrasonic sound rocked him and the sting of an electroshock, taser gun

stunned him senseless. His last thoughts as he slid into unconsciousness
were of his wife and infant son.

A flat metallic taste gagged the Smith. Coughing furiously, he came to his
senses. The cool dell was gone and in its place, he found himself in a
world of shadowy grays, with half guessed at shapes concealed within its
cloak. He lay as he must have fallen, on his side, with his arms
outstretched before him. The coughing fit came again, racking his body
with pain. Forcing himself into a sitting position, he struggled to ease the
ache in his chest. Wincing at the lancing pain in his head, he succeeded at
last. He sat motionless trying to collect his thoughts and to calm the panic
he felt boiling up inside of him.

Try as he might, the Smith could not remember how he had gotten into
this coiling darkness. Dimly he recalled watching the strange light, flashing
over the waste land to the south. He could again sense the strange rhythm
in the pulses and something within him responded, clearing his mind
somewhat.

He could now recall, how his head had bobbed, following the rhythm of
those flashes. He remembered, how his eyes had slowly closed and dimly
the sense of someone's hand touching his shoulder gently at first then with
the grip of panic. There had been a torrent of shouted words, that had
roared into his ears. Most of all he remembered a surge of hot anger. It
seemed as if his thoughts and actions were someone else's. That the things
that happened to him were surrealistic. He could clearly, painfully
remember that he had turned and with thoughtless strength lashed out at
his companion. In his mind's eye he watched as the helpless form of
Rosita flew violently back with the blow, to fall senseless and unmoving to
the ground.

The remainder of his memories were a blur, except perhaps for the brief
echo of a dream which brought with it the momentary glimpse of the face
of a desperate man, haunted with fear and remorse.

The Trumpet of Harmony

A tremendous wave of guilt threatened to upset his reason. If he had killed the girl, but no, she was rugged, surely, she would have survived. The Smith had never felt anything like the hot rage that had coursed through him. Surely there had been times that he felt irritation even anger at Rosita's cavalier treatment of him, but they had become friends while on the road and the Smith could even have wished for a deeper relationship. How could it have been, then that he could wantonly strike out at some one that he had chosen to care for?

A sense of helpless panic ensued as he realized what must have happened. He had been controlled! But by who and to what purpose? He had no conscious idea of how he had gotten here. Instinctively he knew that he should not remain where, whoever, or whatever expected him to be. He scrambled to his feet, glanced around and trotted off into the shadows on his left.

As he crept into the deeper shadows formed by an opening in the long grey wall that had been to his left, he felt the hair on the back of his neck rise. There was a strange tingling sensation running along his skin. It was, as if, he stood in the outer most portion of a fast-flowing stream. He could feel the current as it rushed on its way. That feeling of power carried with it the same rhythmic pulsing that the lights in the waste had carried.

Quickly the Smith stepped back away from that deadly stream. He would not be sucked in by it's currents to be propelled once again along its path. It was then, he realized, that he had gotten away just in time. Something or someone searched along a set path. The path that had lead him to this strange place. He turned and hastened down a corridor which opened up behind the shadows that had sheltered him. He would not chance capture by that strange power again.

It was an alien world in which he found himself. The floor was smooth and even. In the dim light, he could just make out a pattern of dark and light squares beneath his feet. The walls were smooth and straight, unbroken by seam or crack. The ceiling which was scant inches above his head, also displayed a pattern of oblong blocks interrupted now and again by strange translucent panels. He was startled, as he realized that the almost undetectable light which had allowed him even this stunted view of his surroundings came from those panels.

His soft tread echoed with a hollow sound off the nearby walls. Stopping, he listened closely but heard only the rasp of his own breath. Running his tongue over his parched lips, he tasted caked blood laying in their ridged cracks. Thirst, he could not remember drinking during his time of enthrallment. He knew that he must find water soon or parish.

Pushing on now, heedless of caution the Smith soon came to a break in the walls of the hallway down which he walked. A metal strip outlined a door to the right. It stood ajar and in the dim light he could see a thick layer of dust in the opening. Pushing gingerly on the panel he opened it just enough to admit his bulk. As he crossed the threshold a bright light sprang up around him. Frightened he quickly retreated to the corridor.

To his surprise, the light dimmed once again. All was still, nothing moved in response to the odd change in light patterns. Encouraged and driven now by his insatiable thirst, he edged into the fair-sized space beyond the door. The light sprang up once more but he ignored it and glanced quickly around. He viewed an empty room, layered in dust. There were more doors, one on each of the opposing walls.

The illumination came from the same type of panels that he had found out in the hallway. Satisfied that there was no immediate threat, he crossed quickly to the door opposite the hallway. It was closed and there was no visible handle with which to open it. Pushing gently, then forcefully with all of his strength the Smith failed to open his chosen target.

Relenting for the moment, he went to the other two doors in turn. Trying and failing at each, he was forced to admit defeat. Returning to the first door, his throat now an agony of fire, he leaned up against the wall adjacent to the stubborn portal. With a heavy sigh, he slid his back down along the wall and sat exhausted on the floor, with his head cradled in his hands.

The Trumpet of Harmony

A second later the Smith was startled by a soft sighing from the panel next to him. He scrambled to his feet and stared in amazement through the opening in front of him. The door which had blocked his best effort had disappeared. What all of his strength had failed to do was now accomplished by a means unknown to him.

He paused, strength had not succeeded, perhaps he could think this through. Pushing on the doors had proven fruitless. The other two doors had remained closed and even now stared stonily back at him. The only action uncommon to all spots was his leaning and then sliding down the wall.

With some puzzlement, he examined the wall next to the open doorway. There, barely visible, was a small panel with a slight protrusion angled down toward the floor. Carefully, he moved the lever toward the ceiling. Instantly, the door panel reappeared from a slot in the side of its frame and closed the opening.

With a childlike smile, he repeated this course of action several times, until the burning in his throat reminded him of his desperate need of water.

Satisfied that he had mastered the strange manner of the stubborn doors, he cautiously peered through the dark shadowing of the space beyond. Dimly, he could make out objects which seemed to line the room. Nothing stirred. Encouraged, he edged his way through the portal.

As it had been with the outer chamber, so it was with this inner room, light sprang up as he crossed the threshold. Scanning the room, he could see on the wall opposite from him, lined up in three orderly rows, two to a row, what appeared to be shelves. They were extended out from the wall. There was a thick mat laying on each, covered by a layer of cloth. On the wall adjoining these was a series of cabinets topped by a flat surface that looked like stone. Above this was another series of cabinets all with doors that were tightly closed. In the center of the room was a table whose top also appeared to be covered in stone. It was surrounded by a series of six chairs all closely drawn to the table.

The Trumpet of Harmony

His survey completed the Smith moved to the cupboards lining the wall. He could see now that the long counter surface was broken by a deep depression. At the edge of this hollow was a slender metal tube that somewhat resembled the bulky water pumps used in his village to draw water from the deep wells. The strange metal tube was flanked on either side by a knurled knob. The Smith tried gently then forcibly to turn these and was rewarded only by snapping them from their place on the counter.

It was then that he heard the sound of his salvation, the fall of a drop of liquid. He stared in frustration as another droplet of liquid formed at the mouth of the odd shaped, metal tube. Before he could move to intercept it, the drop had fallen, to land with a soft plopping noise in the depression beneath. Looking down into it, he discovered a small pool rimmed with white crystals. From this capture, a tiny trickle of moisture escaped to run down a dark irregular opening in the center of the hollow.

Greedily, the Smith dropped his cupped hands into that pool and drank deeply of its tepid substance. The water had a flat taste but served to slake his raging thirst. Satisfied for the moment he turned his attention to the cabinets above the counter.

He looked closely at the doors covering those cabinets, but could not discern any handles or even half seen switches with which to open them. Running his hand along the lower rim of one such door, he felt a depression which seemed to fit his probing finger tips perfectly.

Pulling outward, with his precarious hold, the panel moved slowly away from the frame which had held it. He heard a soft sighing sound and felt a stale puff of air against his face, as he pulled it away. A swirl of dust made him cough.

The dust settled quickly and the light from the room penetrated the opening allowing the Smith to see several objects. There were rounded oblong shapes with one or two squarish objects sprinkled amongst them.

The Trumpet of Harmony

Cautiously, the Smith pulled the objects out and placed them on the wide surface beneath the cupboards. The containers were made of metal, tarnished but for the most part in good condition.

In quick order, he went to each of the cupboards and removed their contents. For the most, they stood empty. One or two held some more of the metal containers, but most had nothing but musty piles of dust waiting for him.

Gathering all of his prizes together the Smith examined them closely. Apart from a seam which ran the entire way around the top and bottom of each, he could find nothing to suggest an opening. He then faced his next problem, how to get them open to see what waited inside? When he awoke, he had nothing on his person but his clothing. Apparently, he had lost his knife in his nightmarish march to this place.

He hesitated. Being skilled enough in Magic to work on pans and harness fittings did not mean that he could work on a metal that he had never seen before. Still, now that his thirst had been slaked somewhat he knew the beginnings of a gnawing hunger. This too needed to be eased before he tried to solve the puzzle of his prison. He could only hope that the contents of these metal vessels would hold the nourishment that he required.

He picked up each container in turn shaking it gently next to his ear. Some made no noise at all and these he laid to one side. Some sounded as if they had nothing solid in them, but were mostly liquid in nature. These too he laid to the side. Finally he picked one of medium size, to be the first that he would try to open.

The Smith glanced around the chamber and peered out through the door to that section of the outer chamber that he could see. All was quiet. Holding the container in front of him he cleared his mind. In his thoughts he pictured the container as it was and then slowly he imagined how it would appear as the seam around its top began to separate from the metal along its sides. Finally, he pictured the container as two pieces of metal.

The cylinder in one hand and a flat metal disk, that had been its top in the other.

Seconds dragged by but still he kept his concentration until at last the images in his mind remained stable and did not waiver. Opening his eyes slowly, he relaxed, breathing deeply. There, in his hands, were indeed the images of his mind.

Swiftly, for the effort that he had expended had made him ravenous, he dipped his hand into the container and pulled out some of the soft yellow wedges packed inside. They were coated with a sticky liquid which dripped down his fingers. Holding one of the wedges to his nose, the Smith sniffed at it. A fine fruity smell convinced him of his treasure. With delight, he consumed the morsel, licking his fingers with pleasure at the sweet taste of the liquid. Speedily he finished the contents of his find, even drinking the liquid that had remained behind in the container.

With hunger and thirst abated for the moment, he turned his mind to the practical side of his situation. He had no idea where he was or of how long he may have been gone from that peaceful, little dell. He did not even know if he truly wanted to return to that site. Afraid that he might be wrong and that Rosita had died from his blow. The Smith could not bring himself to believe that he had taken the life of someone that he had grown to care about.

Yet, there was hope. If there were the slightest chance that she lived, he would want to be there now to protect her and care for her. His decision made, he went to the shelf like beds which had lined the one wall and with a jerk ripped the cloth covering from the first.

Remarkably it came off whole without a tear. The material was strange to him. It did not feel like any cloth that he had ever seen before. It was soft, yet terribly strong. He shrugged his shoulders, it would do.

He laid the cloth out flat and then piled the containers that he had scavenged in its center. Pulling the corners together, he formed a bag of sorts that would allow him to carry the supplies that he would need to survive. Once more he drank from the captive water in the crystal rimmed pool, draining it. It would be a long time before it would fill again.

Shouldering his pack, he walked back out into the outer chamber. The need for haste was upon him, but he was curious as well. He walked over to the door on the right-hand wall and carefully inspected the surface of the wall next to it. Not surprisingly, he discovered the same type of lever that had allowed him access to the other chamber.

Pushing the lever down toward the floor, the door moved aside. Stepping on to the threshold, a brilliant light flared showing him the interior of a well tiled room. Lining one wall were ceramic devices that glowed white, on the other was a series of boxes that appeared to be metal. The room was small and although strange, did not seem to hold anything of interest to him.

Stepping back away from the threshold, the light dimmed once more. Now he crossed the outer chamber and stood in front of the final door. The same lever arrangement awaited him. Quickly, he moved the lever toward the floor. A whoosh of displaced air followed closely on the heels of his action and a stale musty scent reached his nose. Gagging, he put foot on the threshold. This time the brilliant light did not reveal a clean sterile scene of tile and ceramic but the horror of death.

Everywhere he turned the Smith was faced with the grisly remnants of a long past slaughter. Skeletal remains lay in every corner of the room, bits of mummified flesh and hair hung from them. By their size, he could tell that many of these had been children. He could stand no more. He stumbled out and away from the horror of that room, blindly he reached for the switch on the wall and mercifully the door slid closed once more.

Trembling, he reached the dim light of the outer corridor. The horror receded, leaving only the need for caution. Whatever was capable of such terror, although long past, might still haunt these hallways. Gaining strength, he continued down the corridor, away from his possible capture.

CHAPTER NINE

The exhaustion of their travels had taken its toll on Rosita and she was asleep almost as she settled into the blankets by the fire. She dreamed, as she often dreamed, of the forest and the freedom of the run. Yet in her dreams she began to feel uncomfortable, even fearful. Her dream form came to a patch of forest that her mind had never pictured before. In it was a forest pool choked with greedy plant growth, an oily scum covered what open surfaces that there were.

Even as she imagined herself, ready to turn and take to the woodland paths once more, something disturbed the surface of the mere and a soft plopping sound reached her ears. Hesitantly she approached its edge. The surface had cleared somewhat. A perfectly round opening lay there drawing her eye to what lay below. At first she could see nothing and had made up her mind to leave once more, when the water cleared and small images began to form.

She saw the familiar sights of her peoples' wagons, she watched as they rolled into the Smith's village. She glimpsed the Smith's face as he beheld her for the first time. Noting the look of shear surprise and then a questioning sense of wonder. Now the scenes changed showing her each step of her recent journey until at last she found herself looking back out of the water's mirrored surface.

As she looked down the image changed. The travel worn clothing disappeared to be replaced by the finest of fabrics. Her hair, which she had kept bound, changed to show clouds of soft midnight curls, in which diamonds were caught like the distant stars in the night's sky. Her face filled out and her skin softened with the glow of young womanhood. Eyes which had reflected the hardness of the world, grew wide and innocent.

The image of herself seemed to be sitting, as if at a table and was holding a bejeweled comb in her hand. She appeared distracted as if her attention was split from her present action by something in the room behind her. Indeed, she was moving her lips in a silent conversation.

Turning back from chastising her maid the Lady Rosita glanced back into the mirror, ready to smooth out any stray strands of hair. The image that she saw there froze her in horror. A forested background framed a pitiful, gaunt face. A face she could recognize as her own, in some bizarre way. She watched frozen on her padded chair as the image began to shimmer. Gross deformities appeared on its surface, as if some artist were struggling to mold clay into a different image. The transformation was complete and in the place where the image had stood, a wild wolf paced from side to side.

The Lady Rosita's throat worked spasmodically, trying to form a scream at the horror that she had witnessed. As the screech of shear denial reached her lips, the beast in the mirror raised its muzzle emitting a tortured howl.

Rosita's mind finally had stood all that it could bear. In a terrified instant she was wide awake, sitting up from the tangle of her camp blankets. A cold sweat springing from her shivering body. Gasping she tried to regain her breath and to slow the wild beating of her heart.

What had seemed so real and alien to her quickly faded as she regained her composure. She wondered now, in an objective way, what meaning was behind the vision in the night?

Glancing swiftly about, she became aware of her surroundings. Not too much time had passed since she had wished the Smith a good watch. She could see his tall form, as a darker blot against the dark night sky just on the other side of the fire ring. That darkness was short lived. Rosita was startled by a flash of light arising from the direction of the waste. The light pulsed in a rhythmic way that was at once alien yet somehow familiar.

Rising she crossed to where the Smith stood as still as death itself. Gently she reached out and touched his shoulder. His muscles were ridged under her hand and he did not respond to her touch. With some irritation, she shook him with increasing intensity speaking his name, demanding to know why he did not answer her. At last she was shouting in his ear, real fear running through her. She could dimly see his face in the dark, its expression was blank and his eyes never wavered from the pulsing light.

At last, the Smith moved. With startling speed he turned and struck her with his knotted fist. She was so surprised that even her enhanced reflexes could not save her. The last she saw before his crushing blow landed was the strange light reflected from the Smiths eyes giving them an evil glow of their own.

The heat of the midday sun beat down unmercifully through the open sky of the dell, illuminating the still form of Rosita laying face up in its path. With its heat she began to stir, at first unconsciously, then with returning awareness.

She could taste the saltiness of her own blood in her mouth. The pain that racked her body convinced her that she yet lived. Slowly, painfully she forced her leaden eyelids open and was immediately blinded by the harsh brilliance of the sunlight. Groaning she rocked her head away from that source of torment.

Closing her eyes again, she tried to recapture the memories of how she had come to this sad state. Cursing suddenly, as the image of the Smith returned to her, she remembered. He had, with one blow, nearly killed her.

Sitting upright, she fought against the nausea which that movement cost her. Carefully she opened her eyes once more, to stare at the now deserted dell. A quick glance at the sun told her that it was now mid-day. But noontide of what day she wondered?

Using what strength she had, she managed to pull herself up to stand shakily. Slowly she gained her balance and strength began to flow back into her. She smiled bitterly. Her mixed inheritance had made her more resilient then a normal person would be.

Now that she had gathered herself together, she lent her attention to her surroundings. Moving cautiously, she walked over to the long dead campfire and knelt, running her hands through the ash. A weak smile played over her lips as she touched a still warm ember hidden under that grey pile. So then, it was close to noon of the next day. Now she examined the rest of the camp. Noting the pile of camp blankets that she had abandoned after her startling vision in the night. Then, to her surprise, she discovered both travel packs laying where they had been carefully placed. The water skins, that they had filled, lay untouched beside them.

A sense of puzzlement began to lessen her anger. She knew that the Smith would not leave such behind if he were given a choice. Now at last she remembered the pulsing light filling the night sky and her last vision of the Smith's blank face, filled with eyes that glowed with the same evil light.

He had been possessed! She had often listened to her elders talk around the evening campfire. She could remember the wizened old crone, who served her people as Wise Woman, talk of possession. The taking of the unwary into thrall, so that all sense of their own being would be overwhelmed, leaving only the will of another to dictate what course of action would be taken.

The Smith had been snared. It was the only way that last night's actions made sense to her. She cursed him once more under her breath, for his naivety, yet still she felt a sense of relief.

Leaving the campsite, she crossed to where she had last seen the Smith. Scanning the humus on the dells floor she quickly picked up the trail of his passage. Rosita followed it for a short time, convinced now that he was headed straight for the edge of the waste. His track showed that he traveled at a run, with no care to his surroundings.

She hesitated, undecided as to her next course of action. So far she had ventured with the Smith as a lark and perhaps the need to be near someone that she did not fear, after the sting of her family's parting. Surely she had no other attachment to the man. Yet in her heart she knew that there was something there. She had felt it from that first day in the village.

Even as they traveled she had grown fond of the man and his gentle ways. Perhaps, then it was friendship, of which she had precious little in her young life. It did not matter what she chose to call it, she could not bring herself to abandon him, while he was in the power of someone or something unknown.

Her decision made, she now faced her next dilemma. The Smith had a good start on her, she doubted that he would stop for anything but shear exhaustion. So in her human form she could not hope to catch up with him. Also she would need all the wiles her other form had to offer to face the path ahead. She would go as Were, however she must also somehow carry food and water.

Rosita turned back to the camp. Kneeling next to the packs she emptied their contents onto the green grass. Examining the straps of each, she took out her dagger and with quick strokes cut the thongs. Just as quickly she measured the severed strands and then with swift motions retied them into longer lengths and fastened them back onto one of the packs. She repeated this with the water skins. One would be all that she could carry.

Rosita concentrated on the supplies that lay, spilled out in front of her. She picked out the yellow journey cakes, some of the healing herbs that she had garnered along the way and with a strange feeling of compulsion, the velvet covered chalice that belonged to the Smith.

Her choices made, she stripped her travel stained clothes from her body. Taking up the pack and water skin, she hung them loosely about her in such a way that they would be secured once her transformation was complete.

Now with the discipline of long use, Rosita cleared her mind and the formula of the Ritual of Transformation filled her being. The transformation began. Her mind, which floated free of her physical form, watched with mild interest. She had never found the change gross or frightening in any manner, yet she could not forget the revulsion felt by that dream image, the night before.

The Trumpet of Harmony

Discipline held and soon she was wholly Were. The scene around her had changed. Scents and sounds, which to her enhanced human form, had seemed dull became at once clear and sharp. With a parting glance at the camp she tensed her wiry muscles and sprang quickly out along the trail of the Smith.

CHAPTER TEN

The Smith's trail proved easy to follow, it led straight south. He had moved only to one side or the other as the terrain blocked his way, but he had always returned to the same course. The green forest soon gave way to the dusty grey of the waste. The trail became more difficult to follow but to Rosita's sharp senses the road was well marked.

It had been early afternoon when her chase began, the sun was riding high. The grey sands under her feet grew warm and then hot with the capture of its heat. The ground had remained flat with no hint of sheltering vegetation or shadowed hillock. Rosita paused for a moment to test the air, her paws danced with the heat. She had to find some shelter soon.

Scenting nothing but the aseptic heat, Rosita plunged on at a loping speed designed to cover ground without exhausting her. Surely the Smith, with the bulk he carried could not have managed the searing heat. Then she remembered that he had the advantage of the cool night's cover to make the distance.

Cursing him once more under her breath she ran on. In the distance she at last saw a break in the level plain over which she coursed. A wavering line of shallow hills peered over the horizon, tempting her on to greater efforts with the promise of its cooling shadows.

The afternoon dragged on, the sun made its way slowly down to the horizon and still she had not yet reached the promise of the distant hills. She paused once more, her tongue lolling from her foaming jaws. It had to be a trick. The very land about her was a lie!

Slowly now, with just her determination pushing her onward she continued to follow the trail of the Smith. Late afternoon came and went. The suns rays no longer held the potent heat of midday, although the sand still held the heat. Rosita grew encouraged, she would live to see the night!

The Trumpet of Harmony

Twilight reigned over the desolate plain, as she hobbled onward. Her paws were badly burned and a thirst raged through her, such as she had never known, but she lived. Her head was down as she now walked at a slow pace. Rosita felt a sudden chill fall across her shoulders. Looking up she found herself surrounded now with low laying hills whose shoulders had casted a chilling shadow. She had reached her phantom hills. She would laugh if her form would let her.

The Smith's trail now wound through the hills still heading in a southerly direction but with an occasionally turning which had almost thrown her off the scent. She paused to consider this new event. Each of the turnings had come while at the base of one of the larger hills. That would seem natural except it had gone straight over the top of higher ones before without the slightest hint of deflection.

She was tired. The heat had taken much more of her strength then she had guessed. She caught herself falling asleep where she stood. This would not do. True she could probably follow the Smith's trail in the darkness, but she mistrusted those odd turnings.

Rosita carefully looked around her for a place where she could rest and transform in safety. She needed to drink from the water skin which had sloshed teasingly at her side through the worst of the heat. To do so she would need her hands and in those moments she would be vulnerable.

Looking ahead she saw one of the larger hills. Again the trail turned away from its side. She considered the steep sloping sides of that mound and the advantages that its height would bring in surveying the surrounding area. There at its summit, she could not be attacked without warning. It would allow her time to return to her Were form, if needed, for a desperate defense. Every muscle screamed with pain as she climbed the nearest side of that steep mound. The last of her strength was exhausted as she reached its crest, to collapse in the shelter of a shallow depression which ringed its top.

Her breath came in tearing, racking gasps as she lay there. After a few minutes, the pain began to ease. She was grateful that no nasty surprises had awaited her in this sheltered hollow. It would have been a quick death, she would have not been able to raise a paw in her own defense.

True to the nature of her gift, her pain ebbed away quickly and she recovered enough to look with intelligence at her surroundings. She was laying in a shallow, bowl shaped depression that occupied the entire top of the steep hill which she had climbed. The expanse was unbroken except for a curiously shaped stone which reached up from the center of the hollow.

The block glowed dimly in the twilights gloom, as if it had captured the light of day only to give it back as the dark crept in. The light drew her eye. Quickly she looked away, the memory of the Smith fresh in her mind.

Still, she had not sensed any evil in that glow, or in the hill top itself. Instead she felt, more and more, a feeling of welcome. A wholesome strength, that promised warmth and protection from any evil that the coming night might bring.

Taking this feeling of well being as a sign that she would be safe, at least for the moment, Rosita began the ritual of transformation. Calming her mind, she once again pictured the travel stained, exhaustion pinched woman that she had become. The images flowed and melded until she held her human form steadily in her mind. She stood, her naked frame chilled by the dank evening air.

Rosita scanned the area, nothing moved. Shrugging the pack and the water skin from her aching shoulders, she brought the precious container of liquid to her cracked lips. The water was tepid and tasted faintly of the skin, but it eased the tortured burning of her throat. She stopped drinking long before she wished, knowing full well that it may be days before she could safely refill it again.

The Trumpet of Harmony

Shivering with the evenings chill and in reaction to her exhausting passage through the heated wastes, she pulled her light traveling cloak from the pack It had been her only indulgence to modesty and now it served as protection from the cold. Wrapping herself in its welcoming warmth she sat on the sloping hollow wall and considered the nature of the stone which stood only scant feet from her.

When that contemplation eased into sleep, she had no idea but she found herself starting, awake. Deep night had fallen about the hill top. She edged herself to the rim and peered out onto a sea of fog. She was on an island. Below her, grey-white billows swirled as if they had life of their own. Flashing throughout the fog were streaks of yellowish light that pulsed briefly and dimmed once more.

Now and again the sounds of tortured screams pierced the thick blanket. The horror of those voices made her blood run cold as they rose and fell below her. They had the sound of cornered prey whose screams fell away as their very life's blood fled from their bodies. The fog lapped hungrily at the sides of the hill, rising slowly even as she watched. Fear raced through her veins. Somehow, she knew that once that shroud had drawn over her huddled form, all that made her what she was would cease to be.

With an inevitability the fog crept on, swallowing the hillside, reaching for the lip of the hollow. The yellow flashes of light could be seen clearly now, and in their glow, she knew her doom. For those flashes pulsed with a rhythm. A rhythm that had taken the Smith during the previous night. All around the hill they now could be seen. Almost as if they knew that their prey was cornered. They were toying with her, adding to her fear.

With the subtlety of a greying dawn, an answering glow began to ease its way throughout the hollow. It was a gentle light, hardly noticeable at first. Turning away from the horror of the fog, Rosita saw that a gentle blue light was filling the center of the hollow. She gathered up her pack and water skin and slid down the bowl's shoulder to that haven of promise.

The Trumpet of Harmony

The light came from the stone at the hollow's center. Looking closely she could see, for the first time, carved into its solid frame curious looking markings. They bore little resemblance to any of the writings that she had known. It was from these markings that the blue light arose.

The glow intensified, growing outward from its source. Soon it had filled the entire bowl, edge to edge and to a height twice that of her small frame.

The fog which had not ceased its steady advance, had crested the hill top. At the edge of the bowl it clashed with the blue light of the stone. That light flared angrily and the fog retreated for a short distance almost as if in pain. The blue light remained painfully bright, keeping the fog at bay. Like a flooding stream when it meets an object that can not be swept from its path, the fog rose parted by the light, until at last in a vaulted ceiling it met and joined over her head. She was entombed by a heaven of ugly swirling mist.

From that boiling mass, horrible images began to appear. Faces of men, women and children, all horribly burned. Their skin dripped with yellow pus. Their glazed eyes bled and stared with unholy hunger at her. She shivered with horror at that hunger. Those undead terrors sought more then flesh, they desired to feast on the very essence of her soul.

Still the blue light held, keeping the visions at bay. She retreated now to that source of succor. Forcing her eyes away from those who waited in the night she concentrated her attention only on the stone.

Even as she looked on, the fiery blue symbols dimmed imperceptibly, but enough so to allow her teary eyes to focus on their form. The individual inscriptions which to her at first seem distinct, but terribly remote flowed together now in unbroken lines.

More and more her attention became focused on those tantalizing images. They teased the fringes of her memory but their meaning failed to rise to the surface of her consciousness. There was no fear in her. No alarm was triggered by her senses, as she felt herself drawn ever deeper into the stream of those blue lines.

Suddenly the meaning of what she saw was made clear to her. The images were forming now in her mind. With them came understanding, awe and horror. The beacon had been set here a very long time ago. She knew now, that she had been led into a cesspool of true evil. Yet it was from this den of vipers that her very race had sprung.

In the beginning, they had been as other mortal men, except that here were drawn those who were steeped in knowledge and skill. That shared wisdom had been meant for the good of her kind. It had been a valiant effort to eliminate a great number of the ills suffered by mankind and to liberate their minds, which nature had shackled from birth.

She bore witness to carefully planned studies and voluntary experiments, whose purposes were beyond her ken. Many such scenes flashed before her mind's eye in the space of a few heart beats. Even though she did not understand, Rosita felt the excitement generated by these images, among the wizards of that long ago time.

Chief of these, was a gentle man who, with his love and concern brought balance and control to the people of this place. The man had a son, whose life force burned strong, yet whose body was weak, even to the point of death. Rosita felt the withdrawal of this man into the narrow world surrounding the life of his son. She shared in his despondency, as his efforts to save the boy's life failed and the child sank deeper into oblivion.

So it went until, at last, the concerns of his fellows forced his attention away from his desperate studies. She felt tension and fear mount, as the images continued to roll through her mind. Whole families were withdrawn into the maw of hidden caverns. The ordered life of the inhabitants became hectic. Work was done day and night with no respite.

In this atmosphere of fear and suspense came the glow of satisfaction. The chief wizard had achieved his purpose, the cure for his ailing child. What physical damage had been done could only be repaired in part. The child would remain small in stature, but the treatment would halt any further damage and allow the boy to mature. There would even be some possible benefits that would not show themselves until the boy reached adulthood.

In celebration the man, with his family, left the confined surroundings of the underground shelters. They spent some precious time together in the wonders of the forested land that lay outside of the restrained limits of the town which had sprung up around the labs.

It was during this brief interlude that disaster had struck. Without warning, strange metal monsters had flashed out of the sky, to fall upon the small defensive encampment on the other side of the town. Flames and unholy heat destroyed parts of that quaint little village. Many who were caught outside the shelter of the caverns disappeared in a single flash, but almost all within the caves were safe for the time being.

The survivors struggled to destroy the fruits of their labor, for they feared what might follow. With a dread that was almost palatable, they waited, huddled together with their families in the safety of the sheltered caves.

The scenes flashed together in Rosita's mind as the history recorded in the guardian stone, flowed ever faster. She watched, as the chief wizard was captured trying to regain the sanctuary of the caverns. He had been desperate to reach the material in his lab, which had held the essence of his work.

She trembled, as the soulless metal monster which had captured the wizard delivered its unconscious prisoner into the presence of its master. To outward appearances, the creature looked handsome and well favored. A man of middle age. The only hint of his other worldliness, was the eerie glow of solid yellow eyes and the frozen set of a self-satisfied smile.

The captive man was strapped down to a padded bench. Lengths of thin wire were attached to the man's head and chest. The other ends of the wire were connected to a large, strangely glowing metal box. She watched as the stone generated image of that strange being, threw some levers on the surface of that console. The unconscious form of the captive writhed and twitched in the table's restraints. An eerie glow spread over his form.

After a short period of time the caricature of a man, for she could not in her own mind allow that this thing had once been a man, threw the switches back into their original places. A quiet settled over the work shop, as the being contemplated his captive. With a slow smile of satisfaction, he reached into his belt and withdrew a thin, wicked looking knife. With quick practiced strokes, he slit the throat of his hapless victim.

As the blood gushed from the man's severed arteries, his murderer held an empty vial in that sickly stream. Filling the tube, he placed it carefully in a hollow on the top of the glowing box. Throwing a last switch, he stepped back to watch as the torrent of blood from his dying victim slowed and then stopped altogether.

The images in Rosita's mind flowed even faster now. She watched as the evil one's metal slaves sought out the fugitive families in the cavern complex. Some, the old, the very young and the injured were quickly killed and left to lay were they had been murdered. Others were taken to the lab where they were treated to the metal console. The remaining captives were given drugs that controlled their wills and these became slaves.

Time moved and she witnessed new experiments. These had little of the scholarly air of those she had previously seen through the stones imaging. These were cruel, barbaric rights. Forced matings were common and the get of those unions treated to drugs that altered their growth. These were then mated as they matured, produced and then were disposed of without thought or care.

At the last, two new races were born. These had the capability to alter their shape at will. One had the seeming of mighty stallions, the other powerful, fur covered wolves. With a shock, Rosita recognized that this had been the foundation of her race. They had been made, so to speak, to the order of the demon of her visions.

Even though she had been sickened by the knowledge of the stone, still she watched on, as these races matured and became intelligent slaves. The demon master was now seldom seen, but in his place stood a heartless cowl covered man whose face was never exposed to her view. From him she sensed an evil almost as great as that of his master.

Time passed. As in all in who the gleam of intelligence glowed, the slaves began to recognize themselves as a people. Secret resentment grew and eventually burst out into rebellion. The two new races fought valiantly side by side to win their freedom. They faced the horror of the metal guardians and by their shear numbers beat them back, although at great cost.

The last battle was fought among the dust blown hills that had been the old village outside of the caverns' gates. The leaders of the two races had agreed on a strategy to win at last to the freedom of the surrounding country. Each race was to play its own part, but the plans became known to their enemy and the final battle turned into a bloody massacre. Only a small group of each race escaped the trap at last.

While they had dealt a severe blow to the resources of their enemy, they blamed each other for the final defeat. Swearing blood oaths against each other they went their separate ways to lick their wounds and to establish their race.

In a last image, the stone revealed to her that each had thrived, producing children and assuring their races survival. The center of evil had remained quiet for long years but it still existed. Wise men knew that a warning was needed ere the memory of those days were forgotten and the evil once again would be wakened. Thus the guardian stone had been placed as a sanctuary and a record of history.

The images faded at last from her mind. Fatigue from the day's travel and shock from the rapport of the guardian, sent her reeling into a deep dreamless slumber. The sun had once again risen into the sky when she awoke. It was early morning as far as she could judge. The blue light which had enveloped her the night before had gone. Of the yellow fog there was no trace and no trace of the horrors that the fog had held.

Rosita ate some of the travel rations and took a long drink from the water skin. She knew that she must find the entrance to the caverns by the end of the day. She could not expect protection again if she were to be caught out in the desolate hills this coming night.

Edging close to the brim of the hill she surveyed the area. She did not know with certainty, in which direction her goal lay, but the visions of the night had given her an idea for the lay of the land. Away south in the simmering morning haze the hills looked to be larger and more irregular. It was in that direction the Smith's trail had led and it was into that pool of evil she must travel.

Shrugging at the fates, Rosita stilled her body and let her mind float free. Speedily the incantation of transformation flowed through her mind and her form began to shift. She locked all fears and doubts out of her consciousness. Still a small part of her knew that she had to face the heritage that the stone had shown her.

CHAPTER ELEVEN

The corridor that the Smith walked down went on for several thousand feet. There were occasional doors on either side. All of these had remained sealed and the Smith left them undisturbed, fearful of what might lay behind them.

At last he came to an intersecting hallway. The light panels overhead shone brighter in this passage. Carefully, for he trusted nothing that was to be found in this strange maze, he turned and started down the new corridor.

He soon began to pass openings on both sides of the hallway. These were different in appearance then those in the first corridor. These each had a door for an opening but they also had heavy wire meshed windows of glass facing out into the passageway.

Through these, the Smith saw, row after row of the long, flat topped tables. On several, covered with the dirt of years, lay many boxes of unknown purpose.

As he strained to see into the shadowy depths of the rooms beyond, he failed to hear the quiet whir, whispering down the corridor behind him. It was only the clang of un-oiled metal as the nightmarish contraption raised one of it's appendages toward the unsuspecting Smith, that gave him any warning at all. Turning quickly, he had just enough time to recognize the device from his vision before the paralysis of the taser charge caused him to black out.

Consciousness returned slowly to the Smith. He felt no pain, but his limbs failed to move at his command. Lethargy seeped into his mind but his spirit fought against sinking back into the morass of unconsciousness.

Struggling, he forced his eyes to open and was immediately blinded by the unshielded beams of harsh light coming from panels over his head. Cautiously, with eyes narrowed, he attempted to see his surroundings.

The Trumpet of Harmony

Fear thrilled through him as the reality of his prison became clear to him. He lay bound by metal stays to a flat table beside which stood a strange box which shone of metal yet gave off a cold that he could feel.

A clear, hollow tube lead from the mysterious box to a shunt that had been inserted in a vein of his left arm. With horror, he saw that a clear liquid was being slowly pumped into his body through that tube.

A low throaty laugh echoed eerily behind him. Moving with a gliding motion, a robed and cowled figure moved into the Smith's limited range of vision. From the shadowed, hidden face came a sigh of satisfaction.

"Yes, it has been many a long year since I have had such a specimen to work with. All they bring me are weak, deranged rejects. I needed a strong test subject to withstand the vigor of forced transmutation."

Pausing to gloat over the Smith's restrained form, the cowled figure did not notice the shimmer that teasingly appeared around the metal bands which bound the Smith.

Resuming his position behind the Smith, the evil one continued. "Let me explain the beauty and simplicity of this experiment. For generations, I had to wait for slow mutation to occur in the available laboratory stock. By cross breeding and careful selection of offspring I was successful in creating two new races but they turned away from me and in their arrogance sought freedom." A withdrawn silence followed as if the creature had indeed gone back into the deep past. "Well very few lived to enjoy that freedom," he laughed cruelly.

"I will waste no more time with this subject. I have all the tissue samples I need."

This last comment was directed to a human shaped machine which had padded up silently behind the Smith's prone form. "He is to be given the final transmutation injection and then relocated to the holding cell for observation. Be sure that no damage comes to him until I have measured

Stephen Goodale   85

the effect of the test solution. After that, you may dispose of him in the usual manner."

Without another word, the cowled figure paced away. The Smith, limited in his range of vision, strained to hear the movements of the mechanical horror behind him. Thus occupied, he was unaware of the furtive movements on the other side of the room.

CHAPTER TWELVE

For the most part the Smith's trail had been an easy one to follow. The portal into the underground way had stood mutely open. A testimony perhaps, to the confidence of its master for it had been unguarded. Rosita had quickly discovered the spot in which the Smith had lain prone, his scent was heavy on the dust disturbed floor. From there she had followed his tortured wanderings, never missing a turning thanks to her keen senses.

Her quarry's scent became ever stronger and her pace picked up in the hope of quickly reaching her goal. It was then that she found herself brought up short. The scent of menace strong in front of her, covering the Smith's trace.

Cautiously now she slunk up the dimly lit corridor. Her paws making no whisper of sound. Ahead of her she could, at last make out the form and movement of her worst fear. As she had seen in her visions of the night before, so now in reality moved one of those nightmarish metal monsters.

Fear paralyzed her. Trembling she fought down the desire to turn away from her quest and hide far out of sight of that thing of horror. Yet she could not bring herself to abandon the Smith to the fate that she had witnessed so many others endure.

Breathing deeply she let the fear roll away from her, keeping ever in mind the code of honor that her mother's ghost had instilled in her during her time of trial. It was for the service of her kin that she was to use her powers and although the Smith was not family, he was all that she now had to tie her to those simpler times.

Rosita picked up the hunt once more, now more cautious then ever of any betraying noise. Following the monster's advance she could still discern the scent of the Smith ahead. Indeed, it had grown very strong and fresh. As the two hunters rounded a turning in the long corridor they came at last upon their quarry.

The Trumpet of Harmony

The large form of the Smith could be seen a short distance up the passage. He was intent in a study of one of the heavy wire windows that had from time to time broken the expanse of the monotonous walls. Rosita was about to growl a warning when with surprising speed the metal monster closed on its prey.

With just a small clank of metal on metal to betray its presence the machine raised an appendage. The small sound had drawn the Smith's startled attention, but it was too late. From that gleaming arm arched a flying dart. Piercing the Smith's chest in unerring accuracy. A brief glow of discharged energies followed and then all was still. The Smith slumped silently to the floor of the corridor.

Red fury arose in Rosita as she prepared to defend the body of her companion, but an inbred sense of caution caused her to pause in her assault. Her heightened senses informed her of a barely perceptible rise and fall of the Smith's chest. She harkened to the stillness and could now detect the sound of shallow breathing. The Smith lived!

In the seconds that her indecision had forced her to wait, the metal monster had not been idle. It had moved to a position next to the Smith's prone form. Then in an astounding metamorphosis had uncoiled itself and changed the positioning of its appendages to the point where it now stood as tall as the Smith. Indeed, with two mighty arms of metal it had reached down and had hoisted the Smith's still form into its grasp. For all the world it appeared to Rosita's prospective like a parent picking up its sleeping child for removal to a bed place.

With a whine, the pair rolled down the corridor away from where Rosita crouched in hiding. She rose to her paws and padded silently after her speedily disappearing quarry. They traversed many side passages and hallways until at last they came to sections that were well lit and dust free. Here Rosita slowed and allowed her prey to get out of sight. It would do no good at all to pay so close attention to her target that she failed to take precaution against capture herself.

The Trumpet of Harmony

Because of this Rosita almost passed the portal through which the metal monster had taken the Smith. It was only the sound of a man's voice that let her know her destination was at hand. With as much care as she could muster she sidled up to the partially open panel.

When she peered inside her head swam from the shock of her discovery. For there in front of her was the room in which the Stone's portent had showed the horrible demise of the man in her vision. In the process of hooking up the Smith to that selfsame devil machine was the cowled figure which had overseen the cruel creation of her race or someone very similar to that devil.

Nervously Rosita maintained her post by the door, straining to hear what was being said in the inner chamber. For though the Smith lay as still as death the creature talked incessantly to itself. She stayed quietly in the corridor hoping for an opportunity to free the Smith before someone or something discovered her. She felt the weight of her travel bag against her flank and wished uselessly that she could transform long enough to remove that hindrance to her movement.

When the creature had finished instructing his hellish minion and had moved out of the chamber through a door on the opposite wall, Rosita moved in for the kill. The metal parody of a man had silently slid around to the Smith's side and had for the moment turned its broad flat back to her. She moved with all her skill. She need not have worried, the machine had been intent upon carrying out its assigned duties. Callously, but with precision it withdrew a measured portion of liquid from a tiny vial and injected it into the clear tubing running from the Smith's arm.

Several things happened almost simultaneously. First the still form of the Smith erupted into a pinioned mountain of screaming flesh, hurling vulgar epitaphs at his uncaring host. Then her sharpened senses told her, to late that she was no longer alone. From behind came the whine of one of the metal monsters and before she could turn she felt the sting of a metal dart. As she fell under its paralyzing effect she wished for a quick death and regretfully said goodbye to the image of the Smith.

Stephen Goodale   89

The Trumpet of Harmony

From his vision, the Smith had understood a little at least of what was happening and he no longer doubted that his fate would be death. As the metal monster came around to his side the Smith drew in deep breaths of air and tried to still his whirling senses. By narrowing his attention down to those strange metal straps which bound him, he tried to concentrate his gift to cause the metal to flow and weaken.

He had almost succeeded when an agony like fire spread up his arm from that clear tube. Lights exploded in the back of his skull and pain caused him to arch his back and to coil his great muscles. Amidst his violent struggles he cursed his captor as thoroughly as his limited experience would allow. In one final surge, his weakened bonds broke off and he sprang from his prison.

Immediately he was on top of the source of his torment rending its exposed wiring, tearing at any surface which would yield a hold to his powerful hands. He had succeeded in toppling the mass onto the tiled floor of the room, when a series of pricks eased the torture of his flesh and once again he fell into blackness.

Quiet returned at once and amidst that silence a puzzled voice muttered to itself. "What is the meaning of this, I wonder? Plainly the Were bitch had been trying to interfere with my little experiment, yet what interest would she have of the man?" He paused for the moment over the supine figures of his two unconscious captives. The travel bag that Rosita had carried lay open and spilled out onto the floor. Stooping slowly the evil one picked up the velvet covered chalice, a look of surprise crossed his cowled face. He paused for a moment and then returned the object to its covering.

An evil smile played upon his pale thin lips. "Yes, that would make a most diverting scenario," he said to the still forms.

He outlined instructions to his metal henchmen and then strode briskly down the brightly lit corridor, evil and not quite human laughter trailing behind him.

Time passed. The captives were handled in very different manners. Although both had been given medication which kept them just on the other side of consciousness and both were nourished so that the fatigue of their journey faded. They were separated into different holding cells. The Smith had been left alone to suffer through the agony of the transmutation drug in a bare cell which resembled more a cage fit for a beast, then a prison for man. Rosita was treated to a series of mind altering physiological drugs and a new persona was grafted over the old Rosita. She had become a lady of class, used to the spoils of her position and unused to any hardship. As the days wore on, her body began to soften, the lines caused by her time as a Were disappeared. The very fact of her duel nature was hidden deep beneath the surface of her conscience mind.

When at last the master of the caverns was satisfied that all was in readiness, he caused the two to be transferred to the arena. The arena had been the scene of so many memorable displays of human suffering, triumph and tragedy. It had been set up by his master shortly after he had invaded the underground installation. Through the millennia his underling had learned to appreciate and finally to desire its use. Long had it been since it had served to divert him, he smiled in anticipation.

Fitfully the Smith blinked his eyes open, the light was dim and soothing. He lay comfortably upon a soft yielding surface and was covered by several soft blankets. As he pushed these aside and sat slowly up he realized that under them he was naked. So wrapping one of the blankets loosely around him he got to his feet and surveyed his surroundings. He was in a well appointed room with rich looking furniture. Across the carpeted floor was a doorway closed, by what appeared to be a wooden door. All this registered in his mind along with the odd fact that the room had no ceiling. Space opened up above him and gave no indication of a closure, except that the distant vaulted ceiling gave off a bright, daylight glare.

Hopelessly at a loss, he sat heavily back down onto the bed. Where was he? The last thing he remembered was going berserk and attacking a metal monster that had somehow been hurting him. Everything was dim, but at least he knew who he was and what had brought him here. He also knew that he had to get out.

Quickly now, for he had grown much steadier on his feet, he crossed the room to the curious wooden door. Half expecting to see a slide switch by the door frame, he was surprised to find an old style latch. Unbolting the latch, he slowly pushed the door open.

Outside was a paneled corridor. Moving softly, he walked carefully away from the doorway and down the hall. The murmur of voices caught his ear. He slowly approached a doorway which opened out into the hall in which he stood. Cautiously he approached the portal and strained to hear the voices clearly. After a moment he became frustrated and eased the doorway open enough to peer into the brightly lit room. There with her back turned to him and seated in front of a mirror sat Rosita and near her elbow on the vanity table stood the chalice.

The breath caught in his throat for there had been a transformation in the companion of his travels. All the pinched and lined planes of her face had eased, her hair flowed silkily down her back and danced joyously around the brush with which she stroked it. She had filled out. The soft green gown that she wore, fitted her in a way that defined her womanhood. She talked as if there were someone in the room with her. Her speech was in the manner of a mistress to that of a trusted, yet subservient companion.

Turning back to the mirror Rosita waived a dismissing hand at her maid. As she watched the girl depart from the room she was unaware of the on looking Smith nor did she pay heed to the third door which lay to her right.

At that moment, the Smith was forced to divert his attention to that door. Only the loss of reason could explain what his eyes reported stood boldly in that doorway. There dressed in travel stained clothes with a worn pack slung over his shoulder stood the mighty figure of a man. The Smith recognized both the clothes and the man. For the clothes had been his and the figure was that of himself. Startled he glanced down at his blanket covered body and knew that he did not dream. He stood at this place and in this time, watching his own figure as it crept into the room.

There was no disguising the secretive way in which the false Smith approached the unsuspecting girl. There was a gleam of pure lust in the figure's eyes and that was enough to bring the Smith's nerves to alert. Moving quickly the figure closed the distance between the doorway and the girl. Rosita looked up just as one massive hand was about to clamp down on her mouth. With terror in her eyes and a muffled scream she was jerked forcefully from her seat in front of the mirror.

With a sound of animal lust the man ripped the fabric of Rosita's gown from her squirming body, revealing the velvet expanse of her beauty. That was quickly crushed under the weight of the man's surging passion.

Stunned, disoriented and in shock the Smith had stood in the hallway and watched as the attack had started. Now from some hidden recess of his mind came the need to fight. He wanted to tear the assailant limb from limb. Uncaring, his blanket fell to the floor as he lunged into the room. With amazing speed, he closed the distance to where the struggling forms rolled across the floor. He reached down and grabbed the fabric of his opponent's clothes. With a mighty heave, he pulled the assailant from the quivering form of Rosita and threw him into the dressing table.

The form of the false Smith raised up from the fragments of the table and with a mighty roar charged back at the Smith, huge arms flailing as he came. The Smith looked into the creature's eyes and saw only the need for blood in their depths. Something within the Smith responded to the challenge and with an answering roar he leaped at the oncoming man.

They stood for a moment that was locked in time, the unmoving object had been met by the unstoppable one. Then the Smith felt his opponent's hands wrap around his throat. Soon the air in his heaving chest would be gone and then there would be only death. As the darkness closed in on him, somewhere deep within his brain and blood something powerful began to stir. In a split second his body responded. A powerful surge of energy raced through his arms and he was able to break the death grip which held him. He hurled his opponent back against the wall, momentarily stunned.

The transformation that had started was not to stop. Without the tutelage of the code, his mind nearly broke under the strain of transformation. Finally, as his body changed and his vision blurred and then cleared a small segment of his mind, locked itself away and stood back to watch.

Through slitted eyes and baring teeth the Smith watched his opponent rise and lumber back into the fray. Howling his defiance, the Smith leapt at the oncoming form. With a mighty swing of his massive arms the false Smith swept the Were away and into the wall, but with uncanny agility the wolf turned in mid air and used the wall as a spring. Leaping from the wall with all the force of his body straight for the false Smith. This maneuver had caught his opponent off guard and with unerring accuracy the Smith sank his fangs into the man's throat.

With determination, the Smith held his death grip fast, even as the desperate strength of the man pummeled his flanks. As the seconds drew tight he felt the false Smith lose strength and at last with a mighty heave he tore the throat from his victim. He leapt to one side and with animal lust, he watched his image die.

At that moment, there was a horrible scream from where Rosita had lain, for the moment forgotten by both victor and victim. The blood lust was hot in him and the Smith could have easily claimed a second victim, but that little corner which was the Smith's true self, had seen enough. Exerting control over his mind the Smith unknowingly triggered the retransformation to man. Painful moments later he again stood on two feet, although he knew in his soul that part of him at least would always remain animal.

He stared at the crumpled hulk that had once breathed life and he felt a hardness in his heart. Turning quickly back to Rosita he found her supine form laying before him. She had seen and been through enough to overwhelm anyone. She had fainted. This made the Smith's task easier and in some ways more difficult.

They had to get out of this place as quickly as they could, yet he would not leave her naked. The Smith was determined to find some form of cover for her. Glancing around the mass of splintered wood that littered the room, he saw an overturned chest from which clothing had spilled onto the floor. Walking to the trove he picked out some sturdy travel clothes. Then he moved back to Rosita. With speed, he dressed her and then turned his attention to the dead image of himself.

The horror of what he had done brought vile to his throat but he fought it down. He undressed the corpse and claimed back his stolen clothing and pack. Laying next to the greying corpse was the chalice. With an unsteady hand, the Smith tucked it safely into the worn travel pack.

All of this the Smith accomplished still buoyed up by his battle strength, but instinct told him that this resource would soon run out leaving him helpless. Picking up the still girl, he slung her easily across his shoulders and cautiously edged his way through the hall door. It was as deserted as it was before. He continued on down the corridor until at last it ended in another door.

All this time he saw no one, man, beast or metal. He paused to listen but the silence remained unbroken. With no other choice he opened the door and found himself fronted by the open space of a natural cavern. Across a short distance was an archway hewn out of the solid wall of rock.

With fading strength, he raced with his burden, across the open ground and into the promised shelter of a tunnel. Just as he ducked into its protective shadow and out of the harsh glare of the lit cavern he heard faint but quite clearly the laughter of something that might have once been called human.

CHAPTER TWELVE

The dust was thick, choking him. It made his eyes water, as the Smith tore at the opening above his head. Using all the might of his broad shoulders he levered his body against the fallen ruble on which he stood and with a tremendous surge, freed the rocky slab that had been blocking their escape.

Collapsing onto the mound of debris, his chest heaved as he drank in the sweet, clean air pouring down through the crevice. He had to close his eyes tightly against the unaccustomed glare of the sun. They had been in the tunnels so long that he had forgotten the scent of clean air and the revealing brightness of daylight.

At the thought of their adventures in the tunnels, the Smith wearily sat up and slid his way back down to the base of the pile. There huddling like some frightened wild creature, Rosita sat, with her knees drawn up to her chest. She gently rocked back and forth on her heels. He bent down to guide her to her feet, but she looked up in terror and shrank away from his proffered hand.

With surprising strength, she surged to her feet and scrambled past the Smith, up the rocks to the promised freedom of the open sky.

Slowly he followed, unsure of how to approach her or of what to do next. The horrors of the past days were too real to ignore and he knew that Rosita's mind had become fixated upon them. The savage attack so personal and so base, by a creature that looked exactly like himself. His bestial transformation and the ensuing bloody fight that had left his senses reeling on the edge of insanity. All had left Rosita vacant and compliant, so unlike the girl the Smith had come to know and care for.

It had been her scream of terror which had permitted his return to reality as he stood blood covered and full of animal lust over his victim. His thoughts and feelings of those moments he had locked away, to frightened by them to give them credence just yet.

The Trumpet of Harmony

Had it been two days? Deprivation and exhaustion had left him unsure of the passing of time in the lightless tunnels. During that period, they been driven further back in through the darkened passages until at last the lighted panels had given way to total blackness. Every time they had tried to returned to the more habitual parts of the underground maze, another one of those relentless machines would intercept them and turn them back. He could only suppose that they were to be left, to die of thirst and hunger. It seemed that the master of those machines had no more reason to bother with them.

The Smith cursed the denizen of those halls, as he labored back up the slope to freedom. They had stopped at last, too far gone to continue, when the Smith had espied a faint glimmer of light from the tunnel ahead. So it was that he had found the ceiling of that section partially collapsed and the small opening of welcomed daylight glimmering from above.

As those last hours had dragged by Rosita had said nothing. She had followed his guidance, but would not suffer him to touch her nor would she look directly at him. Lack of food and drink, plus shear exhaustion had taken their toll on her. She had begun to resemble an animal herself and at the last her eyes had gone wide starring straight ahead, unblinking as she had stumbled forward.

His weary musing ended as he crawled out through the opening. Struggling to his feet he was aware at once, of the scent of the open meadow, the sight of soft unmown grass and the sound of rustling leaves. They had at least, left the waste behind, he thought as he turned slowly to survey his surroundings.

The faint sound of a snapping twig was enough to save his life, for as he spun toward the sound his head moved enough so that the rock held tightly in Rosita's hand, glanced off his forehead instead of landing solidly on his temple. The force of the blow, driven by all of the girl's insane fear and hate would have been enough to kill him, as it was he fell to the ground, stunned, unable to move.

The Trumpet of Harmony

For her part Rosita had bided her time, waiting for an opportunity to escape from her horrid captor. She could not even now, as he lay bleeding at her feet, forget the terror of the beast within the man, both two and four legged. She had no idea where she was or where she was to go. All that she knew was that she must get away from this place and that thing which lay groaning on the grass in front of her. She glanced around, seeing nothing but forest glen and the woods edge she just picked a direction and started to run as fast and as far as her exhausted body would carry her.

Soon the cool, green canopy of the forest closed around her. The pillars of greying tree trunks hid the sight of the meadow from her and she began to relax. Strangely the forest felt like a welcoming friend, even though she couldn't seem to remember having ever ventured into the wilds before. Surely her father would not have permitted his only daughter, to travel without her entourage.

Something, hidden in her spirit, responded to the freedom of the forest. She abandoned herself to the feeling and lost conscience awareness of where she was. Instinct kept her to her chosen line of flight and the daylight flew by. Her body which had endured the hardship of travel in the darkened tunnels lost its exhaustion in the exultation that coursed through her veins.

It was drawing into the late part of evening when darkness had began to close around her, that some measure of caution returned to her bemused mind. It was not the impending darkness that had caused her to pull up in her drunken dash through the forest, but rather a curious sense of warning that her newly discovered senses revealed to her. She knew that somewhere ahead there was the presence of man. With slow cautious movements, she crept through the screening cover of the forest.

The first sign that her instincts were correct was the opening of a well worn path at her feet. It trailed from the forest out into a large expanse of open space. Keeping off of the path but staying near its edge she crept to the forest fringe and peered out into the deepening gloom. Her vision was unaccountably sharp for she could still make out the ordered patterns of farmers' fields. The gentle lowing of herd beasts reached her ears, from the safety of their paddocks. In the distance, she could see the outlines of a fairly large village. It was walled in by a high fence of forest logs that formed a stockade which might offer some protection against attack.

As sharp as her senses were, she did not hear the sly approach of several men dressed as hunters, all in forest green. The tallest of these loosened a coil of slender line from around his waist. With unnatural grace he glided to a position directly behind the crouching girl. With a quick fluid snap of the wrist he flung the sliver line out toward Rosita, a circle on the end opened up to encircle his unsuspecting victim.

At the very last moment, Rosita stiffened and sprung powerfully out of her crouch. She rolled to one side as the noose fell harmlessly to the forest floor. Surprise flashed across the face of her would be captor, but he was not to be denied his quarry. Quickly the other men surrounded the girl. With deft motions coiled lines filled the air, and like a spider ensnaring its prey, those lines found their mark. Swiftly they pinned the flailing girl to the ground.

The scent of rich humus filled her nostrils. The fury at being treated roughly began to unleash the power of her inborn gift. Rosita surged and the bonds which held her began to loosen with her strength. Her form began to shimmer with the impending change.

Now the leader of the men was completely taken aback and his eyes narrowed. He barked orders to his men and a curiously pale and fragile looking member of the party approached the changing form on the forest floor. Sure hands reached into a belt pouch and pulled out a handful of withered herbs. The rest of the men shrank away from the man and the girl, being careful to stay up wind of the pair. The man cast the herbs out over the shimmering form. Instantly Rosita stiffened and collapsed. Her form stabilized and once again she was human.

With narrowed eyes the man approached the still form, taking care not to touch the powdery leaves which had been the girl's downfall. With impatience he barked an order to the pale man who had stopped the transformation. Sliding cautiously by his tall burly leader, the slender man dusted off the last flakes of leaves from the girl, he then picked her up. Weak looking arms became knotted muscle betraying the man's strength. He carried the unconscious form several yards away from the scene of the struggle and lowered her gently onto a mossy sward. The leader then roughly shoved the man aside in his haste to examine the face of his victim.

Ignoring the hate filled look of the pale man, the leader looked carefully at the face of the lovely young girl, who lay helplessly before him. Curiously his face did not reflect the lust that might have been there not more then a few moments before. Instead a curious sense of wonder crossed his face. He squatted thoughtfully over the girl for a moment and then in decision straightened to his feet.

In a series of decisive, terse commands he dispersed his company of men. Most to resume their watch on the borders of the land but several he sent on ahead to the village to prepare for their coming. When they had gone and all that remained were his two personal guards and the scrawny man, he again looked at the still form of the girl. This time a wild light could be seen burning in the back of the man's coal black eyes. Slowly he began to laugh quietly and then with a raucous timber, until at last his laughter dissolved into the unnerving howl of a wild animal.

CHAPTER THIRTEEN

In what was becoming an all too familiar manner, the Smith slowly come back to consciousness. He just lay where he had fallen and took stock of his situation. Always a man with a ready wit and a keen sense of humor, he could only laugh at himself. Bitterly he realized how foolish he had been, letting the rush of emotion blind him to the impossibility that he had lived through. He couldn't even place a number on the days that he had been on the road. He had lost all track of time during his trek in the dark tunnels.

The thought of his recent confinement and the manner of his break to freedom, was like ice water in his veins. Had he really been turned, within moments from a man into a wild, raging beast? Had he really ripped the throat out of a living being? He began to shake uncontrollably, that man had been himself! Closing his eyes his throat constricted in the effort to prevent his already empty stomach from relieving itself on the green grass of the meadow. He had been used from the very beginning of this nightmarish trip and worse, his very being had been invaded, changed without so much as a by your leave.

He need only look inward to sense the beast. The knowledge was sobering. He had been controlled, but no longer! What he did from this point forward would be acts of his own choosing. But what would he do? He had given his word to fulfil a duty and even if had he been used, he could not break trust. So it was a certainty that he would continue to struggle along this chosen path. But what of the girl, a major reason for his present predicament? Here he could not make such a clear cut choice. The woman that he had brought out of the underground certainly had little resemblance to the friendly and lively spirit that he had grown to know on the long trail.

Could it be that this person was not the real Rosita? After all he had killed a copy of himself, could not the same evil have befallen her? Again, the Smith closed his eyes and examined the image of the gypsy girl in his mind. He could see her clearly and found, to his surprise a stirring of long hidden passion. Manfully he continued with his mental exercise. Carefully he drew up the image of the changed woman that he had pulled so painfully out of the darkness. The images held steady in his mind. Satisfied that no more detail could be achieved, he drew the pictures together. They slid over each other, becoming superimposed. He held them thus and examined the final image critically. With a growing conviction, he came to the realization that these two images were indeed the different sides of the same coin.

So, he had not left the real Rosita behind. The knowledge of this revelation, caused a flood of relief to fill his soul. He knew with utter conviction that she was indeed free. He also felt that tenuous tie between Rosita and himself tighten, until he knew with a certainty that he would never part from her willingly. She had become a part of him in a way that was both wonderful and frightening.

As thoughts spilled over one another, he realized that he had made his choice. He would try to follow Rosita and keep her from coming to harm. The dual image of the gypsy girl floated in his mind for a second more. There was a thread of hope creeping around the edges of that image. If, these were indeed two sides of the same persona, then could they not be brought together in some fashion so that the two could become one?

The half-forgotten voice of the Conjurer came back to him. "Remember, that the trumpet of harmony could be found in the south. Find it and claim your reward!"

A raucous scream drew the startled Smith's gaze skyward. There circling in low tight patterns, with pinions unfurled and ugly flesh covered heads pointing unerringly at their intended prey, flew the scavengers of his world. In the past he had seen carcasses picked clean by other members of their clan. Unwilling to become their next victim he tried lurching to his feet. The sudden motion betrayed him. He collapsed into an unprotected heap onto the turf, head swimming in pain. A curtain of red blood blocking the dimming vision of his circling tormentors. His final conscious thought was that of the sound of drums.

The Trumpet of Harmony

Over the peaceful, green waves of wind blown grass a gentle sound of rolling thunder could be heard. The inhabitants of this hidden world ceased their endless foraging for food and took notice of the now swelling tide of sound. As one they dove for cover, for the sound had reached a crescendo and riding in the forefront of that tumult ran the powerful form of a stallion. Soft, shadowed flanks of silver barely heaved at the exertion of his onslaught. His nostrils flared red as he breathed in huge gulps of pure air. His mane streamed behind him snapping in his own wind.

Far behind, yet still in sight rode his sub-commanders striving mightily to keep their leader in range. Behind these yet again, rode his personal guard. They were a mere display dressing, yet required by their leader's status as Prince of the People.

As the leagues flew under his feet, Prince Silvermane exulted in the freedom of the run. Out here along the flanks of his emerald realm, he was truly free. The wind of his passage wiped the pressures of the Court from his mind. He had chaffed these past few days under the strict tutelage of his father's ministers. They had tried to reign in their young Prince's energies and direct his mind to learning the task of rule. At last he had seen his chance and had used the excuse of visiting a nearby pasturage to make his break for freedom.

As usual his companion, friend and bodyguard Swiftfoot had seen through his deception. He had been right on his Prince's heels all the way through his madcap run. It was he who had quickly alerted the Prince's guard to follow. It was he who led those who pursued him.

Silvermane snickered into the oncoming rush of air. Swiftfoot did not fool him! His friend had felt the Prince's need to escape and to run the hills of his land. For if Swiftfoot wished, the Prince well knew that he would be able to catch him and bring him to bear. For Swiftfoot was the fastest stallion, that these green pasturages had ever bred.

The leagues flew by until at last a dark smudge appeared on the horizon. The forest which bordered his lands with that of the Werewolves drew near. His people did not often come near the boundary, nor did any live near its dark shadows. There was an age old animosity between the two races.

Clearly now the edge of the forest came into view. Circling high above the trees Silvermane could see several scavengers. Their scaly heads focused on something just within the forest's canopy.

Muscles that had been scarcely taxed by his furious run across the land, tightened in an explosion of speed. Silermane knew that the tight circle of the flying deathwatch, indicated that their intended prey had little time left in this world. He resolved quickly, to rob those carrion eaters of their victim. Why he did so he could not say, except that he believed that any creature deserved a better ending then that of having their entrails picked out as they perished.

The sudden burst of speed did not go unnoticed by Swiftfoot. Instantly giving up his causal pace he sifted into a blaze of speed. The Prince was headed directly into the forbidden zone of the forests edge. Why he did not know, but he did know how headstrong the Prince could be. He feared that in this sudden rush that the Prince would forget his caution and rush headlong into danger.

So it was, that even as the outlying scrub of stunted bush enveloped him, the Prince's guard and lifelong friend pulled abreast of him. No sound of reprimand escaped his friend's lips but Swiftfoot carefully matched his speed to the Prince's.

Together then they broke into a grassy glen, that lay some short distance into the forest. It was here that the scavengers focused their avarice. The meadow was open and unmarked save for a rough patchwork of rock and raw earth that laid approximately in the center of the green expanse. There laying as still as death itself was the ragged figure of a man.

Uneasily they slowed to a trot and then to a stop. They scanned the edges of the meadow, looking for any signs of a trap. Huge lungs drew in the

The Trumpet of Harmony

heavy air. Tasting it for any scent of their enemy. Nothing, but the raucous cries of the frustrated scavengers could be heard. Everything was still and there was no danger to be sensed anywhere near.

The Prince flicked a questioning ear to his friend. Swiftfoot responded with a sweeping toss of his head and a derisive neigh. Yet despite his friend's opinion that they leave this place and the unconscious human to his fate, the Prince stayed by his resolve.

With a final scan of his surroundings the Prince's form fluttered, flowed and in an instant stood tall and proud in his human guise. He was tall and strong with long white hair flowing down his back and taunt muscles bunching as he moved quickly toward the fallen figure.

Lowering an ear to the chest of the prone form, the Prince detected the weak flutter of a beating heart. He felt for broken bones and finding none, examined the ugly wound on the man's forehead. The Prince's lips pursed in thought. Surely that swelling indicated a concussion, if not a fractured skull. Moving the man could kill him, but death would be surer if he was left to the spawn who flew noisily overhead. He must decide quickly for surely others had noticed that circling flock. A snicker from Swiftfoot indicated that he felt the need to depart and soon.

The Prince bent down and scooped the man up into his arms. Not an easy feat because his burden was nearly as large as he, and wore a travel pack as well. A soft moan of pain escaped the mans lips and then he lay quietly in the Prince's arms.

In a few short strides, the Prince approached his waiting friend. As gently as possible he placed the man up onto the back of Swiftfoot. Holding on with one hand he vaulted up behind the placid form. His strong arms circled his captive and his hands laced Swiftfoot's mane in an iron grip.

With a snicker of impatience Swiftfoot turned and made for the safety of the open grasslands. Making good speed despite the double burden that he carried, he broke out into the open. The Prince's guard was finally coming up to the forest edge to meet them. Shocked the Prince realized that they had only been in the trees but for a few minutes.

Silvermane bent down around the form of the Smith and called into the onrush of air from the speed of his friend's passage. "We go as far as the Clear Run, there is a healer there who might help with this wound. Will you bear us there and quickly?"

Any answer from Swiftfoot was lost in the sudden surge in speed that forced the Prince to grip his legs tightly to his friend's flanks lest he be torn from his seat by their flight. The Prince smiled, that was answer enough!

The Trumpet of Harmony

CHAPTER FOURTEEN

Gerlock was more than pleased with himself, as his party approached the gates of the Den. In what was an unbelievable stroke of luck, the instrument that he had long sought to use against the Pack Leader had been delivered almost to his doorstep.

It was well known that the Pack Leader's daughter had been spirited away, low those many years ago, by the Gypsy human who had been their captive at that time. In all the history of the Pack, she had been the only one to leave the security of the Den.

It was also known that she bore the accursed human a daughter and that in so doing had met her death. Gerlock paused long enough to spit, a just end for a traitor he thought.

Now the Pack Leader had broken with the Counsel's edict that all contact with humans be forbidden. By allowing his son to roam wide in search of and in protection for that little band of foul humans that had been Malinda's tribe, the Pack Leader had opened himself to the Challenge.

Of course, the Counsel had been unaware of the transgression, but Gerlock knew. He had overheard a conversation between father and son. Farhunter had just returned from one his long-extended absences and was reporting to his father, in what they supposed was private discourse. Gerlock had witnessed the return of Farhunter and had followed to secretly listen outside of an open window.

Farhunter had described in detail the granddaughter that the Pack Leader would otherwise have never known. He had recounted that she was indeed full Were in blood and in spirit. In fact, he had reported that no further contact need be made, so the desperate risk that they had been running would at last come to an end with no soul the wiser.

Gerlock's lips curled in a feral grin, he had longed these many years to issue the Challenge. He was strong, fearless and cunning, surely he would succeed in combat. But such had to be sanctioned by the Council and that only for major lapses in leadership. As he walked, his gaze shifted to his helpless victim strapped mercilessly to the carry pole strung between his two men. The Council would find what he had to say most interesting.

At the dike his men met him, with the report that everything had gone as expected. The Council had been informed that they were bringing in a captive. They were requested to proceed immediately to the Council Chambers, there the Pack Leader and the Council would deliberate over the victim's fate. Gerlock smiled and ordered a rough sack to be drawn over the girl's slack face.

In confidence, with a look of triumph on his face, he led his caravan across the dike and through the gate. Curious Pack members stared at them as they passed on their way up the narrow streets. Low, one story buildings with round portals faced out at them. Made mainly of native stone, with green grass growing on top of them for roofing, they resembled closely the native rock shelters of wild wolves.

The way wound up to the crest of the hillock on which the Den had been built. There, imposing over the surrounding structures was the only building of any great height. Rising to an impressive hundred-foot parapet, the Chamber of the Council was a great defensive redoubt and the last refuge of the Pack in time of great peril.

At the cavernous entrance, two burly guards blocked their path with crossed lances. With an impatient wave of his hand Gerlock demanded they step aside, for he was there on Counsel's orders. Satisfied, the guards moved away and allowed the party to pass, all the while watching with cold stares of suspicion.

Good, thought Gerlock, they at least were on their toes. He'd would remember their faces after he became the Pack Leader. They or their ilk would make good body guards and he had plans which might not be to appealing to certain members of the Council.

The Trumpet of Harmony

The darkened tunnel of the entrance ramp soon gave way to the lighted expanse of the Inner Chamber. A huge fire blazed in the center of the room, giving a dull yellow, orange cast to those who looked on. Surrounding the fire pit, and ringing the circumference of the rough hewn walls were oblong blocks arranged in rows in such a manner as to radiate out from the fire.

Those who held a position of power took the inner most rings while those whose voices were of lesser importance occupied the outer ones. At the center also stood a huge block, intricately carved and of beautiful hues and shades. On this sat a man whose stature might have once matched that of the rock under him, but now, though still tall, was frail and bent under the weight of years.

Through this garden of stones, Gerlock marched. His men with the prisoner following close behind. As he passed each member of the Council he could hear the mummer of surprise and the sub tones of anger and fear. It was exactly that anger and fear that he intended to work on, to beat the Council into a frenzy until his Challenge would not only be allowed, but demanded!

Eyes full of pride, he came to a halt directly in front of the Pack Leader. Signaling his men to stop and lay their burden down, he gestured grandly to his Leader. "Pack Leader, I am sorry to have disturbed your rest at this late hour but I thought that I would give you the honor of dispensing the Council's justice on this cowardly, human churl."

Here he turned toward the rest of the Council in dramatic fashion he gave them an edited report on the discovery and capture of his "human" prisoner. "Yes, wise members of the Council, I caught her spying out the lay of the land around our Den. No doubt as a forerunner to some invasion from those stinking pits of Hell. The Tunnel Master has been said to be on the move again. Just witness the disappearance of our last two sentry parties, from the edge of his terrible demesne."

He paused to let this sink in. All present knew of the losses, still they never would have conceived of an attempt by their old enemy to actually attack the Den. His statements were having the desired effect, mummers of anger arose in shouted outbursts by those present.

"Of course the Council has long since outlawed any contact with the Human Race. Deeming it, rightly so, a contamination of the true blood. Death is to be the lot of any who break this tenant and I say that death should be the reward of this spy!"

Shouts of Death rang through the Chamber, with some members curling back their lips in unconscious snarls. He turned back to the Pack Leader, who had sat impassively as Gerlock had turned the Council ugly. "Does not our illustrious Leader have anything to say in this matter?"

Grey haired and bent though the Pack Leader might have been he still carried all the charisma of a man in his youth. Slowly he rose to his feet, staring down at the folly that had become the Council's desire for blood. Sadly he shook his head and replied, "Gerlock, I do not know what game you play here, but all present know my feelings in this matter. The taking of any life needlessly, is against the Code. The taking of an innocent life who has not even had the recourse to defend herself, is abominable."

He raised his eyes to the Council and scanned the Chamber, contacting many of those present. A few, very few looked away in shame at his words, settling themselves back down on their stony seats. Most, though had the outraged glare of blood lust in their eyes and the hint of fear. They would prefer, to assuage their feeling of helplessness by killing some innocent who had strayed near their territory, then to listen to reason.

So be it! If he were younger he would take those who thirsted for action on a stealth raid to those accursed ruins. Letting them vent their anger and giving them the self respect warriors should enjoy. Sadly though he was unable to do so.

The Trumpet of Harmony

He had hung on to the Leadership this long only in an attempt to persuade his son to assume the role. Unfortunately, his son had a spirit for adventure and the need to see what lay over the next hill. Farhunter had no interest in the tedious affairs of state.

He had finished his scan of the room, finding this growing disenchantment on the majority of the faces. He knew what would happen to that unfortunate creature on the Chamber floor and he was helpless to prevent it.

Finally his eyes locked onto those of the upstart Gerlock. "I will let the Council vote but be assured that I vote for life!" So saying he sat back down heavily on the great chair.

Gerlock turned, a look of triumph suffusing his features. "What say you, my brothers? Shall we strike down this loathsome wretch, as we should strike down even the heart of the pit of darkness?"

Shouts of life could be heard here and there, but they were drowned out in a tumult of cries for death. Turning back on his heals Gerlock once again faced the Pack Leader. "Council has voted death, Leader. Do you deny them their vote?" Almost absently the Pack Leader shook his head in resignation.

"Then the Council has voted death! Let the time be of the full moon. The midnight hour tomorrow, this churl shall breathe her last." With a quick motion, he reached down and tore the sack off of Rosita's head, picking her up pole and all he held her in full view and listened to the cries for blood.

As the still form of Rosita came into full view, the Leader recognized his granddaughter. He could not be in error. His son had spent hours humoring his father with the details of her face. Now with the morrow's moon rise she would die!

Hoping that he covered his shock and confusion, the Pack Leader looked on dispassionately. His fevered thoughts searching desperately for a way to save his condemned grandchild. He stared coldly at Gerlock. "The prisoner is condemned to death by the Council's will, however I will not allow her to be mistreated in any manner. Is that clear Gerlock!"

If Gerlock had been disappointed at the Pack Leader's calm response, or angered by his implied threat, he did not show it. Instead he replied, "Your words are Law, Leader. She will be placed in the care of your own guards."

With a subtle bend of the waist to his Leader, Gerlock turned and marched out of the Council Chamber. Slowly the rest of the Council followed, returning to an interrupted night of slumber. Satisfied that they had dealt justice at the master of the tunnels by condemning his servant to a sure death.

As the last member of the Council filtered out of the Chamber the Leader's men approached the fallen figure and at a word from him unbound the wretched girl from the carry pole. "Take her to the guest chamber and guard her carefully. No one is to come near except for my son and myself."

Finally he was alone in the vast Chamber. The echoes of his men's footsteps had faded into silence. How could he have come to such a pass? He had watched as the last few years had brought back the old blood lust to his people. It was as if all the history that they lived through had been forgotten. Damn it! They were men, not beasts. Yet they were beginning to forget, in their fear.

"Father." A soft low voice sounded in the Pack Leader's mind. The old man stared into the darkness at the edge of the Council Chambers. "I will not stand by as my kin is sacrificed on the alter of Gerlock's ambition!"

A dark shadow detached itself from the concealment of a council stone and padded silently up to the Leader's rocky throne. "I have sworn kin oath, to protect that child and I will not let her be slaughtered."

The Trumpet of Harmony

There on the sand that lay between the rocks, a huge dark wolf sat watching, the Pack Leader carefully. Golden eyes stared without blinking, no sign of remorse or capitulation, showed in their knowing depths.

Time stretched thin as they stared at each other. One bent by the years of service to his people. His strength almost gone but with a will that was still strong. The other hail and in the prime of his life. Farhunter too, had served his people in his own fashion and his will stood as strong as his sire's.

Thoughtfully, the Pack Leader spoke. "The time of darkness has come again amongst the People. They forget their oath and in so doing forget their humanity. Even if I were to stand in abeyance of their will, they would cast me down. Even you, my beloved son would be overwhelmed by their fear and it would be the same in the end." The grey, aged figure stood to his feet, his bent frame straightening in a mighty effort to regain its lost stature.

"We have lost here, for this time. Yet it must not be that our brotherhood dissolve into the mists of the past." The Leader's face reflected love as he faced his son. "You must take those that are loyal to the oath and together you must save our kin. I will provide the necessary distraction but you must get away and leave me to my fate."

The powerful mind of Farhunter, reached out once again and in the softest touch confirmed his father's wishes. They sat then, father and son and discussed long into the morning hours the logistics of such a departure. They could not stay in their present territory, to be hunted down one by one as enemies of the Pack. Because of this they chose a bold course. They would cross the lands of their ancient foes. The Horsepeople's open meadows would provide scant coverage but they hoped that such a surprising direction would intimidate the Pack and keep them from following.

Their decisions made, they spoke of those amongst the Pack who had held steadfast to the ancient oath of their people. These were few enough and some had young for which to care. In the end it was decided that each member be allowed to decide their own course. Father and son then parted. Each went about their own appointed task. Long after he had physically left his father's side, Farhunter's mind whispered a final farewell to his Sire. In that thought was all the love and respect any man could ever hope for. It was with a lighter heart that the Pack Leader went in search of those who would be faithful to their sworn oath.

It was easier then he thought, the People were outraged at the careless abuse of their ancient tribal laws. Yet they were the few. He dared not approach any of those that he considered marginal risks. He could not risk those loyal to their oaths, for they could easily be accused of treason and executed right along with his Grand Daughter. He personally had no fear of death, which was good, because he knew that he would die by the end of this day.

He had to give his followers enough time to make a clean escape from the Den. With a strong head start, they might have a chance but because there would be young and old in their midst they needed all the time that he could give them. Pursuit would have to be delayed as long as possible. To that end he found himself heading back to the Council Chamber. He had removed all of his garments and went clothed only in the ancient war paints of his people and the knife of honor strapped at his waist. The sun was just setting and it was time to begin his greatest battle.

He went unchallenged through the gaping maw of the entrance way. The guards saluted respectively, straightening their shoulders, in reflex. With a quick stride filled with purpose and strength, he moved through the Council Stones. Going directly to his Throne, the Pack Leader paused next to the grand council gong, a shield polished to a brilliant shine, blinding even in the half light of the fire lit chamber. Loosing his belt knife from it's sheath, he reversed the blade and used the pummel to sound the deep throated gong.

The vibrations of the signal lasted long after the audible sound of the gong had faded. Ensuring, that even those who were out of earshot would catch the message and pour into the chamber. For the gong was the warn call of his people and everyone who could attend to its voice was obligated to respond to its call.

The Door Wards came on the run, eyes wary looking for the implied threat. At a sign from the Pack Leader they settled into flanking positions on either side of the Throne. Next came those of the Council, who were staying at the Chamber of the Council, their eyes alight with suspicion and curiosity. Household members of the Chamber poured in, torn from their duties, happy for the excuse to get away but frightened by the call.

The steady flow of the Pack continued. All voicing demands, all wanting to know why the signal had been given. At last the flow slowed to a trickle and the Chamber had been filled to overflowing. The last member of the Pack to come pushing his way furiously through the door was Gerlock. A look of suppressed anger on his face.

As Gerlock finally approached the Throne, the Pack Leader surveyed his angry and restless audience. Nodding his head with satisfaction. All those who had been chosen to travel out into exile were not present. In the general din, he hoped that their absence would not be noted. If everything went as planned his son, with their followers would be freeing his granddaughter at this very moment.

Gerlock had finished muscling his way to the Throne and stood with his hands on his hips, chest heaving. "What", he said through clenched teeth, "is the meaning of this outrage! Why has the warn call been sounded?"

The Pack Leader eyed his underling coldly, holding the man's eyes long, before replying. "Gerlock, you know that the warn call is to be sounded only in the event of dire danger to the Pack. So, why don't you ask rather, where is the danger that I might help defend the Pack?"

Silence had fallen over the audience in the chamber, as their Leader had spoken. They became glued to the interplay unfolding before them. Gerlock became aware of the uncomfortable silence and chose his next words carefully. "Great Leader of the Pack, of course I stand ready to defend the Pack as is my sworn duty. I was just taken aback on how an enemy could have come so close to the Den without the Out Wards detecting their presence and sounding the cry. I'm sure my noble colleagues of the Council would like to know the reasons, as well as your plan of defense."

The Pack Leader could only admire the skill with which Gerlock could control a situation and manipulate his people. For now, there was a growing murmur from those assembled, demanding to know those self-same things. But as he had intended to answer those questions, the Pack Leader stood unfazed by the surging clamor. Seeing their Leader, cool and resolute before them, the Pack soon settled back down and silence reigned again.

Into this stillness, the Leader spoke. His voice was strong, deep and full of conviction. His bent frame stood tall and proud, as the years seem to fall from his shoulders like unwanted garments. "My people, I have called you here because we do indeed face a threat! One so insidious, that we have allowed it to crawl right past our good Wards, right into the very hearts that beat in each and every one of us."

Dramatically he paused, letting the somber words sink in, then he continued. "So many years ago, that the true reckoning is lost to us, our forefathers escaped their horrid fate through great peril. Thus, freeing our race from the thrall of the Tunnel Master. Yet even as they crossed the desolate waste, they argued amongst themselves. Their concern was about the future of our race. They thought out a plan, by which they and their descendants could live. One which we, as a people, have held to and cherished all these many years."

Gerlock stirred sensing the course of the speech, but the Pack Leader hurried on and did not allow himself to be interrupted. "We have grown as a people. Our lands extend far and wide. Our numbers have increased, greatly through the years. We have lived in peace and harmony, following the Laws of our distant ancestors and those of the Oath. Yet, my people we are threatened!"

Breathing deeply, the Leader came to the crux. "We have allowed ourselves to forget in recent years the basic tenants of those Laws. We have forgotten our Oath!"

Some cries of denial erupted from the assemblage, but most turned grim faces to their leader, hearts cold, minds closed to reason. Time! He must get more time. "People, hear me." The Leaders voice cracked over the heads of his audience. "The Laws and the Oath are all that separate us from the beast within each of us. Should we forget our humanity, then we would be truly lost to all reasoning. We would cease to be a people and would revert to the animals that the Tunnel Master desired us to be!"

Gerlock, face twisted in hate and desire, broke the ensuing silence that threatened to bind the Pack into the shame of realization. "Lies! He lies!" Gerlock threw his arms up and pointed to the now silent Leader. "There stands the true transgressor. The Council has long since passed laws forbidding contact of our people with that of the lowly humans." Gerlock turned to the assembled Pack and shouted. "He spouts on about Laws and Oath, yet in our very prison lays the seed of his own scion. That unholy mix of human and Were, outlawed and sentenced to death, as is proper." Gerlock hurled his words as if they were spears tipped with poison. As they touched the members of the Pack the bemused self doubt and guilt on the upturned faces were replaced by suspicion and hate.

"Yes my friends, we have been deceived these many years by this churl, who spouts the Law and then breaks it at his own convenience. Let him deny this if he can!"

On the heels of Gerlock's explosive announcement came the angry cry of the Pack. The swell of shouting reached a crescendo, shrill with hate. For they had been made to feel ashamed of their own actions only to find out that the one who accused them was, himself an offender. Blood colored the edge of their voices until they were demanding that the prisoner be brought forth and executed immediately.

The Trumpet of Harmony

The Pack Leader looked on horrified, not at the fate that would surely befall him but at the monsters, his people had become. Slowly the crowd noise settled down and Gerlock turned to face his victim. "Do you deny knowledge or complicity in this willful act of law breaking, Leader? Shall we not satisfy the demands of our people and have the prisoner out to face their wrath?"

The Pack Leader stood tall in the light of the crackling fire. Majesty etched his stern face, eyes of glittering coals burned through the thick air as they focused on Gerlock. "Now do you hear me, Gerlock of the Pack. I call you traitor to the people. I accuse you of bending the true meaning of our laws for your own gain. I call you churl and coward. You are the offal of the lowest creature in our world, beneath even the smallest child of the Pack. By what right dare you question the motives of your Leader?"

In a moment that was frozen in time the two opponents stood glaring at each other in the light of the dim chamber. The Pack fell silent behind them. The face of Gerlock became a mask of hate as he at last replied. "Prepare to face your death fool." To the gathered Pack he turned and raised his voice so that all would hear. "I declare, this bastard from Hell a false Leader. I challenge not only his right to lead the Pack, but to draw the next breath into his body. How say you?"

The blood lust that had been hidden so deep within the Pack's breast, burst to the surface as with one voice they roared their acceptance of the challenge.

The echo of that hair raising howl had not reached his ears before Gerlock sprang from the sand of the Council Chamber, a long wicked dagger clutched in one mighty fist. A red film of blood coloring his eyes. This was the way one of his people should feel, he thought in some hidden recess of his mind. This soul churning lust for blood. He knew that this night he would drink the blood of his victim and he thirsted mightily.

The Pack Leader stood, still as the stone on which he had sat these many years and watched the powerful spring of his opponent. Almost, it appeared that he would await his fate meekly, a weary old man at the end of his days. Suddenly when Gerlock had reached mid flight, the Pack Leader leaped out in response, body blurring as he achieved what few could. The transformation took less then an eye blink. Powerful jaws lined with razor sharp teeth met flashing steel.

The Pack Leader feinted and rolled aside in mid air, the wicked blade of Gerlock slicing through the spot his chest had just vacated. Teeth locked onto the tightness of hardened muscles and a howl of pain hurtled off the rocky walls of the Chamber.

The force of their separate leaps was enough to loosen the Pack Leaders hold as they landed on the sandy surface of the Chamber floor. The huge grey wolf snarled around a muzzle tainted with blood. Gerlock glanced quickly down to the tear at his side, satisfied that it was just superficial, he rolled to one side. Switching the knife from hand to hand he lunged at the Pack Leader.

The wolf circled trying to outflank the wiry form of his attacker. As Gerlock lunged, he sprang, his form changing once again. There to meet the wicked thrust of the knife with an arm block, was the grey headed Leader of the Pack. Grabbing the fabric of Gerlock's jerkin he twisted to one side, throwing his powerful opponent forcibly into the rock of a Council Seat.

The breath whooshed out of Gerlock's lungs and he collapsed into a heap at the foot of the stone. A quiet fell over the Chamber as the Leader crept carefully up to the still body of his foe. He was only a few feet from the stone when Gerlock uncurled in a sudden lung. The knife which had fallen woefully short of its target before was not errant now. Straight through the Leader's hasty block the pointed blade came, piercing, mortally into the stomach of its victim.

Impaled on the out flung arm of Gerlock, the Leader was thrown up into the air, while the deadly blade sliced a horrible gash down his abdomen. Blood, spewed forth in torrents as with a final twist Gerlock withdrew the knife from his hated enemy.

The Leader lay, now still, in a pool of his own blood. The sound of a ragged breath the only sign that he still fought for life. Carelessly, Gerlock walked away from his foe. With an eye to the hushed audience around him, he slowly stripped off his own garments. When he was naked, he spoke. "So must end all of my enemies, for I am Leader now." Without waiting for a reply he turned back toward his fallen adversary, his form sifting into a mass of sinew, muscle and razor sharp teeth.

Gerlock, breathed a foul breath upon the moaning form of the disposed Leader. As the old one's eyes opened for the last time, Gerlock saw recognition and loathing but no fear reflected there. With an almost careless motion Gerlock closed his teeth around the helpless man's throat. With a quick flick of his powerful neck, he tore the throat from its owner.

It was the traditional end of a fight for leadership. Gerlock's people cheered their new Pack Leader but Gerlock did not move away from his victim to accept the adulation. Cheers choked off in revulsion as Gerlock locked his jaws once more to the flowing veins that pumped blood from the old one's neck. There Gerlock drank his fill of the blood of his victim.

When at last he raised his muzzle covered in gore, there was a wild light burning in his eyes. A ear splitting howl escaped the Leader's throat and all who heard shook in terror, of the insanity echoed in that call.

CHAPTER FIFTEEN

Death had long been a curiosity for the Smith's race. They held a firm belief, in the human soul and its continued existence past the point of death. Yet these things had never bothered the Smith. He was a young man, full of the confidence that youth brings. Confidence in himself and in the knowledge that his final moments of life were far removed in time. Now, however, he could believe himself dead.

He perceived himself to be laying on a soft rolling carpet of grey, eyes pointed heavenward. A cloudy mist filled his vision. Limbs which had in life, responded to his every command, failed to do so now. He tried to look down at his body but discovered that he could not change his position at all. He was a captive. Alive or dead, all he could do was watch the roiling grey and wait.

Outside of that soft prison, Prince Silvermane bent over the still form of the Smith as it lay, in truth on the soft covers of the Healer's couch. They had arrived only moments before, sweat covered and filthy from the speed of their ride. Even Swiftfoot was unabashed by the exhaustion which claimed him. The Prince had lowered the unconscious body of the Smith from the back of his friend. Feeling for a heartbeat and finding none, had yelled out for the Healer.

That learned man had come out and been apprised of the situation. He unstopped a vial and forced some pale golden liquid down the throat of his patient. He then ordered the Prince to take him inside.

The Prince had laid the Smith on the Healer's couch and then stepped aside. Concern was etched on his noble face. Silvermane was distraught by the words of the Healer. As he had prepared to cast himself into a trance in an effort to contact the wandering spirit of his patient, the Healer said, "He is very near death, my Prince."

"I do not know what you have brought to me. I have read the sign of the wolf in him and he is every bit a Were. Is it your will that I still try to save him from his fate?"

The Prince thought for a moment and then nodded his head in affirmation. Time passed slowly and the silence deepened as the Healer cast farther and farther, in an effort to make contact with the flickering spirit of the Smith. He had just given up the hope of reaching the dying man when a brief flicker of light caught his attention in the surrounding grey of that half land between life and death. Drifting quickly toward it, he soon found himself standing over the Smith's still form.

Casting his own spirit down into that form he wandered freely through the fabric that had made the Smith more then animal. There through many twisting and turning paths, he watched as the Smith's fate was laid out before him. He was astounded by the picture painted there. Hope and great fear filled him. The terror finally won out and the Healer's spirit was cast out from the Smith.

The spirit of the Healer hovered over the form of the Smith, knowing in his heart that there was now nothing that could be done to save the Smith from the hands of death. He hung his head in sorrow, but it was not for the Smith's passing that he mourned. It was for the things that might have been had he lived and for the horror of what will be because he would not.

As he stood there, the feeling of impending doom and utter helplessness began to change. It was like a breath of fresh air in the dank cellars of a dungeon. He became aware of hope beyond hope and the feeling grew stronger, until at last he knew that he did not stand alone. Lifting his spiritual vision, he found himself surrounded by five tall, still forms. It was from these that the feeling of hope sprung. It was from these that he perceived a path by which he might save the dying Smith.

Again, he cast his spirit down into the form of the Smith. This time he ignored the flashing images which bombarded him and instead he focused his attention on the physical damage which threatened the Smith's life. Following the directions of those still forms, he soon traced the trauma to it's source. There pulsing in front of him was a mass of destroyed tissue and blood vessels. Reaching out, in a way new to him, he isolated the torn pieces of the Smith's brain and with a wash of healing light set all back into its normal patterns. Looking again in wonder he could no longer detect the area which had been damaged.

Once more he found himself standing over the image of the Smith. The transition had been instantaneous, caused he knew by those powerful images which now stood looking at him intently. His mind and spirit became filled with their thoughts. Resistance, he knew was useless and unnecessary. For only the feeling of rightness and peace filled him now. Seconds later he was once again free of their power. He had been weighed and judged on scales beyond his understanding, all that was lacking was their judgement.

A vibrant voice filled his mind, "You are the only living creature which is aware of this man's true destiny and as such are a danger to him and his. It would be an easy matter to wipe your mind and furnish you with false memories of this time, but we foresee a time in which your aid will be needed again. Because of this, you must be allowed to know and understand what is transpiring, therefore we will allow you the privilege of retaining your true memories. However, we will block you from revealing these to anyone else. You are now a participant in the most challenging times our reality will ever face."

The voice released him, and he felt his spirit withdrawing back into his own body. Before the transition was complete he heard the soft voice once more. "Go with our thanks. Your spirit is pure and your heart free of fear."

The Healer opened his eyes. He drew in a deep breath, releasing it in a huge sigh of relief and wonder. Facing him across the still form of the Smith was his Prince, whose eyes bore a look of compassion and concern.

Ignoring the Prince's questions, the Healer bent down and examined his patient carefully. Relieved that the man's complexion had regained its healthy pink color. The Smith's ragged breathing had taken on a deep and rhythmic pattern of exhausted sleep. He stood up and faced the Prince. "The man will live. It was a very tight thing but I managed to isolate and cure the affected area in time. What he really needs now is peace and quiet. I strongly suggest that you and Sir Swiftfoot leave him here with me for a time. I will send word when I think that he is strong enough to answer your questions."

The Healer escorted the Prince into a separate chamber for sleeping and bade him to rest the night. The Prince tried to protest but a wave of exhaustion washed over him and he just had time to stumble to the pile of sleeping robes before he collapsed into deep slumber.

When he awoke it was late morning. The Healer had nothing more to report, his patient still lay deep in sleep. Where, the Healer assured him, the mending process was going on at a fast pace. Gathering himself together Silvermane went in search of his friend, Swiftfoot.

The sound of rushing water caught his ear as he left the Healer's door. Mixed in with the joyous sound of laughing water was laughter of another sort. A smile plied his lips. He had wondered where Swiftfoot might have spent the night. That laughter had a definite feminine quality to it.

He followed a well-worn path that lead from the Healer's cot, down to the wide surface of the river Clear Run. There, with one arm held tightly around each of his two tousled haired companions, Swiftfoot soaked his long lanky body in the cool water.

"Awake at last, you slug abed!" Swiftfoot addressed his Prince. "Had you but the verve of youth, you too would have met the sun with open eyes and a spirit full of expectations." Startled the young women looked up and into the eyes of their Crowned Prince.

Clumsily they tried to curtsy while covering their anatomy as best they could. The Prince only laughed as he eyed the firm flesh and pleasant curves of his friend's companions. "I would not disturb you my ladies, but that I need to take council with this randy stud. So, if you will excuse us I am sure that you will be able to catch up with him later, when I have finished with him."

Blushing prettily, the young ladies scurried to the river bank, scooped up their clothes and were gone in an instant, trailing their laughter behind them. Swiftfoot watched them go, a pained expression on his face as he turned to his Prince. "Now why did you want to go and do that for? I was saving the dark haired one for you!"

Without answering the Prince stripped off his own clothing which he had found that morning laid out on the dressing table of the sleeping chamber. Slipping noiselessly into the water he let the cooling current drift lazily over his body. The water washed away the last of his exhaustion from the night before and he felt his mind clear. Turning to his friend and confidant, he asked, "What do you think of our adventure yesterday?"

Swiftfoot took time to judge his friend's reasons for asking, finally he replied. "There would be some in the court who would be distraught by, what they perceive as careless actions. After all you could have been endangering the royal line by your flight into the forbidden zone."

He watched as a frown appeared upon the Prince's face and decided to take another tack. "As for myself I've felt all along that you would tire of the yoke of rulership from time to time and that you would need the run of your land on occasion. That is why you were unable to escape, undetected and I was able to follow."

The Prince stared pensively at the curling rivulets of water flowing by them. Looking up he spoke, "I have acted the fool, my friend. Instead of keeping my place at my father's court, I dash off on a heedless flirtation with danger. And what reward do I get for my foolishness? I'll tell you. I drag a Werewolf from the teeth of death and bring him to the sanctuary of the pasturage."

The startled look from Swiftfoot did little to assuage the Prince's conscious. He knew, as did every foal of his people, the enmity that had existed between the two races. It had been the law of the land, that no member of the Werewolf race be suffered to touch the green grass of the inner meadows.

Now unknowing and with the highest of intentions, he had broken the very laws that he had sworn to uphold. He had brought shame to himself and to his family. There was nothing left to do but to send word of his plight, to his father the King and to await here for the judgement which must surely follow.

"Swiftfoot as I value my life I swear that I had no idea that I was breaking the law, but that still does not exonerate me from my actions." He paused and let the sound of the river calm his frayed nerves before continuing. "Send word to my Father. Tell him what has transpired. In the meantime, I place myself into your custody and I consider myself your prisoner!"

CHAPTER SIXTEEN

Rosita had been unaware of the events swirling around her. The effect of the wolf bane was overpowering and complete. Yet while she did not witness the demise of her grandfather, nor her rescue by her mother's brother, she did dream.

In her dreams, she looked down through her spirits eyes at the memories fleeting through her mind. She watched as scenes opened up to her. She witnessed an idyllic life spent in the manors of her father. In the proper upbringing, she experienced as the daughter and only living heir of her father. Still the more she envisioned the more the picture became thin and frayed around the edges.

There was something wrong with the images that she was witnessing. It was almost like looking at someone else's idea of perfection. Like a background for a painting, all the colors and tones were there but the substance was missing.

She focused on the faces of her parents. They were handsome people, with love and happiness etched on their faces. Smiles that were meant to reassure her only set off growing alarms in her mind. She looked closely at her father but his image remained unclear and elusive. Her mother's face swam before her. Emerald green eyes were framed in a pale face by long flowing blonde hair. Those eyes greeted Rosita warmly. Very fair was the image and very wrong!

Over her mind picture floated the image of someone else. Long dark hair and hazel eyes looked at her with concern. Soft lips compressed with impatience as they moved in speech, conveying words of vast importance to her. She tried desperately to catch their meaning but she always seemed to just miss the understanding of them.

Her frustration became overwhelming. Rosita began to scream in her mind, at the dark-haired image before her. Yet she was unable to make a sound. Then her spirit rebelled against the trap that had prevented her from controlling her actions. As she fought more desperately against the unknown reigns of her paralysis, the images in her mind faded until at last even the dark-haired woman had gone. But before her hazel eyes vanished from Rosita's minds eye, Rosita could swear that she caught a look of approval in them.

Her struggle to defeat her debilitation took on added force with the passing of her dream state. For now, there was nothing and she felt herself drowning in the darkness. Fiercely she fought her way to true consciousness. With a piercing scream that tore at her own ears she breached the surface.

Just as quickly, a rough hand clamped down over her mouth, allowing her breath but effectively silencing her. Her eyes could perceive nothing, in fact she could still be dreaming but for the insistent pressure of that hand. Slowly the darkness began to ease and she could discern shadowy objects in the greater darkness of deep night.

The first thing that she realized was that she was not alone. In the darkness surrounding her was the movement of a large number of people, horses and wagons. All moved with an eerie silence and at a speed that indicated haste and great fear.

She herself was perched on the back of a large horse. A firm strong arm was wrapped around her waist and held the reigns in front of her. The other hand was clamped tightly to her mouth. Fear began to subside from her and she sat quietly watching the strange parade of half seen travelers.

Her captor must have felt the easing of tension in her body, for soon the hand slid away from her mouth and the warm breath of his voice whispered in her ear. "We must keep absolutely quiet we are passing by one of their check points and there will be guards on the watch. Do you understand?"

Rosita answered with a nod of her head. She was suddenly content to follow the lead of her unknown companion. So, she watched as they moved through the night. Trees which had been thick about them began to break up into thinning thickets and then scrub. Suddenly they burst out onto a large open plain. Dimly she could make out the thick grass which covered the rolling terrain ahead of her.

When they left the trees behind the night sky opened up into a panorama of blazing stars. They were so bright and clear that their light lent aid to their passage. Now the silence of their advance gave way to the clatter of wheels and the pounding of hooves as the band broke out into a fast trot. Their speed added a sense of desperation to their journey.

Rosita squirmed around in the saddle and tried to get a look at her captor. The light still wasn't good enough to make out details but she could see that the man was huge, bigger even then the Smith. His face was framed in a cloud of hair the color of midnight. She doubted that even in full light whether that shade would lighten.

They were moving fast but the wind did not prevent her from speaking to her fellow traveler. "Where am I? What has happened and who are you?"

She caught the flicker of white teeth as her captor smiled at the string of demanding, although understandable questions. He answered as best he could. "You are on the back of one of the Pack's sturdy, if not speedy horses. We are entering the territory of our ancient foes, the Horsepeople in a desperate bid to put those who follow off our track."

"As to what has happened, much has passed beyond the realm of life this night. We flee the power of our own people's despotism. What concerns you however, is that you were caught on the outskirts of the Den and were accused by a false man of spying. You were sentenced to die a horrible death and at the last were rescued by those you see around you."

Rosita sat still as a stone, trying to digest his words and put them into some form of reality. She could remember fleeing from the Smith after they had come out of the underground prison of the Tunnel Master and her subsequent discovery of the stockade town. From that point on her memory failed and she said so.

Her companion answered. "You were under the power of the wolf bane herbs. They caught you in the middle of transformation and so the effect was doubly strong. You have only just now recovered consciousness."

Stunned, Rosita felt her grasp loosen on reality and the horse. A strong hand lent her support and kept her from physically falling to the ground. Her mind reeled from the importance of the man's words. If she had been able to transform in the manner of the Smith then she must herself be the same kind of monster that she accused him of being.

She felt the denials flooding from those memories that lay just below the surface of her thoughts. Horror and unreasonable fear fought to send her mind over the brink of madness. Yet, that which had made her struggle against the bonds of darkness surged to the forefront. Other memories flooded into her thoughts, as if the gates of a damn had opened. They tore the final shreds of those false memories away until at last she knew and understood who and what she was.

Her body trembled uncontrollably in the protective hold of her companion. Tears welled up and fell unchecked down her cheeks. She could remember at last, that the image of the dark hair woman had been her mother. It was an image that she had never seen in waking life but one well cherished from the mind link that they had shared so many years ago when Rosita had learned herself to be a Were.

Those memories stood her in good stead now, for she realized that she was indeed no monster. She had lived by the Code all of her adult life. That code was much more civilized then the lawlessness by which most humans lived.

At last Rosita's mind, stabilized. She knew that she had been used somehow by the Tunnel Master. To what end she could not know but she could guess that it had to do with that creature's evil sense of pleasure. The one memory that she regretted with all of her soul was that of the

The Trumpet of Harmony

Smith, whose form had lay bleeding at her feet. Helpless and perhaps mortally wounded in the confines of an unfriendly forest, the chances of his survival were slight. So, it was that she sat quietly and wept openly for a time. Surprised at the strength of her emotions. She had to admit that she had come to care deeply for the Smith.

Her companion did not disturb the silence of her grief. He only continued to guide the horse at a ground eating trot. When at last her tears subsided he spoke. "I am not sure that this is the time to answer your final question but it might help you now, to know that you are not alone in this world. My name is Farhunter and I am your Uncle, Melinda was my sister."

CHAPTER SEVENTEEN

The earth shattering howl had barely ceased its fierce echoes, when a guard burst into the Council Chamber. He glanced quickly away from the fallen figure of the dead Pack Leader and looked uncertainly around him.

Gerlock strode quickly to the man and grabbed him by the shoulder spinning the guard around to face his new Leader. "What is it, guard?" growled Gerlock.

"M-m-y-y Lord," stuttered the unfortunate guard, "it's the prisoner. She's gone sir."

Red rage filled the Pack Leader's eyes. "What do you mean gone!" He tightened his hold on the guards shoulder until the man was driven to his knees in front of him.

The guard's face was deathly pale as he answered. "We heard the Warn Call, sir and we ran to the Council Chamber as fast as we could. As we ran I remembered that my sword lay next to the guard table in the room next to the cell. I thought only to run back to retrieve it in case of trouble here in the Council Chamber. By the time I had gotten back and grabbed the weapon, I noticed the cell door hanging open. The prisoner was gone Lord. I ran back up here as fast as I could to sound the alarm."

These last words were gasped out, as Gerlock's hands had moved from the unfortunate man's shoulder to his throat. A loud grating noise was heard as the guard's neck broke in his Leader's hands.

In disgust Gerlock hurled the dead man from him and with a low threatening voice called for the Captain of the Guard. It was clear to him now that he had been tricked. While the old one had fought him, Farhunter or his men had slipped down to free the prisoner. Well it would do them no good. He would use every man, woman and child in the Den, if he needed them to track down and kill the traitors. Kill them all, except for Farhunter and the girl. For them he had some special plans of his own.

The Trumpet of Harmony

The Captain of the Guard came in through the round archway of the Council Chamber and marched straight to his new Leader. Bowing slightly he said, "You have sent for me Leader. I am prepared to take full responsibility for the prisoner's escape. Before you kill me though, hear me out. The prisoner is not the only one to have left the Den under the cover of the Warn Call. Many who held loyalty or fealty to the past Leader have fled. They have taken wagons and horses from the stockade. The supply house has been raided as well. It seems to have been a well organized escape."

Gerlock's features suffused in anger and the Guard Captain gave a silent prayer for the care of his soul. However his Leader's mood changed once again. A smile seemed to creep over the corners of his mouth. He turned to the on watching members of the Council. "How say you, my friends? Shall we allow these insignificant fleas to boldly walk all over the edicts of this hallow body or shall we not gather ourselves together and march out after the traitors?"

There was an enthusiastic growl of agreement. This new Leader was decisive and he fed their need for blood. So, it was that the members of the Pack who streamed from the Council Chamber, resembled more a hunting pack then the gathering of men who once held up the law of the land.

Although Gerlock had urged them on to instant action, they had not forgotten all caution. First a band of trackers were sent out to pick up and follow the trail. Then the Den was stripped so that a large assemblage of hunters could be supplied and readied. Other and darker preparations were performed. Those who could not or would not make the journey either fled or were slaughtered. Their blood drunk in foul ritual. A darkness crept over the soul of the Pack. They had submerged themselves in the animal side of their nature, giving it full reign so that the laws of the Code were completely forgotten.

When the tracking party had reported back that they had found the trail, Gerlock signaled the abandonment of the Den. He did not share the apparent destination of their quarry with his people, but allowed the Pack full throat to their blind need for blood. The Weres boiled out of their long cherished home no longer sane with their desire to rend the flesh of their prey.

From his hiding place in the scrub surrounding the Den a thin figure watched the mad departure of his people. He had just been able to save himself, from the ruthlessness of Gerlock's commands. He had counted himself lucky to be without kin, for the blood that had been spilled that day had been appalling. He was luckier still, to have been forgotten by Gerlock, in the general insanity that had ensued.

Still, as the silence of death closed down over the once thriving Den, Mandrake could not bring himself to forget his people. He had been in the Council Chamber when the old one had given his impassioned plea for a return to the laws of the Code. He had been impressed with the genuine concern and love that the old Pack Leader had shown for his subjects.

He had been an outsider, traveling in the company of a very close nit clan. Although he been born the son of true Were blood he had never demonstrated the ability to transform, as could any of his people who had come of age. He had been the object of much curiosity and occasionally of scorn. Still he had been treated kindly by most of the Pack.

Yet he had longed to be someone, to do something that would make his mark. So it was that when Gerlock had come to him whispering of friendship, courage and power. Mandrake had been a willing listener. Soon he found himself deeply involved in plans to overthrow the Pack Leader and the Council. Since Mandrake had no reason to be loyal he went along, thinking these were only the words of a braggart and a bully. However of recent months he had seen the light of insanity begin to shine in the eyes of Gerlock. Fear and contempt had begun to color his view of the man.

Finally he had begun to realize that he was not a friend to Gerlock but a tool. A tool to be used when needed and carelessly laid aside once his usefulness was done. For he alone of all the Pack, was capable of gathering and using the dreaded herb, wolf bane. He had served so ably in the capture of the old one's granddaughter. He had also seen his reward, the virtual destruction of his society.

Mandrake chewed on his lip a moment in indecision. Finally in his mind's eye, he saw again the contempt on Gerlock's face as he, Mandrake, had subdued the girl. Enough was enough! His people had been ruined because of his preoccupation with his own feelings. Now he must somehow atone for his sins.

Quickly, for night was coming on once again, he moved away from the concealing cover of the scrub. He had heard the Captain of the Guard say, that all of the horses and the draft animals had been taken or released by the rebels, so that they would not be used in the pursuit. Still there must be one or two wandering around the fields and he must find one so that he might catch up with the Pack.

In the dim light he could see no better then a normal human, another sign of his cursed birth. However he had another sense which he had hid from all the others. As he grew he became aware that he could sense the thoughts of animals. He could not read their minds but he could receive general impressions from them and in some part he could let them see his thoughts.

So it was that he came to stand in the now abandoned fields of the Den's pasturage. He cleared his mind of thoughts and allowed it to drift in search of that which would give him aid. His mind touched the edge of many creature's thoughts, but none were those for whom he quested. After long minutes he had begun to draw his mind back, when at last he made contact.

Close, very close was that response and of such clarity! Still he could not allow himself to waste time on wonderment. Carefully he tried to build a mind image of himself standing in the gathering twilight of the meadow. Then he constructed an image of himself mounted and riding on the back of a sturdy horse. He held this picture steady in his mind and then sent an imploring plea out along with it, hoping that the strength of the contact would allow the beast to understand and accept him.

For long moments, he held contact with that other mind, then the link was broken. Mandrake almost fell over with exhaustion. The mind probes had always taken a great deal from him, but never before had he poured so much of himself into the effort. Perhaps that had explained the sharpness of contact, but had he succeeded?

Moments later a soft nicker broke the evening silence. The sound of steady hoof falls told Mandrake that he had succeeded in at least this much, the beast had come. Over by the stone fencing he caught the glimpse of a dappled shadow. The furtive movements suggested caution. At last the shadow moved out into the awakening moonlight and Mandrake caught the glimmer of a red mane on the sleek shape of a roan filly.

The grace of his new companion mesmerized him. The filly approached, coming to stand directly in front of him head up, liquid eyes gazing steadily at him. Mandrake did not move but once again attempted to reach out with his mind.

Mandrake put all of his energy into his thoughts. All of the terrible things that had transpired over the past two days filled his mind. He put all of his resolve to help out the remaining members of his Pack. Those that had chosen to follow the Law of the Code out into exile rather then suffer the debasement of turning their souls into the beasts that the others had become.

Somewhere in his attempt to communicate his urgency, Mandrake realized that the mind he was trying to reach was instead reaching out to him. He felt the intrusion of thought go deep within his own conscious and subconscious minds. All that he was, all that were his dreams, fears and hopes were laid bare to that mind.

Deep within his soul he knew that he should try to resist this invasion, but something stirred in his heart that would not allow him to fight this testing. It was the first time in his entire life that he allowed himself complete honesty with another being. Even if he was found wanting, at least he had been given the chance to demonstrate his true nature and not be ashamed of himself.

How long was he locked in that mind probe, he could not say, however he soon felt that hold lessening. With a final surge of power the mind withdrew leaving only the memory of understanding and perhaps a hint of sympathy.

Mandrake swayed on his feet and wiped his hand crossed his brows, in an effort to clear his mind. A soft breath blew across his cheek as the red roan gently nuzzled against him. Clearly he had found acceptance by at least one other traveler in this crazy world.

He no longer concerned himself with the how or the why of it. He only knew that the resolve which had drawn him to look for aid in his quest remained firm and strong. Without hesitation, he threw himself up onto the back of the filly. Mandrake grabbed a hand full of mane, more to steady himself then to guide the horse. Then they turned away from the lonesome sight of the Den and began their pursuit.

CHAPTER EIGHTEEN

It was another day before the Smith regained consciousness. The grey swirl of his delirium lifted, leaving him staring at the ceiling of an unfamiliar room. Try as he might, he could not bring himself to recall how he had gotten there. The last thing that he could remember was the screeching cry of the death birds, as they circled in for their feast. He shuddered, for he knew that he was to have been the main course of that repast.

Thanking what luck had brought him out of his peril, he tried to raise himself out of the thick blankets which had been covering him. He struggled vainly against their coiling grip, before a wave of weakness overcame him and he was forced to ease back into the softness of the couch on which he lay.

Feeling helpless he tried to think through his present predicament. Deciding that if he were in real danger his captors would have long since dispatched him and seeing nothing else that he could do in his weakened state, he decided to call out for help.

His voice cracked on the first effort and the sound was very low. Gathering his strength he put all of his energy behind the next effort. Although little better, he did hear a response from beyond the curtained door. It lay along a wall that was in his limited field of vision. Soon the footfalls of someone or something, approaching sounded from without.

With an effort he propped himself up on his elbows and held his head erect as the curtain parted allowing the egress of two unlikely looking characters. The first, was the taller of the two and although his hair swung down over leather clad shoulders there could have been no doubt of his powerful, masculine physique. The man's eyes swept the Smith and then were diverted to stare at a spot over the bed and fastened there.

He stepped aside to allow the second and older stranger through the doorway. Even as the first man had dominated the room with his physical presence, this newcomer caught and held the Smith's attention. His was the charisma of power. Confidence and comfort radiated from him as he stood looking over the Smith. A knowing smile played upon the man's lips.

No one spoke. The feeling of suspense was thick in the room. Finally the Smith could stand the silence no longer. He said, in a steady enough voice, "If you two could please explain where I am and what I am doing here I would be grateful."

The young man continued to avoid looking at the Smith, as if in fear of acknowledging his existence, but the old one had no such compunction. He stood for a moment longer in silence, as if he were rehearsing what to say in his mind, then he smiled warmly at the Smith and spoke. "I am the Healer of the Clear Run River, this rash but noble young man is Prince Silvermane. It was he who raced you here as you lay on death's door, in the slim hope that I might be able to save you."

The Healer held up a warning hand as the Smith began to sputter his thanks. "You must hold your thanks for you may yet be luckless and not truly have found your succor. The Prince, in his enthusiasm, brought you here as he ought. Had you been of any other race than that of the Were you would have been welcome amongst us."

"For you see friend, our two peoples have been at odds for many a year. You are now to be held in judgement by the Lord of this land. The King of the Horsepeople has been notified of your existence and we expect to hear word from the Court at any time concerning your fate."

The Smith was stunned by the gross unfairness of the fates. Here he was saved from what he was sure would have been a terrible death, only to be accused of being something that he had never been, had never wanted to be. A thing that had been forced upon him with no knowledge of his and almost at the cost of his life. Not to mention the loss of the one girl that he had ever come to care for.

The Trumpet of Harmony

The anger that had possessed him before the world had gone dark on him the last time, once again boiled to the surface. This time he would not let it submerge again. He was going to control his own life and he was going to start right now!

Propped carefully on the soft cot the Smith's eyes caught and held those of the Prince. Slowly but clearly the Smith spoke. "I thank you Prince Silvermane for my life, now that I am in your favor I beg one more boon."

The Prince became attentive. He felt the spark of power flowing around the Smith. A look of astonishment crossed his face, yet he answered as a Prince should. Proud of bearing and regal, but something deep inside of him began to realize that his helpless prisoner was far more then he appeared to be. "Speak for now we both are truly equals. Know this, I am as much of a prisoner here as you. The penalty for breaking the old laws could be death!"

The Smith relaxed a fraction but the determination and the power did not lessen. "Prince, what I say is the truth. I speak and swear it before all of the old gods. I, not that long ago, was a simple village smith. I wanted for nothing and I lived happily serving my people, but for a reason that is more personal than practical I left my village. After some pleasant times on the road I and my companion found ourselves captives of a strange manic being, who lives underground in a maze of tunnels somewhere in a wasteland near here. I have no way of knowing in what direction you have brought me out of peril, but it must be nearby.

"During that captivity I was altered, in what manner I can not say but in our escape from the tunnels I discovered my body capable of changing its form. I did not do this voluntarily and I don't mind saying that I'm scared to death of the wild emotions that I felt and the deadly things that I was capable of doing in that changed state. But I swear that I was unable to do these things before I was captured."

"I hope that you think I'm sane, for if I were you, I would think me a mad man." With that the Smith fell silent and watched the faces of the two

Stephen Goodale   140

men in front of him. The Healer's face mirrored understanding and compassion, but the Prince looked unconvinced.

The Prince broke the strained silence that ensued. "It is plain to me that you have not the strength to travel much less escape. So I will leave you to your own devices until the messenger returns from my father the King. This much I will say now, you have not convinced me of the truth of your story, yet I will keep my eyes and mind open. You may yet be able to persuade me." With that the Prince turned and left the room, heavy curtains swaying in his wake.

The Healer followed the Prince out with his eyes and then turned back to face the Smith. "The Prince is a proud man and a good leader of his people. I'm afraid though, he has blamed himself for breaking trust and will not now, be easy to convince. He believes that he has committed a crime by bringing you here."

The Smith looked curiously at the Healer. There was something about the man's casual tones that made the Smith think that the Healer had believed his story. "What I have said is the truth," said the Smith. "Up until I awoke from my delirium, I had no idea that you or your people existed." He paused as a look of puzzlement crossed his face.

"You seem to know of others like myself. Have there been many prisoners of the Tunnel Master who have escaped after they had been changed, as I?"

The Healer looked closely into the Smith's eyes. He was searching for something of those others that had aided in healing the Smith. "No lad." He replied. "There have been no others like you. However there is a race of beings who had been bred and molded much the same as we were, many centuries ago. These also have the ability to change their guise, from man to wolf and back at their will."

At the Smith's puzzled look the Healer went on to explain the origin of the two changeling species and the history of their escape from the horrors of the Tunnel Master. "So you see lad it was because of the destruction of most of the rebelling forces, some say accomplished mainly with treachery that the enmity of our two races began. That is why the apparent breach of our laws by the Prince is so serious."

The Smith tried to cope with the information given him so freely by the Healer, but it was too much for his weaken mind to grasp. He felt himself growing faint and once more collapsed down into the soft folds of the couch.

The Healer stood looking over him for a moment, bending quickly to slip a small scroll of parchment onto the pillow next to the Smith's head. Satisfied that he had for the present done what he could, the Healer walked quietly out of the room leaving the Smith to his dreams.

When the Smith awoke, the dull ache in his head was gone. He could feel strength flowing through his body. Raising himself easily up from the couch, he caught the sound of rustling parchment. Glancing down he saw a small roll which had been laying next to his head on the pillow. Curiously he leaned down and picked it up.

Using the couch for a table he spread the thin sheet of paper out flat. Smoothing the edges, he read the words printed there. As they unfolded, his mind began to grasp their meaning and a look of wonder crossed his face.

There before him lay the Law of the Weres. It was a code by which all of the Were race could live. It also was a pattern of safeguards which could be used to prevent madness during the transformation. It seemed that those who came by their changeling heritage honestly, were not monsters at all but were well aware of the double edge that their beastly demeanor gave them. They used the Laws found in the Code to control the beast within and stay human.

It was great relief that he rerolled the parchment, at a loss to know how it had gotten to him but grateful that it had. Now as he looked around the healing chamber he could see a set of clean clothes laid out for him by a dressing bench. Moving to the bench he quickly dressed, because another problem was making its presence known. He was ravenously hungry.

The Smith had barely finished when once again he heard the sound of approaching footfalls. This time when the curtain parted, the Prince faced him alone. "The Healer said that you would soon be rising from your couch. He sent me to bring you to the table."

The Prince stepped out in front of the Smith and led the way down a short passage. The welcoming aroma of fresh baked bread reached them as they came to a wide arch. Bright light from open widows showed a large room with a baking hearth on one wall and a number of long tables, set up for meals, filling most of the remaining floor space.

There were no other diners there at present, but as the Prince led the Smith down the aisle between the tables, several of the Healer's household followed them in through the arch. As the Smith settled into the table, serving wenches came in and set deep, fragrant platters down in front of them.

There were slabs of warm bread, ewers of honey, huge salads and plenty of mead. The fare was simple but tasted unlike any food the Smith had ever eaten before. He kept at his plate without wasting time on conversation. After a bit, the Smith became aware that the Prince had stopped eating and was beginning to eye him with something that resembled awe.

At last the Smith slackened his pace. Finishing the last bit of salad on his plate, he pushed himself away from the table. "That was the best meal I've had, in many a day," said the Smith. "Tell me Prince Silvermane, is it possible to take a short walk and enjoy the taste of fresh air for desert?"

The Prince smiled at the Smith. "That is an excellent suggestion, Sir Smith, but we must be careful to watch each other, after all we are both awaiting the King's justice!"

The Trumpet of Harmony

Excusing themselves from the company of those who still supped, they walked the short distance to the Healer's front door. Here the Prince turned to the Smith. "I don't know why I should trust you but there is something about you that lends itself to trust. Also the Healer keeps a high place in my father's kingdom. He has assured me that you are not only no threat to my people, but may in some way that only he can see, be of extreme importance to us."

The Smith looked at his host, a startled expression on his face. The Prince stopped any attempt by the Smith to deny the Healer's words. "Don't try to forestall the fates, what will be, will be. Meanwhile, let us at least be companions in misery. If I give you my word that I will not try to escape then I will accept your word that you will not. Are we agreed?"

The Prince extended his hand in a tradition so long in use, its origins were forgotten. Taking the Prince's hand in his the Smith squeezed firmly and shook their joined fists. "My friend," said the Smith. "You have no idea how long it's been since I've felt as welcomed in a place, as I do now. Thank you for your trust, I will not let you down."

From the door of the Healer's cot the sound of rushing water once more caught the Prince's ears. Turning to the Smith, the Prince broke into a grin. "Let us follow the sound of the Clear Run to where its banks draw close to this house. There is a man there, that I'd like you to meet."

Puzzled, but happy to be free for the moment to enjoy the cool air and the warm midday sun, the Smith willingly followed the Prince. Soon they could discern a sound rising above the murmur of the flowing river. The sound acted in disharmony with the sweet singing of the river. It was immediately apparent that someone was shamelessly voicing a nameless song at the top of his lungs. The voice was in total disregard for anything that might have been called a melody.

Rounding a final bend in the path the Prince and the Smith came out on the banks of the river. There standing in the shallows of the Clear Run was a tall lanky man not much out of his youth. With a final bellow the man finished with his song, and bent down to examine his roguishly handsome visage in the still shallows.

The Prince smiled and then shouted. "Hail and well met Sir Swiftfoot." As Swiftfoot looked up he waved a hand in a motion, which said come join the fun. "Friend Swiftfoot allow me to present the Smith, a traveler from a far village, on a quest of his own keeping. Vast wonders and many close escapes has he seen. Let us now convince him to soak in the cooling waters of the Clear Run and forget the troubles of his road."

They scrambled down the steep bank and strode out onto the sandy spit where the gentle backwater of the Clear Run formed the bathing pool of Sir Swiftfoot. As they came Swiftfoot strode from the shallows and stood looking curiously at the Smith. Finally he said to the Prince, "You know he does look a lot better once he is conscious. Not much of a threat to the Realm, I'd say. I hope that we didn't over do it a bit by sending word to your father."

Silvermane was about to remind his friend that the situation was nothing to joke about. But he caught the serious set of Swiftfoot's jaw and decided that he knew, as well as the Prince himself, how bad things could get. Still there was no need to think gloomy thoughts. They were all young, even this Smith fellow was just out of his first fuzz. Why worry about those things that they had no control over.

So with a lighter heart, the Prince decided that they should join his friend in a cool, after lunch soak. Stripping down he launched himself at the startled Swiftfoot, but as usual his friend regained his balance and dodged the assault without a problem. However, he did not count on the speed at which the Smith joined in the melee.

A broad smile painted the young Smith's face as he had quickly stripped off his own clothes. Then with an unaccustomed dexterity, he threw himself behind the triumphant Swiftfoot just as the Prince regained his balance.

The Trumpet of Harmony

Seeing at once what the Smith was up to, the Prince lunged again at his friend. As expected Swiftfoot moved quickly backwards, only to find that he was tumbling head over heels while the Smith cut his legs out from under him. He landed on his back in the Clear Run's wet embrace.

Swiftfoot came up sputtering, cursing and swinging his fists wildly. The two men watched from a safe distance, laughing at the absurd antics of the dripping victim. For a moment he looked as if he were about to reprimand his two antagonists but he caught the humor of the situation and joined in their merriment.

Calming at last the trio, settled down to a long soak. It was only when the Prince noticed the slightly blue tinge creeping into the Smith's pallor that he called a halt to the celebration. Shivering but invigorated they made their way up the bank and quickly dressed. The evening was setting in and the air was definitely turning colder.

Unwilling to end the night so early, the Prince suggested that they retire to his room, for a mug of warm mead. "Apart from that, I want to hear more of our gallant Smith's adventures. It is so boring being in court all the time. I don't get many chances to escape my duties to my people."

"Yes and it's a good thing too," chimed in Swiftfoot. "That way I don't have to keep pulling you out of the messes you make."

The Healer met them at the door, a worried look crossed his face, as he examined the Smith. Satisfied for the moment that his patient was not going to expire immediately, he suggested that the Smith would do well to turn in early. "After all," he said, "you have only just risen this afternoon from a terrible wound. It would not due to have you relapse before the King has decided what's to be done with you!"

The Prince hurriedly explained that they were just headed for his sleeping chamber for a mug of mead and that he would personally see to it that the Smith gets his rest. "Well, as long as you don't make it more then another hour, I can not see the harm. But no more then an hour," admonished the

The Trumpet of Harmony

Healer.

They moved aside as the Healer walked past them and on down the hall to his study. The Prince held a kindly smile on his lips as he watched him go. The Healer was truly one of the gentlest men that the Prince had ever met. Yet it would do no good to antagonize him, for the man could be a stern task master when it came to handling the sick.

Quietly he led his small entourage to the room that he had been given while visiting here. Ringing for a serving wench they waited in companionable silence until she had come and gone, leaving them steaming mugs of honey mead.

"Now then." The Prince broke the silence. "Let's hear your story from beginning to end. I'm especially interested in all that you can tell me of the Tunnel Master and his complex. It has been time out of mind since any of our people have entered his darkened realm and returned to tell about it."

They sat enthralled as the Smith, for the first time, told his whole story. For some reason he did not hesitate to speak of his quest nor of the events that had unfolded for him. He did, however feel a little embarrassed in talking of Rosita and his feelings for her. However their reassurances led the Smith to believe that he was not such an isolated case after all. Even these carefree men had at one time or another felt the sting of love.

They made him go over those final days in the tunnels again. Traveling as he had with no guide and with the burden of a changed Rosita. They did, much to his relief agree, that the girl he had brought out of that maze was indeed the same one that had gone in after him. It seemed that they, or their histories were somehow acquainted with the strange transformation that had befallen Rosita.

"Yes indeed, although it has been many generations of our people since we have seen one such as you describe." The Prince paused in thought. "It once was a favorite trick of the Tunnel Master, to take one of the People hostage and then return him to us, unharmed but changed so that he

Stephen Goodale   147

would not even recognize his own family."

"What happened to them?" Asked the Smith.

"Well, it was quite by accident, but once a long time ago the Tunnel Master did such to a son of the King. Every known method of cure was summoned up to aid in the healing, but to no avail. Finally distraught, to the point of madness, the King took his son and went up onto the high mount, which lies on the very southern edge of our borders, in order to pray to the gods. Asking only aid for his son and offering his life for that of his heir."

The Prince paused in his narrative and Swiftfoot took up the accounting. "It was then that the King heard the sound of a distant trumpet. It was the sweetest sound that he had ever heard. Its voice was so poignant that the King had to cover his ears or be driven mad by its beauty."

The Prince looked up from his introspection and finished the story. "When at last the King had removed his hands from his ears and could once again hear, the trumpet had fallen silent. In that silence the sound of his son's voice could be heard calling out his father's name. With tears of joy the king held his son to him and the light of recognition dawned in the boy's eyes. Crying, he clung to his father."

"It has been from that day to this, since the Tunnel Master has tried that particular trick. I wonder why he has attempted it now. For he surely knows that the last attempt had failed even though both he and our people have no idea why. The People just say it was the intervention of the Gods and as such could not be counted on to happen again."

As the Prince spoke the Smith felt excitement run in his blood. He asked how long ago it was that this miracle occurred. The Prince replied with a puzzled frown that it would be approximately a thousand years since the King won his son back on the high mount of The King's Hope, as the mount had come to be known.

The Trumpet of Harmony

When the Prince started to ask the Smith why the year might be important, the quick mind of Swiftfoot supplied a guess. In a quiet voice he said, "You think that this story somehow relates to your quest and the first of the four symbols of power that you've been enjoined to retrieve."

The Smith turned so that he faced the two men and nodded his head in agreement. "But it is now much more important to me that I find this Trumpet of Harmony, since I know that it might be used as a cure for the one I love."

They fell silent as each contemplated this latest development. The Prince had grown very fond of the Smith in the short time that he had been with him. He no longer doubted the Smith's story. In fact he found it fascinating. With a surge of emotion, he decided that no matter what else happened, he would see to it that Rosita was found and the two of them reunited at the King's Hope Mount. Who knows, they might even find the ancient cure and break the evil spell laid on Rosita by the Tunnel Master.

For now though, it was getting late and the Healer would be furious that they've kept the Smith up this long. Still there was one more question that the Prince wanted to ask the Smith. Breaking the reverie of his friends, he said to the Smith, "Why is it that you do not use a name, my friend. It seems awkward to call you by that which you did as a profession."

The Smith thought about the question for a moment. Then he asked his host if there were any metal object in his room that either needed repair or that could be modified without damaging its basic use.

Curiosity peaked, Silermane looked about him until at last his eyes fell to the scabbard of his sword. It lay where he had thrown it, after one of his aides had caught up with him and given the Prince his personal effects. On the scabbard, rough usage had battered the metal filigree which formed the linage of the weapon. He had meant to have it repaired but he seldom even carried the thing, so it kept slipping his mind.

The Trumpet of Harmony

Now he retrieved it and handed it to the Smith. Describing what the problem was and what he had intended to do with the thing, he sat back watching his new friend.

The Smith, for his part, settled himself comfortably and closed his eyes. In his mind he pictured the scabbard as it was and then built an image of the completed filigree. With practiced patience, he brought the images together in his mind and then he ran his hands over the damaged area. Soon all that remained of the picture was the image of the completed scabbard.

Opening his eyes, he moved his hands away from his work and heard gasps of astonishment from the two men next to him. For there, brightly polished as if newly forged, was the completed scabbard down to the last detail of the Prince's description.

The Smith felt a wave of exhaustion pass over him. The Prince noticed the shutter that passed through the big man's frame. With the aid of Swiftfoot, the Prince supported the now slumping Smith and they managed to get him to his own chamber. Making the man comfortable, they left him in deep slumber.

Back in the Prince's room they sat and looked at each other. It was Swiftfoot who managed to break the stunned silence. "My Prince, I think that some providence is looking down over our shoulder. For of all the poor wretches in the world that we could have possibly been called on to save, we saved one who could perform Magic!"

"Not only that my friend," replied Silermane, "but we seem to have found one whose destiny might be that chosen by the Gods themselves." The Prince then told his friend of his resolve to aid the Smith.

Swiftfoot did not reply, but in his heart he knew that his friend had already decided on this course of action. Once the Prince made such a commitment, Swiftfoot knew that there was nothing in the world that would deter him from his vow.

Sighing, Swiftfoot arose and bowed, in mock respect to his friend. "I am, as always your humble servant my lord, and as such will do my best to make sure you survive your decision. At least long enough, for your father to have you hanged anyway." Shaking his head he left his Prince alone to contemplate his rashness.

CHAPTER NINETEEN

Darkness had given way to the bright light of early morning and still they raced on. The deep emerald grass clung around the hooves and wheels of their horses and wagons. Rosita had long since begun to weary of the uncomfortable pace of Farhunter's horse. She longed to be free to range the meadow land in her Were shape.

She had thought that an added guard would be a wise and prudent precaution in their flight. She said as much to her Uncle. How strange it was to find a kinsman from her mother's family! However he quickly denied her the idea. It would seem that the land they traveled through now had long been forbidden to one of their race.

"Rosita, it would be death for any of our race to be discovered this far into the pasturage of the Realm. Our only hope of being unmolested lies in the speed of our passage and the allusion, that we are just another of those scattered bands of humans who travel the countryside in search of a better life."

His words were scarcely out of his mouth, when the alarm was sounded from up ahead. Urging his mount to greater speed, Farhunter quickly brought them up to the head of their flying column. From there Rosita was able to look out far over the terrain ahead. There in front of them and to the right, standing proudly on a grassy knoll, was the form of a large stallion.

The magnificent creature calmly watched the large caravan of her people. He appeared completely unafraid and stayed still as stone for many long moments before rearing up high on his hind legs and disappearing down the opposite side of the hill.

Farhunter pursed his lips in worry. There would be no way to make a full run for it, there were too many oldsters and children in their midst. Even so they could pick up the pace and close up the gaps in their line.

So, Rosita and he rode slowly down the line of refugees urging a greater speed and more care in their spacing. Farhunter also arranged to put outlying scouts around the line of wagons, in the hope that they might have some measure of warning before their foes could reach them.

"It is fortunate that the Horsepeople have withdrawn into their winter quarters, at the foot of the White Mountains and have left their summer abode here in the outer pasturage." Farhunter fell silent as they rode up and down the line of their march. Rosita could only imagine the pressure the man felt, but she thrilled in the knowledge that this brave man was her mother's brother. To break the silence and ease the tension Rosita asked Farhunter to tell her of the Horsepeople.

Farhunter took another look at his people in their flight and then looked at his sister's daughter. He smiled to himself as the thought crossed his mind that she was to old to be telling stories to. Still he had nothing but time right now and it might make the girl feel more at home with her people.

So, he spoke of the other race that was created to serve some unknown purpose of the Tunnel Master. He told her of the great palace of the king tucked away under the skirts of the tall White Mountains, down away to the south and west of where they stood. "In many ways," he said, "they have established a well ordered and peaceful life for themselves. They are tied very closely to their land, loving it almost as much as they love their freedom."

Then he delved deeper into the past until he came upon the time of revolt and death. Here Farhunter's tone of voice grew harsher as he spoke of the secret alliance between the two races. They had stood united against the Tunnel Master in their bid to win freedom from his enslavement.

It had been a desperate and bitter fight. Many of both races had fallen to win them freedom, but at last they fought free of the tunnels and had struggled into the waste. Their scouts had brought them hope. For they had come upon the lands to the south, still lush and green.

They had camped in the burned out remains of the old ones' town. There they licked their wounds and discussed the future when the forces of the Tunnel Master fell upon them again.

How the Tunnel Master had found them became apparent when, during that last struggle a spy of the Horse race was caught among those dreaded machines. In fact he had been observed to direct some of the slaughter of the Were race personally before he was killed.

When the battle finally was over and the forces of the Tunnel Master lay in smoldering ruins, almost one half of the survivors of the flight from the tunnels lay dead. They were in sorry shape, but in their breasts the hatred of the Horsepeople was strong. This was aided by the fact that the Horsepeople had come crying vengeance, for they claimed that they had proof that it was a member of the Were race that had in fact directed the last assault upon their camp. They called us traitors.

It would have been a struggle to the death had it not been for the wise council of two elders, one for each of the races. They cried truce instead of battle. For know this Rosita, our numbers at that point were so low that had we lost many more of the people we would have become extinct.

So it was that the land to the south was divided between the races. The Were's laid claim to the wooded forests and the Horsepeople to those rolling grasslands that had opened up in front of them. To each race was given the task of patrolling their borders against any attack from the tunnels.

"From that day to this we have hated and distrusted those who ride the meadows and they have hated us. It always seemed a shame but the betrayal cost so much of the blood of both races that no common ground could later be found and after a time they stopped trying."

Farhunter fell quiet, apparently finished for the moment with his narrative, but Rosita was puzzled. Finally she broke the silence. "Farhunter, I thought our people had discovered the truth about the betrayal. Isn't that why our ancestors put the protection stone on the outskirts of the tunnels? To tell the future generations what had truly happened?"

Farhunter looked at his niece without comprehension. Rosita caught the look and became impatient at his lack of understanding. "I guess it would be better to tell you my whole story and you can judge the value of what I've seen in the light of your experience with the Tunnel Master."

Rosita picked up the threads of her story from her first encounter with the strange wolf who had come to her in the forest glen right on through the moment that she awoke in the saddle, held there by Farhunter's strong arms. It was a lengthy tale and the morning had long passed the mid afternoon hour when she at last finished.

There were times during her tale that Farhunter smiled sadly to himself. Rosita's description of her mother was like a balm to him, for a long unhealed wound. Her apparent affection for the Smith became obvious, at least to him, although he suspected that she had not yet realized that she was truly in love.

All of that paled in comparison to her description of the protective stone. The story it told was identical to the oral and written history of his people except that part which had shown the duplicity was actually a plot by the Tunnel Master to drive a wedge between the two allied races. The tactic was brilliant. It had worked for hundreds of years.

Even the part of the story in which Rosita had not been truly herself aided Farhunter in understanding the Tunnel Master's methods. If a person could be duplicated and that duplicate used in such a manner, then it was fully possible that they had hated needlessly all of these years.

As the silence between them lengthened Farhunter felt more and more the fool. How could they have allowed themselves to play the part so well? He had always carried a certain respect for the Horsepeople in his heart and now it was just possible that his feelings for that brave folk had been right all along.

He must be certain though, that this was not yet another trick of the Tunnel Master. He resolved in his heart that he would make the dangerous journey back through the Were land and then into the Tunnel Master's domain to stand as Rosita had stood. If he could believe the stone then there would be a reconciliation with those who should have been their brothers all these years.

Rosita broke the silence by asking a simple question. "Was it you those times in the forest? Were you watching over our band?"

The eyes of Farhunter sparkled in mischief as he looked at his niece. "I kept you and your's out of trouble, until you were able to take over the role. Believe me it took most of my time, too."

CHAPTER TWENTY

Mandrake could almost believe that he was dreaming. The smooth sure pace of his new friend and companion could lull him into sleep, if he let it. Still he busied himself by developing the mind touch that allowed him to communicate with the filly.

It seems that she was one of the Horsepeople but like him had been different enough to have been considered an outsider in her people's lives. She had always been treated well and her parents were very close to her, but there had always been that which had kept her apart. Even though her voice sang warm and mellow in Mandrake's mind it would be the only place that he could hear it. She had been mute from birth. Born, her parents had been told, without even a vestigial remnant of vocal cords.

Shadow had been loved but had grown up lonely, so terribly alone. Unable to tell anyone her thoughts, or wishes she was reliant on others to survive. Finally, she ran away unable to be a burden on another soul.

It was when she had wandered in the wilds that a strange talent had begun to manifest itself. There were times when she could hear whispers in her head. At first she feared that the loneliness had toppled her reason. Slowly as she began to listen she discovered that the voices belonged to the wild animals that had shared the woodland around her. What was amazing to her was that no matter what the animal was, she was able to understand the voices.

As Shadow concentrated on the words that would have been hers had the gods not been so cruel, she found that she could communicate in return with the wild animals around her. Forming the words carefully in her mind and focusing on the creature that she wanted to reach, she found that they heard. They heard her!

She had been on her way back to her people when she had caught the desperate plea being cast by Mandrake. The need in that call had been so poignant that she was forced almost against her will to respond. She, of course, knew that he was one of the Were folk, but it did not matter. Because the depth of his feelings, the amount of pain in his soul and the quality of his character had been laid bare to the probe of her mind.

Shadow knew that he had the power to block that invasion. His mind was powerful. But he had chosen not to do so, instead he had invited her in, to share completely all that he was and all that he had been. Even though it could cost her the chance to be with this terribly complex man, Shadow knew that the only way to really become part of his life was to let him know her as deeply as she had come to know him.

Her pace had been swift in the pursuit of the Pack, but she was not as large and powerful as most of her people. She soon began to tire under the burden of Mandrake's weight.

He was no horseman, he trusted to her to care for him as they rode. Meanwhile Mandrake had been striving to improve the quality of his mind link with his beautiful companion. Now he could sense the strain that came into that link. His mount was growing weary and was unable to maintain the pace that he had set.

Mandrake was torn with indecision. If he were to stop now it would mean that he could scarcely reach the refugees before the hunting pack caught up with them. However if he did not give pause to let his mount rest, then he would surely cause her harm and that he could not abide.

With a silent prayer that somehow those that he cared for would be delivered from their horrible fate, he pulled up gently on his hands at the same time broadcasting the need to stop and rest. His mount snickered in denial but her own legs betrayed her as she tried to stumble onward.

There was a sheltered grove of trees ahead of them. Mandrake guided them into the cool shadows under the tree's thick boughs and dismounted quickly. It was a comforting place that exuded peace. The sound of a bubbling spring could just be heard over the gentle rustle of the leaves.

The Trumpet of Harmony

Mandrake filled the water carrier that he had stolen from one of the farm holds and then stood back to allow the filly to drink her fill. He sat in the tall grass looking at the fiery roan. She was gracefully drinking from the rocky rim of the spring.

He noticed that there was something strange about the appearance and the set of those rocks. Mandrake studied them, looking for he knew not what. The filly had long since finished and had wandered off into the copse, probably in search of better shade. The mid-afternoon sun was warm and he could feel the sweat on his own brow, but still he sat. He let his mind wander aimlessly over those stones.

Suddenly he realized that those rocks had been laid out in a pattern. Excited he arose to his feet and began to pull at the concealing overgrowth that surrounded the spring's basin. It came away easily, as if their roots had not really found anchorage in the stone. They seemed to have doggedly held to the surface soil that the winds had over the years deposited around the spring.

When he had at last finished, sweat poured in rivulets from his face, but he scarcely noticed. For there in front of him was the image, untouched by the years of a five pointed star. The pavement under the thin layer of soil shone in an outline of dusky silver. Almost as if it gave off it's own light instead of reflecting the bright glare of the sun.

The spring was centered in the very heart of the star and it picked up the glow from the pavement. It began to shine in its own light. A noise from behind him, caused Mandrake to turn from his fascinated study. There Staring at him with apparent unconcern was a slim woman, whose long flowing red hair scarcely concealed the softness of her curves.

The truth dawned on Mandrake as he fought to take his eyes off of the beautiful creature next to him. He waited for the expected race hatred to flare through his veins. Finding, not much to his surprise, that he had no hatred for this woman. After all, she had seen into his very soul and still chose to bear him hence with no animosity.

The Trumpet of Harmony

She turned to face him and her voice filled his mind. It was a soft warm voice, almost shy. Yet it carried a strong self assurance, that left Mandrake little doubt about the determination of her spirit.

"My name is Shadow," she whispered to Mandrake. "I am of the Horsepeople and I too know the shame of being different."

Mandrake thought he knew what she meant. The horsepeople, although much kinder then most of the Were race, had a absorption with physical beauty. Especially when it came to that of the body. They admired sculpted perfection, strength and form. Any one that might be thought of falling short of their ideal was looked upon with sympathy, it's true, but with little else.

Shadow, as lovely as she was, would be considered imperfect. Someone to be cared for, but apart from the basics, ignored. Sad for her experiences, Mandrake was overwhelmingly joyous to have her as a companion.

Carefully Mandrake reached out and tilted her chin up. With a look that expressed a million words he gazed for a second into her eyes and then gently kissed her full red lips. His hands reached out to brush the modest curtain of her flowing hair aside. Her long slender arms reached out and held him about the neck as she willingly yielded to his kisses.

They held each other for a moment that stood outside of normal time. Their passions transcended any question of race or origin. There they made love in the brilliant fire of the silver star. As they reached the heights of emotion so too did the flood of silver light. Its intensity was that of a small sun hiding, them from prying eyes.

Tenderly they held each other as their passions ebbed. The silver light of the fountain danced around them and they lay content in each other's arms. Content to watch that ever changing flow of light.

How long it was that they lay so, Mandrake could not say. When at last the light began to fade from the fountain they discovered that they no longer lay in the copse of trees. Instead they stared incredulously at a well appointed sleeping room. There was a shaft of silver light beaming down on them from a window high above.

The room was framed by sharply angled walls. A cool white covered those walls picking up the radiance from the window. Mandrake sprang from the covers and Shadow joined him holding tightly to his side. "What has happened to us", she whispered nervously to her lover.

Mandrake did not answer but busied himself with a thorough study of the room. It was unlike any other sleeping chamber that he had ever seen. Its lines were sharp and clean. The furniture was sparse but functional. Most of it made from metal.

Against the far wall, a door was framed and it was ajar. There seemed to be a light shining through it and from beyond it came the sound of voices.

Mandrake motioned for Shadow to quietly follow him to that portal. They reached the door without raising an alarm. Gently Mandrake nudged the door open further. It opened effortlessly.

The sight beyond the door made Mandrake and Shadow blink in disbelief. Surely they must be sharing some dream. For there, across from their door, stood a being. They were unable to make out any details of the creature's appearance because it too was shrouded in the silver light that had enthralled them a moment earlier.

They perhaps could not see the creature in front of them but it became immediately aware of their presence. A soft voice echoed in their minds. "Do not be alarmed. You have been transported to a place of safety. We have waited long for both of you."

Mandrake screwed his eyes up to get a glimpse of their captors but to no avail. The being shifted slightly and once again its voice came clearly to their minds. "You are not prisoners. You have accidently activated one of the old transport devices. It is gratifying to know that they can still function after all these millennia."

"You can of course leave and return to the spring, but I would like to talk to you briefly about the future before you make up your minds. You were destined to come to us. It was foretold long ago that two of the new races would seek us out. They would come willing and be apt pupils for our dying knowledge. We, who are the spirit kin of this the planet Marintha, could teach you much."

Mandrake slowly closed his mouth, which had been hanging open in astonishment. Shadow who had clung nervously to his side straightened her shoulders and stood tall next to him. Her mental voice broke the prolonged silence. "Our time is not our own to give. We travel to warn my love's people of their doom. Even now we may be too late to save his kin."

The tall being faced them calmly and its measured voice filled their minds in response. "There is nothing that you could have done to stop the course of events transpiring in the world above. The future is wide. Many things that, may for the moment seem horrible and devastating are in reality a form of growth. Mandrake's people will survive their current crisis and because of it become a strong nation."

Mandrake cleared his throat and interrupted the creature's explanation of events involving his people. "How do you know these things? The future is one thing all must face with the same lack of knowledge. No one can claim the ability to foretell its course."

Gentle laughter filled their minds. The creature's thoughts once more reached out to them. "Well put my young friend. Yet there are many things in this universe that do not fit into your well thought out order. There are those who can pierce the future in thought, if not in physical form. There are also ways to manipulate the stream of time. Not to change the course of events mind you, but to allow those events to flow at different rates. We who occupy this plane of existence are no longer flowing down the stream of time at the same rate as the world above."

The creature paused in its thoughts and examined their emotional and mental responses to his words. He was amazed at their rapid absorption of new concepts and ideas. He was just as pleased by their growing sense of curiosity. "We who were once rulers of a million different races now rule only the natural order of our planet. We are not ignorant of events that occur beyond the boundaries of its space. You were destined to come to us so that we might share our knowledge with you. Yet there is a higher destiny waiting for you."

"The events that are occurring on our planet are causing ripples throughout the fabric of the physical universe. Soon those ripples will reach those who would have been better left undisturbed. A terrible fate will await all, if those who struggle now on Marintha should fail in their goals. There are those who you might aid, that hold the key to a bright and wonderful future. Yet the only way to help them is to stay now with us and learn what we can teach you."

"Time will move much quicker for you here, then for those who await you. We will give you what we can and allow you to see some of the future. But it will be through your efforts and not ours that the future will be wrought. What we can do we have done. There are other concerns which draw on our strengths and need our attention. The decision is yours. We await your answer."

Mandrake let the words flow through his mind. He weighed them against his desires and found that he hungered for the chance to redeem himself to his people and to his world. Here he was being offered a chance to gain knowledge and experience that would enable him to achieve his desires. Shadow had never desired knowledge or power but hungered instead for love and happiness. She had sensed the depths of Mandrake's soul and knew what her love's answer would be. Still in her heart she felt there was a reason, separate from his desires, that she should accept this creature's offer. Suddenly she knew, but she buried that knowledge deep within her soul until such time that she would be called upon to use it.
The two lovers turned and looked into each other's eyes. As their eyes met

their minds joined and they knew each others answer. United they turned to the waiting creature and responded in unison. "We accept your offer and will become your students. Teach us and we will serve those who struggle above."

CHAPTER TWENTY-ONE

The dark of night was still upon the world when the Smith was awakened by the sounds of excited voices. The door to his room opened and the light of a shielded lantern revealed the tall form of the Prince and the slighter form of the Healer.

Moving quickly to the Smith's bedside, the Prince leaned over to look down on his new friend. "Sir Smith, a messenger has come unlooked for in the night. He has brought a message from my father that concerns you in many ways. First let me tell you that although displeased by my breach of faith by not following the letter of the People's Law, he was not all that put out. As a matter of fact, I've been enjoined to return with you to the Palace so that he might hear your story personally."

The Smith was wide awake now, as he lay looking up at the Prince. He felt a growing excitement stir in his veins, though he could not say why. It was plain that the Prince had more news to tell and he soon broke the brief silence.

"There is other more important news, my friend. It seems that late yesterday morning, a scout on routine patrol deep within the heart of the pasturage found a large band of humans traveling through our land. This has been unheard of since we claimed this land many centuries ago."

"The scout soon realized that the band was unswerving in direction and moving with great speed considering that they were burdened down with oldsters, women and children."

The Prince paused once more. His eyes were lit with the excitement of the unknown and the thrill of challenge. For it seemed that his father had commanded him to take Swiftfoot and his personal guard to intercept this band of interlopers and to determine their purpose.

"You are to go with us my friend, for I've been instructed to take you to my father once I've seen to this problem. With us will go the Healer, for you must arrive in one piece or my Father will truly be mad. He loves to hear a good story and I've assured him that yours is an epic."

Laughing, the Prince turned away from the bewildered Smith and spoke to the Healer, who stood quietly by his side. "We leave as soon as you can get your affairs together here and we get a little breakfast in us. It will be a long run."

Turning away from the Healer and the Smith, Silvermane put the lamp down on the corner of a table and left without another word. The Healer looked curiously at the Smith. "How do you feel this morning?"

The Smith stretched his huge frame, smiled at the older man and answered that he couldn't remember feeling better. "I am a little confused, though. It seems, that through no choice of my own, I've acquired a curious ability to transform myself into a powerful, frightening animal. I've never thought about being a wolf and I certainly can't ever remember wanting to be one. Now however I find that I can be one."

The Smith looked up at the Healer and continued. "At first I thought that nothing but horror and self destruction could come of this peculiar power. Then yesterday morning when I first awoke, I found laid carefully under my head a packet of aging parchment. On them were the written Laws that the Were race, my new found race, were to live by."

"Now you may laugh but there was much in those Laws that humanized the Were race for me. Would you know anything about those Laws and how that parchment managed to get under my pillow?"

The Healer gave a quick prayer to those unknown powers lurking behind the scenes and then reached a hand down urging the Smith to rise to his feet. "I have found that there are many areas of knowledge that are not necessarily looked at with favor by those who rule us. Yet they are vital to know so that we can use that knowledge to aid our cause."

The Trumpet of Harmony

"That parchment is such. I believed your tale from the start, although I can't tell you why. Suffice it to say that there are powers at work here that are so far above our normal understanding that it would be impossible to put their purposes into words."

"You are going to need full understanding of that which abides within you. It was left to me to help you realize this portion of your future."

The Healer stood back away from the Smith. The Smith's strong body lay bare, now that the sleeping blankets he had clutched in knotted hands had fallen to the floor, in his acceptance of the Healer's words. "I am ready, Healer. Guide me through the transformation and stand by to kill me if I can not control the beast within me."

The Healer agreed and drew his belt knife. He knew that the Gods would not let him use that weapon but then he knew in his heart of hearts that he would not need it. "Do you remember the Code of Transformation?"

At the Smith's nod of affirmation, the Healer continued "You must recite the Code in your mind and never lose sight of it's meaning. You must reach down into your very soul and release the beast that lays within, but you must stay in control. The two parts of your soul must become one. Do you understand?"

The Smith once more nodded. He no longer felt afraid. A curious excitement began to rise in his veins. His head throbbed slightly with the unaccustomed effort but he soon felt himself sliding down into the hidden reaches of his soul. There he looked straight into the eyes of his other self and knew with all the certainty of his being, that this was right.

In his mind, he recited the words of the Code and knew at last the feeling of transformation. Under his mind's direction, he slid into the shape of the Wolf. He was as huge as his human form had been. He felt far more alive then he had ever felt in the past. His senses were extremely alert. Sounds from around the Healer's cot could now be heard, the early morning darkness became grey light to his eyes.

Stephen Goodale   167

The Trumpet of Harmony

He looked up into the eyes of the Healer and saw a smile in the eyes of what should have been his enemy. He waited for the anger and hate of the beast to form. Much to his surprise he remained in complete control with the cool reasoning of his former self.

The Healer let the Smith adjust to his new trappings and then lowered his voice so that the Smith alone could possibly hear. "You must return to your human form now, but in those moments that you can do so without jeopardizing yourself, practice the transformation until it becomes as second nature to you. One other thing, remember that although you can change shapes your clothing can not. Do not allow yourself to become entrapped by them in a moment of desperate need."

The Smith gloried in his new-found form for a few more minutes and then allowed the transformation to occur again. This time it felt more as if he held a fist full of sand and slowly that sand slipped from his grasp. He was quickly himself again. The transformation took only a few seconds but he knew that during that time he would be completely vulnerable.

There was one benefit from his new talent that he noticed immediately. His senses, although dulled by the standards of his Were form, remained much sharper then those he held previously.

The Healer had stepped over to the chest that lay against the wall and removed some tough traveling clothes. These he threw to the Smith, who hurriedly pull them on. For the first time in his life, he felt a faint distaste for being clothed.

The Healer also pulled out a rough looking pack that had been battered but was still serviceable. He looked over to the Smith and said, "this was the pack the Prince found laying near you, when they pulled you from the forest. Everything is as it was and only I have looked over its contents."

The Smith accepted the pack and slung it over his shoulders without another thought. The Healer's face still remained puzzled though. He questioned the Smith, "I don't mean to pry but that heavy chalice is made up of some strange metal that I have never seen before. It has a feeling about it, that gives off a sense of energy. Energy waiting to be released. Of what metal is it made?"

The Smith shrugged and replied with the truth. "I don't know of what metal it is composed. It's nothing that I've ever seen before. Until recently, I made a living at working metals. This chalice came to me just as you see it from my father and his father before him. So, it has been for many generations of my family."

A smile creased the old Healer's face as he shrugged his shoulders in return. "Let the fates keep their secrets. We who are mortal have our own problems to worry about. Come let us hurry or our headstrong Prince will be off without us."

As they left the Smith's room, there indeed striding impatiently up the hall to meet them was the Prince. "Come my friends let us be away. You, that were slow in coming to the table, will have to eat on the way. Sir Swiftfoot and I will serve as your mounts. The royal guard will follow with provisions and gear."

Curious the Smith followed the Prince down the hall and through the dining room. Here the Healer and he were allowed to grab up hand fulls of food and were then quickly hustled out through the front door of the cot.

There already waiting was a sleek looking horse, well muscled and handsome, the Smith guessed, as horses go. The Healer went directly to the horse and threw himself up on it's back with practiced ease. The smith could only guess but that this handsome beast was Swiftfoot in his equine guise.

The Smith could only marvel. This beast was larger then Swiftfoot could ever be in his human form. Weighing, what must be almost three times his normal body weight. The history of changeling species had been laid out for him by the Healer. But the Smith knew that there was more to this magic, then the equations of an insane killer.

Fascinated he watched as Silvermane closed his eyes and slowed his breathing. The transformation of Prince to majestic equine was an awesome sight to witness. Instead of a slow melding of flesh into a new pattern. The Prince's form wavered. His outline became misty and his form actually expanded as it changed its aspect.

The body of the Prince soon coalesced into a magnificent form of power and grace. His guise reflected his human characteristics, but magnified them into heroic proportions. He was a Prince of his people no matter which form he took.

With an impatient toss of his head the Prince indicated that the Smith should mount. Clumsily the Smith complied and wrapped his fist tightly into the mane of his friend. He needed that hold, for the Prince leapt away from the Healer's cot with a surge of speed that underlined his desire to start this new adventure.

The Smith glanced away from the press of the onrushing wind, so that he might see where the Healer and Swiftfoot had gotten to. There was no need for him to fear the loss of that duo, because Swiftfoot strode lazily along side of his Prince. There were no signs of strain in his lean, well muscled body and the Smith came to understand that his name was well placed.

Turning back to face their line of flight, the Smith struggled to get a good look at the lay of land. All that was visible to the naked eye, were the rolling hills of ever present green grass. Content for the moment at his part as an impassive spectator, he leaned his weight back into the hunches of the Prince and closed his eyes. He did not sleep, but he soon became lost in thought and those thoughts turned to the dark-haired Rosita.

How long had it been since he had looked into the laughing eyes of Rosita? He let his mind drift back down the course of their adventures, savoring every moment of the precious time that they had spent together. He realized, not much to his surprise, that there would never be another woman to take her place. His feelings had been strong at their meeting and they were right!

He wondered idly, what Rosita would think of him now that he had full control over his Were powers? Her hate and fear, were forever etched upon his memory. He could only hope that someday, in some fashion, he could bring her back to the Rosita of old. Then and only then would he be able to take her rejection to be her honest feelings and not those of someone controlled by the Tunnel Master.

The leagues flew by. They did not stop for any length of time. Occasionally one of the Horsepeople would gallop up and then the Prince and Swiftfoot would ease themselves back into their human shapes so that they could communicate. After a brief exchange the Prince and Swiftfoot would revert to their equine form and press on.

As the Prince stepped away from the last of these, he signaled the Smith to his side. Lowering his voice Silvermane spoke, filled with worry. "It seems that we are not alone in this hunt, my friend. There has been a large force of Weres seen, traveling in their wolf shapes. They were spotted crossing the boundaries of our land and run in blood lust, uncaring if they are discovered."

He looked into the wide eyes of the Smith. "They are closing on the group of refugees. My father has instructed me to make all haste and catch the fleeing band of humans before the Weres reach them. We must find out what has occurred to bring the Pack across our borders in violation of our long standing peace."

Quickly the Prince and Silvermane, transformed once more and speedily the Healer and the Smith mounted. As impressed as he was before by the ground eating strides of the Prince, he now marveled at the speed of their passage. Sparks flew from their hooves as they struck the ground. Even Swiftfoot had broken into a flowing pattern of sweat in the mad dash.

CHAPTER TWENTY-TWO

The grasslands rolled on in an ever present and endless horizon. It was the third day of the refugees maddening journey through this land. Every nerve was keyed up. All the travelers were alert and still they pressed the strength of their mounts. The expected call had not yet come to show that the Horsepeople would impede their progress.

Several times on far off hillocks they had seen the scouts of the equine race but still they had not been brought to halt by their ancient enemies. It could be that they had been able to deceive the Horsepeople into believing that they were only a band of humans and as such of no threat.

Still the horses were tiring and it would do them no good to run the poor beasts into the ground. Farhunter was forced to call a halt to rest the horses and allow his people a chance to stretch their legs.

It was during this rest stop that the nature of their true doom became apparent to them. They had left scouts to watch their back trail, and one of these arrived at full gallop. With gasping breath he reported a vast stirring in the plain behind them. It had been difficult to tell, but allowing for an error in judging distances, the Pack would arrive in not more then a few hours.

Hastily, Farhunter called his people together. When they had assembled quietly around him, he told them that their worse fears had been realized. The Pack had crossed the borders of the equine race in a effort to track them down.

They knew as well as he, that if they were acting so carelessly then all thoughts of surrender had best be forgotten. It was plain that they had abandoned the Code completely and had let the blood lust rule their reason.

Farhunter had them remount their tired beasts. They ran them as hard as they could in the direction of the southern edge of the Horsepeople's

Realm. There he hoped that they could find some protection in the steep mountains that marked the end of the grasslands.

The dark smudge of the distance mountains began to show on the far horizon before the next alarm came in from their outlying scouts. This time the flanking guard reported the approach of a small band of Horsepeople.

Farhunter pursed his lips in thought for a moment and then ordered the band to continue on in their flight. In the meantime, he had Rosita dismount and join one of the already overcrowded wagons.

When she offered protest, saying that she wanted to stay by his side, Farhunter looked at her long and replied. "Rosita, this may be the last time that I will be able to speak to you so please listen. Your family was always a close knit clan and it hurt us to lose your mother to outsiders. But never did we forget that she and then her daughter were family."

"We have always done what we could for you and now it's time that you returned the trust that we gave you. You, Rosita must lead the people into a new land where they can bring their children up in accordance with the Code and never allow them to yield to the beast."

"If your grandfather were here he would be proud to have known you as his granddaughter. Don't let his sacrifice go for naught. Lead your people to a better life and remember that we always loved you."

Without another word, Farhunter turned and left his tearful niece behind to ponder his words. As he went back down the ranks of refugees he gathered to him a small force and then galloped off to meet the oncoming Horsepeople.

Rosita watched as he left. Her heart burst with pride for the brother of her mother. Pulling herself together she looked to the distant mountains and willed the column of horses all of the strength that she could lend.

The Trumpet of Harmony

Farhunter kept the pace of his beast to a slow trot. It would do no good at all to approach those of the equine race with horses, half dead from fatigue. Although there was no real relationship between those of human extract and those of pure horse ancestry, he knew that natural equines formed a strong bond with their human counterparts.

It won't be long, he thought before the Pack would overtake the defenseless band of refugees. His only hope lay in convincing the Horsepeople to aid in their defense. If he could only convince them that his people were just innocent victims of the Pack's hunting madness. Then there was a chance that he could succeed in his appeal for that aid.

The ground rose in front of him sloping up to a hill in the grassland. There standing tall and proud on the brow of the hill was a magnificent member of the equine race. Unaccountably mounted on the broad back of the horse was a man. His appearance fit that of his companion.

Farhunter reined in his own horse as he watched that huge man dismount. They stood for a moment eyeing each other over the distance until Farhunter broke the spell by raising his hands high over his head in the universal sign of surrender.

There were two men standing by their mounts now but as he watched, those horses blurred and shrank into the images of two large, handsome warriors. He had never seen any of the Horsepeople transform before and he now found it much more mystifying then his own race's appearance in the same moment. Well, each to his own magic, he thought as he urged his mount to move slowly uphill. He signaled the rest of his men to stay where they were but to be alert for trouble.

As he crested the hill top he noticed that these four stood alone with no weapons visible. Carefully he pulled his horse to a halt and slid off it's back, never taking his eyes from his stoic opponents.

"Greetings," he spoke in the universal language of the people. "I am Farhunter, leader of a large group of refugees, fleeing through this land. I

would seek parlance with any who call this land their own."
One of the tall Horsepeople moved forward, his long hair flowing over his shoulders in a wave of glittering silver. With him came the smallest of the four. His face was lined with care but his eyes held a weighty look, that bespoke of long wisdom.

The tall man spoke softly in the same universal tongue that Farhunter had used. "Hail Farhunter, I am Prince Silvermane, heir and son of the King of this Realm. I speak with his voice and deal his justice."

The silence between the men lengthened until Farhunter under the press of events, broke out. "My band and I ride with no malice to you or to any in your land. We seek only to pass through to the southern mountains and hence to the lands beyond."

Before the Prince could respond, the old Healer stepped forward and eyed Farhunter. "Why does the son of the Pack Leader ride the lands of his mortal enemy, seeking the aid of his avowed foes? Why does the Pack swarm after you, forgetting in their blood lust the ancient rules of order that have kept our peoples at peace for a thousand years?"

Farhunter thought furiously of a deception that would allow him to deny this oldster's seeing eye but he quickly decided that these who stood before him did not deserve deception. "Know you of the Ancient Code of the Weres?" He answered with a question of his own.

If he had hoped to deceive the group in front of him he would have failed and perjured his cause. As it was the Healer looked at Farhunter and answered that he was well acquainted with the Code.

"Well then you know that from early youth we are sworn to uphold the truths that are to be found in those pages. In recent years a division has crept amongst the Pack as to the strict interpretation of the Code. There were even those who chose to abandon the Code completely and live by the law of the beast instead."

The Trumpet of Harmony

He had their attention now, he could only hope that he had the time to convince them of his sincerity before those who hunted closed in on his helpless band.

"Four days ago, the matter came to a head. My father was out voted in the council chamber and the Code was to be broken openly for the first time." Farhunter's voice broke but he managed to continue. "We who hold the Code dearer then our own blood could not stand in conscious to witness this breech. We arranged to escape from the Den under the cover of the Warn Call, leaving my father to delay the Pack."

"This I swear to you Prince Silvermane. My Father spent his blood in Council Duel and is no longer amongst the living, yet his sacrifice gave us much needed time. We have come this close to our goal. Now I must beg from you the boon of passage at the very least and aid in defense if you can lend it."

Prince Silvermane could make quick decisions on matter of policy but he was forced to pause and access the implications of the situation. On one hand, he had sworn to keep those of the Were race out of his Kingdom. So, the matter of defense against the Pack was moot. Yet if he were to intercept those who hunted the trail he would in turn be aiding a band of Were refugees. Again, a position against the Law of his people. He turned and took quiet council with Swiftfoot and the Healer. The Smith for the moment stood forgotten watching with interest the Leader of the Weres.

Farhunter noticed his studied interest and in turn examined the tall Smith. A sense of puzzlement and then of incredulous understanding and recognition flashed through his eyes.

Moving close to the Smith's side, he whispered, "I am glad to see you whole, Sir Smith. I was led to believe that you had left this world of woes."

The Smith stared openly at the tall man beside him. "I beg your pardon, Farhunter. It is true that I have recently passed through the vail of the Reaper and come out once again into the land of the living, but there is no way that you could know this."

Farhunter smiled at the Smith's puzzlement. Here at least was a bright spot in the darkness surrounding his people. "Sir Smith, I know of these things because I was told of them. In fact the tale was laced with many tears and much deep remorse."

The open face of the Smith passed through a remarkable series of emotions as he thought about Farhunter's words. At the last, realization painted his face with an incredulous joy.

Quietly Farhunter confirmed the Smith's unspoken guess. "Yes, Rosita is with the group of refugees that I lead across this land. In fact, she now leads them in my absence."

The Smith was dazed by the twist of fate which brought his beloved Rosita so close to him. Yet he was confused by the image of the slim dark haired girl leading a desperate band of Weres out through the unknown, pursued by deadly danger.

"How is it that she comes to be with you and how can it be that she leads a group of Weres in flight?" Asked the incredulous Smith.

Farhunter paused before answering to look over at the Prince. Seeing him still talking animatedly with his two compatriots, Farhunter decided to risk a short tale. "Rosita was the cause of our break from the Pack. You see she was captured by a cruel member of our race, whose name is Gerlock. Suffice it to say that this man has long aspired to the leadership of the Pack."

"Until now he had little support among the members of the Council, but recently some of our border patrols have disappeared near the waste land of the Tunnel Master. Gerlock had been agitating for an attack against the lair of that foul being, but my father had been opposed to it. He feared waking the forces that lay within those darkened halls."

The Trumpet of Harmony

The voices of the three Horsepeople rose just then in angry debate. It seemed that Swiftfoot now stood alone in his stand against aiding the Pack. Farhunter continued his narrative, quickly now for the press of events were about to fall around them again.

"That is when your Rosita was captured almost on our doorstep. Gerlock accused her of being a spy for the Tunnel Master. Which of course was sheer nonsense, since Gerlock was aware that his prisoner was in fact the granddaughter of the Pack Leader."

At the Smith's startled glance, Farhunter nodded his head in affirmation. "Yes, my friend, Rosita is my sister's daughter." He hurried on to finish his tale, for the conference was breaking up and the Prince was walking over to them.

"We rescued my niece from the Den's dungeon. Then, with those that had kept strictly with the Code escaped from our Realm in an attempt to keep our race from falling into the abyss of animal terror."

The Prince now faced Farhunter, his Royal visage dark with worry. "I have been reminded that some of my decisions of late have not conformed with the laws of my people. Now this is a very serious offense. Especially from one who would one day bear the weight of the crown."

He looked into the closed face of Farhunter and then into the imploring eyes of the Smith. "However I am forced to make a judgement in this case, as befits the future ruler of this land. I believe that you, Farhunter, speak the truth. I am willing to aid your folk through to the southern borders of my Realm."

The Smith broke into a broad smile, but the Prince was shaking his head. "Do not be overly cheerful my friend. I have been constrained, all be it against my will to wait here until my guard can be assembled and a message sent to the Palace informing my father of my actions."

The Trumpet of Harmony

"It seems even a Ruler must bow to the will of his people. My friend and companion Sir Swiftfoot will not permit me to foolishly charge to the aid of your people unprotected. We must wait and in the ensuing hours the Pack which stalks your folk will surely catch up with your band. We can scarcely hope to reach them before they come under attack."

Farhunter drew himself up to his full height and in a formal tone addressed the Prince of his people's ancestral enemy. "To Prince Silvermane, I give the thanks of my people and myself. I recognize the wisdom of your course of action and applaud this abridgement of our past hates. I will never forget you and what you do here today. If we both live to see happier times I and my people will be proud to call you and your race friends."

The young face of the Prince blushed with pride and even the cautious Swiftfoot displayed a broad smile. Farhunter continued, "I would bid you come as soon as you can gather your force, but in the meantime my people need my leadership and strength in battle. Therefore, I would beg you to release me to rejoin them. Even now it may be to late to reach them before they come under siege."

Without hesitation the Prince agreed, but before Farhunter could step away the Smith spoke up. "Prince Silvermane, friend, I too must ask the boon of being allowed to join Farhunter in his effort to reach his people."

The Prince looked shocked and Swiftfoot was shaking his head. "The King has deemed that you be brought in front of him for judgement and you are not free to leave the care of the Prince. In fact, I had thought of sparing a guard or two and having you sent on ahead to the Palace while we took care of this matter."

Before the Smith could muster a denial, the Healer stepped between him and his two friends. "I must interfere with your judgement Sir Swiftfoot. With my respects Prince, I strongly urge you to allow this man to pursue this course. I can not tell you how I know this but I know that he is tied up inexorably with the fate of many and he must be allowed to follow his fate."

A strained silence ensued while the Prince thought over the Healer's words. There were many things about this affair that had moved without any conscious will on his part. He sensed that there was some kind of pattern developing. He was a wise enough man to know that he had no control in the way that pattern moved. Even though he and his people had become entangled in its web, still he knew in his heart that they were playing a very small part in the events that were to follow.

Slowly he bowed his head, covering his eyes with his hands. Then in a moment of decision lifted his eyes to face the Smith. "I find in myself, a poor choice to lead my people. Once again, I must bow to the fates. Sir Smith, friend, I find that I really have no choice but to allow you the freedom to follow your destiny. All that I ask, and I do so now as your friend and not as the Prince of a people. Please come to the Palace as soon as your duty will allow. Go with my blessing and my friendship."

Swiftfoot looked as if he would protest and then he drew in a huge lung full of air, letting it out slowly he relaxed. Until he too was smiling sadly. "My friend, I think that from the start the Gods have looked over your shoulder. I could no more stand in your way then I could change the fates once they were set in motion. Take care and go with my friendship. I hope that when battle is joined, that you and I can stand side by side and serve both of our races with honor."

He too walked away leaving the Healer to say a few final words to Farhunter and the Smith. "I hope that all of us will come out of this in one piece. If so I think that I will then have lived to witness the beginning of a new world. One where our two races will be friends and comrades. Go with my blessings and those of the Gods."

Farhunter looked at the Smith, a knowing smile on his face but a puzzled frown soon replaced it. "How can you hope to keep up with me, my friend as well as escape the detection of those who block our way?"

The Trumpet of Harmony

The Healer looked at the Smith and nodded his head in respect to Farhunter. "I have come to know this young man better in the short time that we've been together then perhaps I know any other living being. He has a will that is strong and a heart that is true. He also has an amazing talent for adapting to new situations that will in time prove startling even to himself. For now, however he can run by your side as full Were, completely in control of his nature."

Farhunter looked skeptical, but could afford the problem no more time. The Smith would have to do the best he could under the circumstances. Farhunter took the reins of his horse from the hobble where he had been tied. Then turned away without a further glance at the three Horsepeople, watching from the crest of the knoll. He walked back down to where his men waited for him.

The Smith was about to follow when he felt the hand of the Healer restrain him. "You can not carry that pack with you when you run in your wolf guise. If you trust me, then leave it with me and I will bring it when we come to join you in battle."

The Smith smiled sheepishly and answered, "I trust you Healer, as would any who had their life spared by your efforts." He then shrugged the pack from his shoulders where it had lain unnoticed and handed it to the Healer. Then he smiled sadly once more and turned away down the hill to follow Farhunter.

He found the Leader of the refugees surrounded by his small knot of men, giving them last instructions. "I want you to pair off in twos. Your groups are to infiltrate any of the Pack between you and our people. I do not want you to engage them. We must avoid detection and reach our people with news that the Horsepeople will lend us what aid they can."

He turned as the Smith came up to the group. Farhunter turned back to his men and introduced the Smith to them. They were all curious to see this man who had escaped from the Tunnel Master's grip and who, all be it untried, had become one of their race.

"You will come with me Smith, I don't want you to endanger any of my men because of your lack of skill. Besides my niece will have my head if I don't return you in one piece to her side."

With practiced motions, Farhunter's band stripped saddles and blankets from their horses, releasing them to find their own fates. Then just as efficiently they stripped off their own clothing and weapons. These they made up into bundles and covered them with sod in the hope that they could be retrieved after the day had been won.

When all had been set into readiness they paired off and transformed. When at last it was the Smith's turn he felt the eyes of the entire group upon him, but curiously he felt no panic. The Code of the Were's flowed smoothly into his mind and the transformation was over in a blink of the eye. He was once more all wolf.

At the mental signal from Farhunter the group ran off. They took somewhat different directions so that they could run through the opponents ranks from as many different angles as possible.
When at last Farhunter and he stood alone, he felt the keen mind of his mentor giving the order to run. For the first time, he was in the open air stretching his legs at the ground eating pace of his animal cousins.

The Smith's senses were all alert. In his mind he knew excitement, for he was going to his beloved Rosita and this time he would make sure that she understood exactly how he felt for her. He heard Farhunter's amused laughter echo through his mind.

CHAPTER TWENTY-THREE

The long day was drawing down to a cloudy, gloomy evening. Rosita had driven her people as hard as she dared but the line of mountains tantalizingly close, still stood many hours march away. They had tried to angle their path of flight close to the base of a very tall peak which stood out from the others. It stood alone as an island in a sea of green.

The Guards who watched the back trail reported occasional sightings of some careless scout of the Pack. As of yet they were safe, but as night closed down Rosita's fear and apprehension increased.

When the wagon, carrying those women who were near their birthing time, broke an axle she was forced to call a halt to their travels. They stood now under the very shoulders of the high peak. Its presence cast a cold shadow, a precursor of the night, across their band.

Rosita eyed the sides of the mountain carefully. In the deepening gloom, her enhanced sight was a blessing. For there high up on the ridge in front of them she could make out a thin half hidden path trailing up the steep flanks of the mountain. It wound in long lazy loops. It would be difficult but she dare not let her people face the night on the plain under the eves of that towering rock. In the open they would be surrounded and over run in short order.

The evening drew into to the darkening night and a thick cloud cover flowed in from the mountains beyond to block any help they may have gotten from the moonlight. In the darkness, they desperately readied themselves for the arduous trek up the side of the peak. They unpacked the wagons and divided the food and water amongst themselves.

Rosita had the emptied wagons brought together to form a rough barricade at the base of the trail. The horses were hobbled behind the wagons, in the hope that they would be spared to aid further in the band's flight.

The Trumpet of Harmony

Nervously the guard kept a lookout for the attack that they were sure
would come. Chewing on her lip, Rosita hesitated to order her people up
the steep path. As the night grew darker the howls of the hunting Pack
came to her ears. Now she ordered the oldsters, pregnant women and
children to begin the ascent.

Those women who had no family or who had men by whose side they
refused to leave, stayed behind to add their strength to that of the rear
guard. Rosita decided to keep half of her force in their human guise.
These she had man the barricade. The other half she had transform into
their Were shapes. These she kept in reserve at the very base of the trail, as
a secondary defense against any of the enemy who broke through their
lines.

The night deepened. Rosita ordered that torches be set up and lit. She
knew that the Pack could see her defenses clearly despite the gloom and
she needed to give some aid to the enhanced sight of her guards. The light
flared and reflected red on the metal of the drawn swords of her people.

Into the pools of sputtering fire light step the naked form of Gerlock.
Rosita knew him instantly from the description given her by Farhunter.
The rouge Leader of the Pack stood quietly looking over the barricade and
the defensive line of men and women ranged against him.

In a voice that carried without effort Gerlock spoke to those who were
once his people. "I have come to bring the criminals Rosita and Farhunter
to justice. There are many of you who do not deserve to die, defending
these traitors. I will pardon you, if you step forward now and surrender."

Gerlock paused, allowing his words to sink in, then he continued. "There
are none left in the Den or the Pack to protect you once the attack has
begun. The Pack runs with one mind and to one purpose. We will
revenge those who have fallen to these traitors. There will be no mercy!"

Rosita could feel her cheeks getting flushed with anger. From the shelter
of her hiding place she yelled out into the night, loudly, so that those

The Trumpet of Harmony

others who had come under Gerlock's sway could hear. "You talk of traitors and cowards, Gerlock! You need not look any further then yourself. You have brought the Pack to the brink of barbarism. Why have you undone all the good our people have strived for over the long centuries? Why do you make my people less then the beast of the woods? Less, for at least the beast is ignorant of man's law!"

Gerlock growled in his throat, his eyes lit by the fires of insanity. "Bah! Laws are for the weak. I have not disgraced my people. It is they who were tired of the words of the spineless. The Pack knows that it is strong. We will crush our enemies and we shall crush you."

With another snarl of animal rage Gerlock slipped out of the light of the torches. Rosita, watched him go, a sense of doom shadowing her soul. Turning slightly in her position she could see her people looking quietly to her. Drawing a deep breath, she smiled and told them to keep a sharp watch. "We are in the right. Somehow we will survive to keep the faith of the Code."

The darkness grew all encompassing as the clouds thickened and a trace of rain began to fall. Rosita has just ordered the torches shielded from the dampness when a wild howling broke out all around the perimeter of the barricade. She caught a sudden rush of movement from the corner of her eyes and then all hell broke loose.

In waves of grey furred fury, the Pack leapt out into the fire light and charged the barricade. There were a few bow men in the ranks and Rosita had dispersed these throughout her defenders. An answering rain of arrows fell amongst their foe. Some fell crying piteously with arrows through their hearts but the bowmen were to few and the Pack soon beset the wall itself.

Red swords flashed into the torch light leaping out to meet the fangs of their brothers. It was a horrible battle. They killed and were killed. Brothers, fathers, sons all dying at the hands of each other. Several of the Pack broke through the line of defenders and those who waited in wolf

Stephen Goodale   185

shape as a second line of defense leapt into the fray. teeth snapping and throats howling their rage.

Not one of the first wave of attackers reached the base of the trail. Many of their bodies lay lifeless behind the overturned wagons. Many, too, were there of Rosita's trusty folk. They lay mauled. Faces and throats ruined in the fierceness of the Pack's onslaught.

Rosita, herself stood fiercely in the torch light. Her face was covered in blood and her sword dripped a bright crimson. The attack broke back and at some unheard signal vanished beyond the light as quickly as it had come.

The defenders stood or lay panting with the exhaustion of their efforts. Those who had any strength walked among the dead and dying. They gave surcease where they had to and tried to console the seriously wounded where they could. Rosita had those in the second line of defense come and retrieve the wounded. Ordering them drawn up to the foot of the path.

Curiously the attackers had died to the last man and woman. Rosita shook her head in dismay at their fanaticism. These were not the people that Farhunter had described to her. These were driven animals in who the humanity had almost vanished.

The next attack was sudden with none of the wild howling of the first wave. These stole up to the edge of the torch light and massed there waiting again for an unheard signal. The onrush was silent and deadly, only the alertness of one of Rosita's guards gave them any warning at all.

The slaughter was on. In the bitter fighting, no mercy was asked and none given. The two sides flowed around, through and back out of the barricade. Rosita, with some part of her mind that wasn't given over to the defense of her self or her people, observed that it was like some sort of stately dance. A dance of death. She actually laughed, her voice rising in her humor as she slew with abandon.

The Trumpet of Harmony

Those who fought around her wondered at her careless laughter. Those of her people, in awe and those who chose to be her enemies in deadly fear.

The defenders grew weary and their numbers dwindled. The light of the torches began to falter as one by one their stanchions were knocked down by the attackers and their light extinguished. Rosita ordered her people to fall back away from the barricade and toward the base of the trail.

Those who pressed the attack, howled in blood lust and lost any of their orderliness as they charged after the retreating defenders. Rosita smiled and let them come. When they had extracted themselves from the cover of the defender's barricade and stood in the open space beyond, Rosita barked a sharp order. The echo of her shout resounded in the minds of her people and the secondary defenders slipped down behind the attackers as Rosita had planned.

At a loud command from Rosita the defenders who had feinted a retreat suddenly charge their over confident attackers. Those of the Pack who had kept any semblance of reason, stopped for a second in fear. Then the defenders were on them, a fierceness in their eyes enough to match any of the blood lust of their brothers.

In great confusion and fear the Pack retreated only to find their path blocked by a second front of the enemy. They fell into the defenders in a wild frenzy. Fear written in every line of their canine forms. They fought madly and because of that many of Rosita's brave people fell. They had taken a terrible toll of the Pack that had once been their brothers, but at the last their line was broken. The Pack retreated back through the barricade and into the shadows of the night.

Rosita was exhausted. With what little strength remained she ordered her people to abandon the barricade and to retreat to the narrow opening of the path. The dead and dying were left to their fates. She now had fewer then twenty men and women who were able to raise swords. Sadly, she knew that the next wave would break them. Those who toiled up the path were doomed as the lambs to the slaughter.

The Trumpet of Harmony

The night remained quiet, except for the moans of the wounded. Rosita posted guards and let the others fall into an exhausted sleep. They took turn and turn about and still the night remained quiet. She could not hope that the Pack had given in so soon, but she wondered why they did not press their advantage.

Sleep must have crept over her as she stood, because suddenly Rosita woke with a start. All was still and quiet about her. The stars had at last broken out of the cloud cover and with the waning moon, they gave her a little light by which to see.

There was a stealthy sound of padded paws and the roll of a stone knocked from it's place. Rosita was suddenly alert, she waved to the nearest guard who sluggishly joined her in the dark. Rosita whispered for the guard to listen. As they stood there the sound was repeated, but before they could raise the alarm a pair of golden eyes appeared from out of the darkness. Catching the dim glow of the moon and reflecting it back to the waiting pair. Then a quiet, assured voice filled her mind and she wept for she knew that help had come.

Farhunter padded down into the small knot of on watching defenders and behind him came another. This one she recognized from the nightmares of the Tunnel Master. With a cry of great joy, she rush to meet the huge wolf. In one swift motion she knelt in front of him and swept her arms around his neck, hugging him. All the while tears fell about her face.

Farhunter, transformed and stood watching the scene. A bitter yet contented smile playing on his lips. At last he spoke, his words slow and measured. "He has come for you, my sister's daughter. He has told me all of his tale and I believe him to be a honest, trustworthy fellow."

At last Rosita pulled her arms away from the furred throat of the Smith. The tears glisten on her face and the smile on her torn lips was warm and loving. The Smith allowed the ritual of transformation to sweep through him. A moment later he stood in front of his love. The smile in his own eyes told Rosita all that she needed to know.

The Trumpet of Harmony

She stepped up to the Smith and touched the forelock of his hair which dangled down over his forehead. "I feared that I had killed you my love. I have grieved in my heart ever since I broke free of the bonds laid on me by the Tunnel Master's spell. Now I know great joy in the midst of death and I am content."

The Smith stood solemn and still, just drinking in the sight of his beloved Rosita. Then carefully, as if he feared that she would deny him, he reached out and took her in his arms. Gently he kissed her swollen lips and then held her tightly to him, burying his face in her hair. Softly he whispered, "I love you. With all my heart and all my honor, I love you."

One of the Guards brought out some rugged clothing for Farhunter and the Smith. They donned them quickly. Then Farhunter questioned Rosita on the state of defense and the nature of the battle. Quietly he stood as Rosita related each attack. She added her observations of the enemy and her wonder at their single mindedness.

Farhunter replied, "I am afraid that I can add some hint as to what is going on. We wormed our way through their lines to get here but in doing so witnessed a sight straight from Hell. There on the plain, not more then three leagues distance, the Pack has set up a small camp. Alongside the camp we watched as a strange noiseless bird landed. The thing was huge but that's not what frightened me. The side of the thing opened and metal monsters rolled down a ramp to the ground."

"Gerlock was there and he seemed to be talking to the things. After a few minutes, they disappeared into the one skin tent that had been set up for the camp. Then one by one they brought the Pack through that tent flap. As they came out they stared straight ahead and did not seem to care where they were."

The look of dismay on Rosita's face told how shocked she was at this turn of events. They had barely managed to stave off two attacks by their own people and now they had to worry about defeating those metal monsters of the Tunnel Master. She knew very well just how tough those things were.

Another thought was nagging at the back of her mind. She recalled what Farhunter had said about the fateful show down in the Council Chamber. It had been Gerlock who had accused her of being a spy for the Tunnel Master. He had enraged the Council by reminding them of their recent loses along their border with the Tunnel Master's domain.

Rosita asked Farhunter about the patrols that had been lost. It was not much to her surprise that she learned it was Gerlock or one of his close group of cronies that had led each and every ill-fated mission. She watched the light of comprehension appear in the face of Farhunter as he came to the same conclusion.

"What fools we have been!" Growled Farhunter. "It was right there for us to see. How could we be so blind? Gerlock must have been in league with the Tunnel Master for a long time now. He has delivered our entire race into the hands of that evil incarnate."

Rosita leaned, wearily against the Smith. "He has not yet fulfilled that contract my dear uncle. We still have a few stout arms left to turn him back."

The Smith spoke into the silence that followed. "If we have to face those metal things in open battle, we had better make some plans. We can not go up against them with sword in hand, for they can kill or capture from a distance."

He paused to look around them at the darkened slopes. "It will soon be light. If they hold up their next attack, we can spend the time preparing some nasty surprises for them. I suggest that we set up some dead falls. If we can trap them in the cut of the passage through these rocks, we can attack them from the heights above. They will be at our mercy!"

Farhunter surveyed the slopes, a smile crossing his thin lips. "Yes, it could be done," he said at last. He then walked down the path toward the tumbled barricade and the carcasses of the fallen.

With a piercing whistle, he called the rest of his men out of hiding from the surrounding rocks. With an apologetic look to his niece he said, "I had to be sure that we were not walking into a trap here, so I held my men in reserve."

As his men joined him, he quickly discussed strategy with Rosita and the Smith. It seemed that there was a perfect place for their ambush not more then a hundred feet up the path. The way became narrow and the walls enclosing the path were steep but scaleable by determined men and women.

Farhunter sent most of Rosita's people up through the pass, to act as a secondary force in case their plans went awry. He also suggested that Rosita go with them. She could be sure that they rested in the brief respite that had been given them. Rosita made it plain that she would have nothing to do with parting from the Smith again.

She tilted her face so that she might look into the eyes of her beloved. "I have found my destiny and I will not be denied the comfort of his company again." Her warm smile sent a thrill through the Smith's frame and he held her tighter to his side.

Farhunter looked at the two of them as they stood lost in each others eyes. The sight gladdened his heart. Even in the face of death there was still hope for the future. He turned his attention to organizing his people into work groups. The men he had brought with him were still fairly fresh. To these he gave the task of setting up the dead falls at each end of the cut.

Fortunately, there were many lose rocks of usable size to be found on the upper slopes of the pass. These were stacked into large piles on either side of the pass. His men disguised the rocks to look like natural formations. At the base of each pile they rigged a key stone that when pulled away by hidden ropes would bring the entire mass down to seal off the path.

The few people who had survived the attacks under Rosita's command and who were still capable, he set about positioning rocks along the upper fringe of the path. The others he sent along higher up the path, beyond the range of the trap. These he commanded to rest as best they could and to be ready for a last defense if their trap failed.

The Trumpet of Harmony

CHAPTER TWENTY-FOUR

The day broke, fine and clear. The hours of intense preparation were behind them now as the last defenders of the Weres waited for their doom. Some lay where exhaustion had claimed them. Some had crawled off to sit huddled with their fellows, using each other for physical and moral support.

The Smith and Rosita had spent the time holding each other close. There were no more barriers to their love. As short as their remaining lives might be, they knew that their love was precious. At first, they spoke of the past days, together and apart. So, it was that they came at last to understand what had transpired in the rapid flow of events.

Rosita looked up into the Smith's eyes as she lay with her head cradled in his lap. "You know of all the wonders that have transpired to us, the one I find most exciting is your transformation into a Were. We had spoken many times of the world and the patterns of nature on our trek. Now that you've experienced the enhanced senses at your command, what do you think of it all?"

The Smith smiled fondly at the memory of her teachings. Looking back now over what seemed to be years he could understand fully, the meaning that she had tried to give to every bush, tree, stream and flower. He had been blind, deaf and mute but now he was alive. Even in his human form he was able to sense things that never would have caught his attention before his transformation.

"I have told you now of the quest. You, my beloved had smitten my poor defenseless heart and I would have given my soul to the Conjurer rather then go on living without you."

Rosita blushed. They had spoken openly about their feelings from their first meeting and she recalled the way she had dismissed the Smith as a bumbling, gangly youth.

The Trumpet of Harmony

The Smith continued to reminisce. "The Conjurer said that I must learn your magic. That I would have to come to join you in its practice and love it with all my soul."

"I have come to know wonders that are hidden from man, even as he walks wide eyed in the world about him. I would no sooner give this up then I would pluck out my eyes. I have fulfilled the first part of my answer."

"And what of the other part of your answer my Lord?" Rosita whispered coyly to him. "You must ask me, my Lord but know that once it's given your heart will never find room for another!"

The Smith's face was flushed but his voice was steady. "Rosita, I have come to the crux of my problem and my great shame. For although you willingly tell me your greatest treasure I cannot return the trust."

"You see, on my birthing, my mother was taken with fever. I was set aside and in the hours that followed, a old crone from the village, tended to my needs. When my mother died the next day, my father picked me up in his arms and held me to the sky. Yelling defiance to the Gods for taking his love, he swore never to give me a soul name. That if the Gods required a name, they would have to revel it themselves to me."

"Rosita from that day to this I've been truly nameless and although the Conjurer said that in a time of great peril I must reveal my true name to you, I can not. For I do not know my Name."

Tears rolled down Rosita's cheeks, she too had lost her mother on her birthing, but her father had given her the name that was chosen for her. It had always been her pride and a source of reassurance to her in times of doubt. Now she meant to give it to this man, someone who himself was nameless. Pain had bred the contempt of the Smith's father for tradition. It had bred a greater hurt within the man child that was his son.

The Trumpet of Harmony

It was time to show the Smith the depth of her love. It would be given with all the passion of her gypsy soul. Let it heal, in part the wound in her man's heart, she prayed silently. "We may not see the night sky again you and I. There may not be another dawning to shed its light upon the world. But no matter where you go you'll always have the light of that one bright star seen just at the edge of morning. My love, I am Dawn Star and my soul always rests within that soft glow."

As she said her name in the quiet of the morning, the Smith could feel the presence of her spirit enter his heart. Forever he would have the comfort of her love. He cried and long racking sobs shook his body. Never had he felt so alive and never had he felt so ashamed.

When at last he could control himself, he lowered his tear streaked face so that his lips could brush those of his beloved. "Darling, the universe is vast and in its depths lies the secret to my soul. You have given me the strength to find it. I will never rest until I force the Gods to give us the Name and make us complete."

He was holding her to him. His lips crushing hers in his passion, when the alarm was passed through the waiting ranks of the defenders. Those who had lain somnolent in their exhaustion were awakened with speed because their doom already trundled up toward the narrow corridor of the pass.

Reluctantly they parted. The Smith was to lead the assault from above. Rosita was to head the ragged remnant of her valiant guard as they stood to defend the upper pass in case of a rupture in the trap. They said no word to each other but then they had said all there was to say. They were bonded mates for life and beyond.

Farhunter took a few volunteers to defend the opening of the pass. These were to lead the enemy up the narrow opening of the pass, feinting resistance in their retreat. It was a suicide mission, for the metal enemy could strike at a distance. But they could think of no other way to lure them into the trap.

The Trumpet of Harmony

The bright morning light and the crisp winter air remained empty and silent. The minutes stretched into an eternity of waiting. Sweating hands rested on the hilt of swords. Nervous guards waited to yank the ropes setting the dead falls into motion. Still the Smith and Farhunter stood tall and proud in plain sight of those they lead. If there were any signs of fear, they had hidden it well and their followers took heart from their stout defiance.

The Smith for his part scarcely felt apprehension. His mind and soul still thrilled with the love Rosita had given him. He knew that the fates would no more cut him down this day then they would yield control of his destiny.

Farhunter stood on the rock strewn floor of the path. He felt no confidence in his future. He could only feel anger. Hot passionate anger. He would avenge his father and all those of his people that had died. He would not rest until his fangs drank the life's blood dry from the throat of the betrayer, Gerlock. If that was to be in the body he now posed or in the vengeful form of his spirit he did not care.

The peaceful morning air was shattered by the rumble of metal on stone. Down the path Farhunter's men could still see the distant line of the wagons. Behind these were the few horses that had survived the first two attacks. Rosita had ordered that they be released. Yet they had refused to go out into the plain and short of mounting them, Rosita's people had no choice but to let them remain. It was their doom.

The distant shapes of the crawling metal forms could just be seen in the haze. Of the Pack there was no sign. The barrier of over turned wagons had been ripped apart during the first two attacks. Now as the monsters drew closer a high-pitched whine could be heard. Then the entire barricade burst into flames. Loud explosions reached the ears of the defenders as the wood in those wagons vaporized in the enormous heat.

The horses behind the wood turned foaming mouths to scream and they too burst into flames. The stench of burning flesh wafted up the path and

Stephen Goodale   196

the Smith retched. Quickly he ordered his men to place themselves behind thick protective rock as they waited.

Farhunter too, had seen the uselessness of his position. He ordered his men to retreat to aid those who waited in the last defense. He moved down the pathway, to turn and stand alone against the horror of the oncoming foe.

It wasn't long before the defenders could hear the approach of the enemy. The machines whined as their gearing took the uplift of the slope. They came in ordered ranks. Ten brightly burnished nightmares with one larger unit bringing up the rear. That one differed, on it's back sat a metal cage. It was empty now but waited to take captive, the victims who survived the onslaught.

At the opening of the passage those machines in the front raised long metal arms into the air. Tube like devices protruded from those arms and these were pointed squarely at the rocky slopes above them. At some unseen command, they unleased the hell that had engulfed the barricade below.

The Smith hunkered down as far as his frame would allow. He prayed to whatever Gods still listened to men, that his rocky shield would be enough to protect him. He had been the closest to the edge, so when the hellish wash of those weapons broke over his hiding place he knew that if he lived, his men would too.

When it came, the heat was awful. Its intensity ripped the air from his lungs and he covered his mouth with his jacket sleeve. The rock around him began to crack and pop as pockets of moisture heated beyond steam and exploded. Time stretched thin. Just when he could no longer stand the heat and knew the terrible realization of impending death, it was gone.

The Smith squatted for painful seconds before raising himself up to look around his shield. Most of his people had survived. He could see them stirring from behind their life saving rocks. One or two were not so fortunate. They lay were the heat had taken them. Their bodies smoldering with their death. The Smith knew a grim surge of pride, all had died without making a sound. Their stubborn determination stayed with them through a horrible end. The Smith whispered a prayer for the care of their souls.

He turned to give the command to lose the trap. Those metal monsters had moved further up the cut. Then a tortured scream cut through the air. Peering out over the edge of the slope he was just in time to witness one of those metal hunters reeling in its prey.

Farhunter had stood his ground, in plain sight of his enemy as they started their attack on the pass. With a horrible realization he knew that nothing would survive long under the path of those beams. Screaming his defiance, he had leapt down the cut toward the soulless, metal monsters. His voice distracted the flowing energy of those weapons and all ten lead machines advanced on him. They made no attempt to cut him down but approached him, in an almost leisurely fashion.

Farhunter slowed his own advance and then began a cautious retreat up the pass, waiting for the bite of death at any moment. Still the ten monsters advance steadily to him. Farhunter's lips curled in a smile. His prey now lay within the jaws of the trap, if only some of his people remained alive to set it in motion.

He stole a glance at the slopes and this proved his undoing. Circuits closed with a speed that far surpassed that of a human mind. Powerful taser darts leapt from the ranks of the advancing enemy and they found their target. Farhunter screamed once in agony and then lay still as death.

The claws of one metal monster closed none to gently over the outstretched leg of Farhunter. With no care to the damage it caused, dragged the unconscious man behind it. The unit retreated back down the valley to where the machine with the metal cage waited. Pausing briefly, it then raised its victim, to be dropped without ceremony into the waiting maw of the prison.

The Trumpet of Harmony

The remaining units had pulled to a halt about one third of the way up the pass. The Smith, infuriated over the treatment of his friend, nevertheless held his command until the ten units were once again moving up the valley. When they had reached the midpoint, the Smith gave the command to seal the pass.

Within seconds the air was filled with the roar of falling rocks. In that narrow passage, the sound was picked up by the sides of the slope and amplified. The ensuing vibrations kicked off a series of avalanches higher up the mountain. The Smith looked up and saw their danger. He signaled the retreat by hand and then dived back under the cover of his rocky ledge.

The Smith never saw what happened in the valley below. It would have been his death had he moved from his chosen cover. As it was, he would learn later he lost a full half of the remaining defenders on the slope, to the avalanche. Below him the ten machine units caught in the pass were thrown about like toys. Their shielding both metal and electronic held briefly and then flared into violent subatomic death.

The unit with the holding cage had remained outside of the pass and caught only minor damage for which its shields could not compensate. Its captive remained unconscious throughout the nightmare of rock and dust. Briefly the unit paused, all telemetry trained to catch any signal from a survivor of its command. Then receiving not even a beep from an emergency beacon it rotated its tracks and retreated down the slope of the path.

Rosita squatted behind a handy rock outcrop as she waited with the rear guard for the dust and the noise to settle. She had grown distraught by the news from Farhunter's retreating squad. Farhunter had decided to face the menace alone. Using his life as bait for those who hunted.

Then came the awful wash of heat pouring through the gap of the pass. Farhunter's men had told her of the death rays which wiped out the barrier along with the horses. She knew that her people and her love faced that weapon now. Suddenly the heat was cut off, soon after her mind vibrated with the terror and the pain that had taken Farhunter.

She was about to set her force, small as it was into the battle, when the warning rumble of the dead falls filled her ears. They dove for cover as the noise of falling rock set in motion the whole side of the pass. The noise was unbearable and seemed to last forever.

When the rock fall ceased and the air cleared enough to allow Rosita to examine the pass she knew that they would not be able to go back that way. She could only hope that the Smith had survived the death which filled the cut in its many forms.

Her hope brightened as one by one the survivors of that horror pulled themselves down the slope to the waiting aid of her guard. There were broken bones, torn gashes and some horrible burns. Out of the six people who survived the pass she guessed that they would lose two to their wounds and there would be several missing limbs after they were treated.

She questioned each as they arrived. Most knew nothing after the retreat signal had been passed down the line, just after the release of the dead falls. The last man to make it through was one of those who would not live. But in a brief moment of lucidness he told Rosita that he saw the Smith dive for cover just as a huge ledge fell from its perch above him. He could not be certain but he thought that most of the rock had slid on down into the pass leaving the Smith's hiding place relatively unscathed.

Rosita caught her lip as she watched the man she held cradled in her arms, die. She let the shattered body slide from her hands and laid the mans broken arms gently across his breast. She knew that she must think of her people now. They were terribly few in number and she could not even guess what that rock fall had done to those who had gone ahead.

Rosita ordered the wounded readied for the trek up the path. Then she turned her back on the tomb of many she had called friend and perhaps to the man that she had given her soul to.

CHAPTER TWENTY-FIVE

The dust choked the Smith and blotted out the light of the sun. The ominous rumbling of falling rock seem to go on forever. Yet fewer boulders flew past the ledge where the Smith had taken shelter and after a few minutes the rumbles ceased. The slope stabilized and the air began to clear. He was still alive!

The Smith remained crouched under his sheltering rock for several more minutes, just to be sure. Then he scrambled out of the crevasse kicking loose stone and rock away from the opening and his freedom.

Rising to his feet, he looked over a vastly different landscape. The narrow cut of the pass was no more. Instead a slope of loose rock and shattered shale lay below him. Of the metal beasts, nothing could be seen. Most of the damage lay in the cut. Below he could still make out the outline of the path as it wound down to the burned-out barricade.

Of the machine that carried the cage in which Farhunter had been thrown as captive, nothing could be seen. The Smith could only hope that it had escaped the brutal punishment unleashed by the rock fall. He thought of Farhunter trapped and held captive by the Tunnel Master and knew in his heart that he would not rest until the Were Leader was free or dead.

He could do nothing about his resolve for the moment. There were still the survivors of the refugee Weres to think about. They may yet be threatened by another attack from the Pack or more of those metal monsters. He shuttered at the thought of those heat beams unleashed amongst the helpless women and children who had sought refuge up the shoulders of this lone mountain.

Somewhere ahead he knew that Rosita waited. That she had survived the avalanche he knew, because he sensed her life force burning strongly in his heart. He wished that he had been able to give her the same comfort, for she must be worried about him. There was no way that she would know of his survival. In fact, by the amount of damage around him, she might be certain of his death.

The Smith moved slowly across the slope, now treacherous to his footing. The loose scree slid from under his cautious steps and he fell many times in his effort to cross. It was slow work and the morning passed into afternoon before he came across a final barrier that blocked his path.

A huge slab had fallen from the heights and slid like a gigantic wall across the slope of ruble. The Smith, tired and aching with his effort, leaned against the smooth surface of the rock. His touch told him that it would be impossible to climb over the frustrating barrier and he mistrusted his strength to slide down to the foot of the block.

The way up the slope, along the slab's side seemed easier to him. If he could just reach the upper end and then slide down the other side, he was sure that he could reach the top of the pass and thus regain the path.

It was a nightmare struggle, each step more painful than the last. His lungs burned from the dust still floating in the air and his vision blurred causing his eyes to water.

Through the film of tears the slab appeared to go on forever. If the avalanche had tripped this huge monolith, then surely it would have split the mountain in its fall. It seemed more likely that the slab had been there under many layers of dirt and rock. The force of the avalanche just sloughed away the layers, like peeling an onion, leaving this spine of rock to cut him off from his goal.

He had reached an area where the rocks grew fewer and the way grew easier. It was then that he noticed a series of indents in the steep slope, under his feet. These quickly grew uniform in their spacing and height. He was climbing a stair!

The steps were even and polished, running along the sides of the wall he had sought to overcome. He was to exhausted to go back and to stubborn to quit and rest. He continued up the hidden stairway, soon noticing the side opposite the wall growing steeper as he went. Soon he was in a narrow cut with walls on both sides. Then the walls closed over his head in an arch.

He now traveled underground, still going gently up the slope. The darkness was relieved by a dull glow from mosses he found hanging from the walls of the tunnel, like tapestries. Seeing where he was going had eased his nerves, the last time he had been underground he had been pursued by the Tunnel Master's toys.

Now the steps disappeared leaving him in a flat hallway. With what was left of his strength he stumbled on, doubting now even his sense of direction. The passage did not last long and the bright light of full day could be seen ahead, where it terminated in an arch.

The smell of growing plants and of water, wafted through that opening on a gentle breeze. His spirits lifted and he almost ran the last few feet to that promise of freedom.

Blinking back tears, the Smith looked out from the archway. His eyes widened as he realized from what perch he peered, for he stood now on top of the world. Below him spread in glorious panorama were the plains of the Horsepeople. The shoulders of the lesser mountains that lay nearby and the darkened smudge of the Were's forest away in the distance.

Drawing his eyes onto the slopes just below his feet he could see that the steps started again in an even march down the side of the mountain. Pausing only to enter small level area some hundred feet below him.

There, sheltered from the harsh environment surrounding it, was a smooth sward of grass encircling a bright, flowing fountain of clear water. The fountain was held captive by an intricate pattern of stone work, its out flow hidden by the distance. In the center of the fountain a clear pool lay reflecting the image of the surrounding mountain.

The Trumpet of Harmony

Bone tired, the Smith started down the slope toward that promising patch of green. The sound of cascading water reached his ears almost at once and the air held the taste of clean water. Licking his parched lips, he forced his legs to respond to his urgent commands and he soon covered the distance.

The entrance to the dell was guarded on either side of a narrow opening by two pillars, standing straight and tall. They were unblemished by time. Made of pure white marble, they were columns of flame as they caught the afternoon sun. Passing beneath their shadow the Smith felt his exhaustion leave him.

The sorrows of his mind and the deeds that he would do did not abandon him, but they carried less weight and were no longer a stain on his soul. He stood in the healing shadow of those pillars for a brief time. Before pressing on he whispered a prayer of thanks for his easement.

The grass beneath his feet was a green, so brilliant that he wondered at its pure color. It was as if it had come into the world just at that moment whole and fresh, untainted in any manner. The marble of the fountain was white like the pillars but was shot through with the green of the grass. The water was colorless of itself but picked up the surrounding mountains, grass and sky and reflected them back in a spray of rainbows.

At the base of the fountain lay three wide steps. The Smith mounted these, coming at last to peer into the quiet of the central pool. The mountains were once again reflected clear and poignant in the pool's surface but here they looked fresh drawn and sharp as they might have seemed in the dawn of the world.

The Smith began to feel as one in a dream. The scenes before him were those the mind would paint, if given the chance to project perfection. At the very center of the pool rested a small island of marble. A narrow bridge crossed over the water's surface allowing the Smith to cross. He moved freely now. There was no fear, no hint of danger. Instead he felt the rightness of what he did, as if he were preforming the steps in a dance that had its origins in the roots of time.

Crossing the narrow span easily, he found floating in a small bowl of the white, green marble a broad leafed, gold veined plant. Its leaves stayed on the surface of the bowl with no apparent support. It was not this wonder that caught the eyes of the Smith, for in the center of the plant, rising gently on a single stalk, was a flower. It was shaped like a simple trumpet and its flesh was the color of pure purple.

It was when he understood that he was witnessing the vision of his first quest, that the Smith realized that he had been holding his breath. Exhaling hugely, he drew back a fragrance, at once familiar and yet unknown. Its perfume filled him with peace, his doubts disappeared. He was one with himself.

Here he knew rested the Flower Trumpet of Harmony. Now he must somehow harvest the gentle perfection that was the flower without damaging it, or allowing it to spoil. He was at a loss. He had come so far, there must be a way to succeed!

Looking desperately around him, he noticed a small pedestal lying next to the bowl holding the flower. On the pedestal was a small box made of the pure white marble with green veining. The Smith knew only that his prayers were being answered, for he quickly stepped to the box and with exaggerated care lifted it down. There was a hinged lid which he lifted to reveal a space big enough to hold the flower.

As if trained in the dance, he returned to the bowl and carefully touched the flower, cradling it gently by its throat. At his touch, a brief pulse of light flowed over his hands and through the plant. When it passed he held the flower and all trace of the plant which had born it were gone.

Speedily he placed the flower into the waiting box and closed the lid. As he did so the feeling of welcome that he had experienced as he entered the glen, vanished. It was replaced now by the need to leave. The force of that desire had him running back over the narrow bridge and through the

Stephen Goodale   205

gate of the pillars before he even realized what he was doing.

As he crossed through the shadows of those guardians, he came under a compulsion. He could not move back up the slope to the tunnel, but was allowed only to move down the stairs into the waiting mists of the lower valleys and the oncoming gloom of the evening. When he tried to turn and face the vail again, he found his will totally gone. He was being lead and there was nothing that he could do to stop his flight.

The stairs wound down the long flank of the mountain's side. His downward march was steady and neither impending nightfall nor his own exhaustion, would stop its relentless progress. In the evening's gloom he caught the brief glimmer of small campfires below and to the right of his present path.

The stairs took a turn to the right and ducked down into a short tunnel. The other end of the tunnel opened up on the old path. The road that the refugees had traveled lay at his feet. After several steps, down toward the campfires the compulsion under which he had been driven vanished. Turning quickly, he tried to trace his steps with his eyes. But where the opening of the tunnel through which he had just come should have been, lay nothing. There was only a solid wall of unyielding stone.

The Smith clutched his cold marble box tighter in his hands. There lay the proof that his reason had not fled from him. He had just started back down the path when he was hailed from the shadows by a sentry. Mentally he admired Rosita for keeping her people on alert, even this far up the mountain side. He answered the hail and was pleased to hear a muffled oath sworn to the Gods of the Were's.

The guard separated himself from a hidden niche from which he had watched the trail. Coming close to where the Smith stood, the guard unshielded a small lantern and shone the light in the face of the Smith. After a few seconds, the light vanished leaving the Smith blinking from the glare. "Come with me sir Smith," whispered the guard. "The lady has been praying for your safe deliverance."

The Trumpet of Harmony

Again the Smith could only wonder at the tone of respect, that he heard in the voice of the sentry. Rosita seemed have been accepted by the refugee's as Leader. One in whom confidence could be placed.

The light from the campfires let the Smith know that they were getting close to the makeshift camp. Twice they were challenged on the way in. Both times there was a sense of relief to be heard in the voices of the guard. Relief that the Smith had at last been found.

The camp was quiet. There were tarps set up as rude tents, to shelter the old and the young. Fires burned brightly, throwing those faces that he could see in sharp relief. They were pinched faces, etched with bitterness and sorrow. These were a people that had been pushed to the edge and now stood there fiercely determined to survive.

At the center of the camp, set apart a little from its neighbors stood a large tent. It was to this tent that the sentry took the Smith. His guard paused outside of the tent flap and scratched softly at its folds with the edge of his hand. There was a soft command to enter and the sentry stood aside, pulling the flap open to allow the Smith egress.

As the tent flap slid softly back into place behind him, the Smith's eyes adjusted to the dim interior. There laying in a small pile of soft rugs and skins, was Rosita. She raised herself up on her elbows and the skin that was serving as a blanket slid down off of her pale shoulders.

The Smith stood silently, not daring to disturb the fire that raced between them. Then slowly he advanced to the foot of Rosita's sleeping rug. Carefully he knelt, never losing contact with her eyes as she looked quietly up at him in the darkness.

The seconds drew into minutes when at last Rosita spoke. "My Lord, I feared that I had lost you forever. I have prayed to those who sit in judgement on our souls that you would live. That you would return to me."

As she spoke, her voice filled with unrestrained emotion, she came to the Smith and knelt facing him. The Smith reached out and with his hand gently pushed back some stray strands of hair from her face. Then his fingers caressed Rosita's cheeks, pausing to raise her chin a little. Then with his eyes fastened to those of his beloved's he kissed her gently.

Rosita's arms circled around the neck of her Smith and with all the strength in her wiry frame, she clung to him. Determined for this moment in time not to let go of his powerful body. They held each other for a long time before they parted.

Holding each others hands they swore a bond that would last past the death of their bodies. Their souls would now, never be alone. In the quiet of the night they made love. Joining body and soul. The world lay forgotten outside of the thin walls of their shelter and the men who guarded their new Leader kept the press of her duties from ruining the magic of this night.

When at last, the Smith and his Dawn Star lay quietly, exhausted in each others arms, they spoke softly of what happened in the pass. Rosita could not hide the tears that welled from her as she spoke of the unbearable pain, reverberating through her mind when Farhunter was attacked. She had been unable to reestablish the mind link with her uncle since and feared the worse.

The Smith could at the least convince her that Farhunter yet lived. For he had seen his capture and his dream memories supplied him with the method used in that bondage. "Your Uncle yet lives but for what ungodly purpose, I do not know. My love, I swear that I will pursue his captors and free him!"

"No, my love, I will not allow you to part from my side again. I do not want to lose you now after all we have been through." Rosita pleaded with him but the torment in her eyes showed him that she was torn. At last she said, "I will go with you and together we will once more enter the darkened realm of the Tunnel Master.

The Trumpet of Harmony

The Smith knew better then to try and argue with her just now. Rosita's feelings swelled high and engulfed them again in her passion. When at last she collapsed from her trials of the past days and her release of pent emotions, the Smith held her until she was fast asleep. Gently he laid her down in the warmth of the sleeping robes and covered her with the soft furs.

He looked down at the face of his beloved, relaxed now in sleep and smiled to himself. With exaggerated care, he made himself comfortable and soon joined her in dreamless slumber.

CHAPTER TWENTY-SIX

The harsh shouts of alarm tore the Smith and Rosita from their sleeping robes. It wasn't long before there was an insistent scratching at the tent flap. The night had not yet fled but there were hints of dawn creeping over the rim of the world, as the two lovers threw open the tent's door and stood looking down the side of the mountain slope.

There, like the ghostly marsh lights one could see over bogs at night, floated hundreds of torches. The enemy had scaled the sloping walls of the lower mountain and now stood at the foot of the slope on which their camp rested.

A white faced guard captain ran up to them as they watched in horrid fascination as yet another group of lights appeared behind those that now faced them. "My lady," he bowed to Rosita. "They came out of no where. The flanking scouts had not been sent out far, for we have few men to lose, but these swear that they had seen nothing before those torches were lit."

Rosita drew her breath in and stared out over hopeless odds. She dare not show any hesitation now or those she led would lose heart and become useless in their own defense. Quickly, in sharp commands she set the invalid, very young and the women close to their time back against the wall of the mountain. Then she ordered the remainder of her people to form a semicircle around these.

This would be their last defense and she swore under her breath that her people would not die alone. She knew in her heart of hearts that each would die fighting rather then surrender to that non-death that had taken the others of her race. With a wild look at the Smith she moved to the front of her guard, ready to take the brunt of the first assault while leading her people.

The Smith for his part felt nothing but admiration for his Dawn Star. Surely, she had been born to lead these people. He knew that he would take his own place at her side to fight and die with her. He did not know fear at that moment, but he could not help feeling that there would be another ending for them.

These people had been deceived and then betrayed by that monster, Gerlock. Farhunter had been certain that the mad Leader of the Pack, had been dealing with the Tunnel Master for some time. This attack and decimation of the entire race of the Weres must somehow figure into his scheme.

The mindless way the Pack had attacked the refugees at the barrier had allowed Rosita's people to survive. But that same mindlessness would overwhelm them this time. Unless that spell could be broken there would be no hope.

Anger welled up in the Smith's soul but from somewhere deep in his mind the cool words of Prince Silvermane came. "It was then that the King heard the sound of a trumpet." Excitement raced through the Smith's frame.

The Smith ran back to Rosita's tent. Ducking inside he looked furiously until he found the marble box. It had lain where he had placed it absently the night before. He had not even mentioned it to Rosita. They had been busy with other things. The Smith smiled as he came out of the tent. The first light of day broke over the edge of the world.

The guards must have thought him a little touched but they said nothing as he took his place next to his Lady. In the sky, the Dawn Star winked brightly hanging there despite the oncoming glare of morning. With his free hand the Smith reached out and squeezed the hand of Rosita. In her other hand dangled the naked blade of a sword.

The attack came from below, as the slopes beneath them swarmed with bodies. There was no sound, as the remainder of the Pack attacked in their human forms. All their faces were empty. Their bodies naked in the morning sun, looked thin and gaunt. Behind them in the distance the smith could just make out the tall forms of the second wave coming up the slopes.

If his plan did not work then this would surely be his last day on earth. The Smith whispered a brief prayer to the Gods, in thanks for the night he had spent in his lover's arms. He could feel Rosita tense and he released her hand.

Quickly he opened the box and with great care removed the purple flower from its resting place. The first wave had just reached the crest of the hill and were scrambling to attack Rosita, when the Smith put the narrow end of the Trumpet to his lips.

He pursed his lips and blew, his great lungs straining with the effort. The sound that issued from the horn of that flower broke over the onrushing forces like a wave of purifying water. Everyone, everything stopped, the sound held all captive.

Never had the Smith heard such pure beauty. The voice of the flower reached out and caressed all within hearing. It cleared minds and brightened hearts. The sound reached down into the soul of each man, woman and child and made them whole.

The echoes burst down the slopes of the mountain washing over even those who had stood below as a second assault. Then the voice died. The flower withered in the Smith's hands as the vibrations of the echoes faded. A brief flow of light passed over him and the Trumpet was gone.

Time seemed to stand still as the front lines of the two opponents stood facing each other. The light of humanity began to flow back into the faces of the Pack. A curious scene of bewilderment, and dawning realization occurred. All the remaining members of the Pack burst into tears, their souls filled with the knowledge of what had transpired and the healing power that had brought them back from the depth of the abyss.

The Trumpet of Harmony

Rosita's force, small as it was dropped their weapons and walked amongst their brothers and sisters, holding and hugging each one. Many had been friends. Many had died. The Were race was one again, but at a very high price.

The Smith had stood back holding Rosita close. Together they watched as the remainder of her people became one. They were very few. Most of the attacking force was starving. Many had open wounds from their previous battles. Seeing these poor helpless souls, Rosita's eyes flamed with indignant rage.

She called her people to some semblance of order and began to direct their efforts at aiding their brothers and sisters. The most seriously wounded and deprived were taken into the tents for treatment, the rest were given what succor could be had.

The Smith had watched the reclamation of Rosita's people with a solemn awe, but his mind had not slipped into the apparent forgetfulness of the defenders. That second wave of attackers had paused at the trumpets sounding but had soon resumed their march up the steep slope.

The Smith watched impassively. He knew that if these newcomers were to attack now, then all would be destroyed. The guard had vanished into the organized effort of saving their fellow Weres and he alone stood to witness the oncoming doom.

Fascinated he watched them come, but he soon began to see subtle differences in this assault. These were organized and disciplined soldiers. Their hair flying in the breeze. Their armor of dark leather showed no patch or stain. Joy suffused the Smith's face as he realized who approached. The silver white hair of the foremost warrior, recognizable at last.

As Prince Silvermane crested the slope under the Smith's feet, the Smith reached down and lifted him into the air, with a warriors hug. "My friend you are a sight for these tired eyes. You have come as you had promised and none to soon. The people of the Weres are in sorry shape. I beg of you the boon of succor for them."

The Prince stood panting, trying to regain his breath after the Smith's enthusiastic greeting. His guards stood by with smiles on their faces, for it was an oddity to see their Prince treated so.

When at last the Prince could speak without gasping he managed to give the Smith a weak smile. "I had come expecting a battle. We thought that we were to late to save your wretched hide, friend Smith."

The Prince paused and looked the Smith over carefully. "I had the opportunity to hear first hand how well you've mastered your Horse Lore. Tell me Smith, if that was the trumpet of the King's Mount that sounded over the mountain side?"

The Smith's toothy grin was all that the Prince needed to confirm his guess. "Well now, sir Smith. Since you've managed to rescue yourself without my help I find myself in your debt. These people are a sorry looking lot, and so few." The Prince shook his head in sadness.

"Perhaps friend Prince, you had better come meet my Lady, Rosita. It may be that she could find a use for your errant help."

Blushing the Prince followed the Smith, to the tent where the sorest hurt were being treated. Rosita smiled at the Smith and then catching sight of the Prince paused in her string of instructions. Rising she curtsied formally to the Prince and the Prince in turn bowed gravely to her.

"My good Prince, you have caught me ill prepared to honor such distinguished Royalty. I am hard pressed to offer you hospitality but what there is, I give to you."

The Prince was about to respond curtly that he had come to help, when he caught the mischievous look in Rosita's eye and the exchange of smiles between her and the Smith. "My Lady your generosity becomes you.

Please allow me to offer my humble services and sincere apologies to you and your people."

"You are well acquainted with responsibility, Lady Rosita. You have served your people well. I too must bear the yoke of honoring my people's demands before indulging my own honor. Because of this I broke trust and arrived too late to save many of your people from death." The Prince looked solemnly around him and sighed.

Rosita could only nod her head in understanding and the three leaders stood quietly for a moment in the midst of suffering. Then the Prince pulled back his shoulders and smiled at his two companions. "Well, be that as it may, I am glad that in all these dark times, the Smith here, has managed to find his way to your side, my Lady. True love often has a way of winning out!"

Rosita blushed and the Smith laughed out loud. "I am afraid, my love, that the Prince has unmasked us."

Rosita smiled and replied, "Prince Silvermane, I want you to know that any friend of this scurvy knave is a friend of mine." She pursed her lips and continued. "Seriously though, we do need your aid. Most of my people are in a bad way. I am not sure that many of them could make it back down this path and over the blockage at the end.

"In the meantime, supplies are very short and the nights up here are very cold. If we get any bad weather, then I'm afraid that nature will succeed where that bastard, Gerlock failed."

The Prince eyed the care worn young woman and nodded his head solemnly. "I anticipated, such a need. My second in command, Sir Swiftfoot, should be joining us shortly with supplies and proper shelter for your people. While we wait I will send some of my men out to scout the path ahead and behind to try and find an easier way down."

The Trumpet of Harmony

Silermane turned looking at his friend and said, "You must know sir Smith, that I am not the King, only his beloved son. I can not guarantee what he will have to say about all of this. But I will give my word in the Pack's defense and plead for succor of its people."

Rosita, interrupted the Smith's reply. "We graciously accept your word, my Prince and are forever in your debt. Now if you two gentlemen will excuse me I must see to my people's needs."

As she walked away the Prince shook his head in wonder. "I don't know if your aware of this my friend, but you've gotten a real filly, in that lass!" "Now if you would be so kind, could you please tell me what has occurred since our parting? Swiftfoot, that stickler for detail, forced me to stay safe and secure waiting for my guard. In the meantime, you've been having all sorts of high adventures. I insist that you tell me everything."

The Smith looked at his friend and understood the eagerness that the Prince felt. To be restrained from doing what the heart dictates is never easy. To be a leader often means that the responsibilities far outweigh the freedoms.

"I have not yet told anyone the complete story of these past two days but this is your land and you have a right to know." So, the Smith filled the empty minutes, with the tale of the events surrounding the King's Hope Mount.

Time spun by quickly and the Prince did not interrupt the tale, although his eyes widened at the tale of Gerlock's duplicity with the Tunnel Master. Then they narrowed when the Smith spoke of Farhunter and how the Pack Leader was captured.

"Sir Smith, Farhunter is such a man that the people would honor highly in the Palace Halls. We can not allow him to become fodder for that monster. We must rescue him!"

The Trumpet of Harmony

The Smith did not doubt the gallantry of his friend but knew that the only Prince of the Realm would not be permitted to stick his long silver tresses into the monster's den. "Silvermane, let us speak plainly. I have already given my word to rescue the Pack Leader. In fact, I think that it's the only way I will be able to truly reclaim my Lady."

The Smith looked into the eyes of the Prince. "My friend I am bound by my very honor to continue the quest. Rosita would accompany me to the ends of the earth, but look around. These are her people, they depend on her now in their time of need. She would no sooner leave them then you could leave your people if they were in the same situation. Yet she would be torn, her spirit decrying her desires."

"Now if I were to go to the rescue of her uncle from the Dark Tunnels, then she would be free to allow me to continue with my journey. She would support this, although she would worry herself over me, but it's the only option open to us."

The Prince seemed to accept this logic and said nothing more about sallying forth to the Tunnel Master's domain. The Smith finished the story, including descriptions of the battles and the reasoning behind each of the tactics used. The only thing that he left unsaid concerned the night, just passed.

The Prince, being who he was, did not fail to notice the lapse, but he was certainly more of a gentleman than to ask. He did look puzzled over one thing. "My friend." He said to the Smith. "If you feel compelled to continue on your quest, that is your affair. But I fail to see the purpose. If the Flower of Harmony had stayed safely ensconced in its marble box, then yes. Yet it is gone. Its voice stilled for another thousand years, why go on? Your quest is over before you've truly begun."

The Smith was stricken. The thought of falling so far short of his word was a burden that his soul couldn't bear. He cast his thoughts back in an effort to remember the words of the Conjurer. He could hear the little man say, "Each must be whole not a petal out of place."

He shook his head. There was no way to recover the Flower of Harmony, yet his mind kept saying there must be one. The Smith's heart also argued for the quest. At long last, he just shook his head.

"I can think of no solution to this puzzle my friend. Still in my heart of hearts, I know that there is one. I must go on and since I've no way of knowing the location of the remaining Flowers, I will attempt the rescue of Farhunter and pray that the Gods show me the way."

The Prince looked at his friend for long a moment. In his heart, he knew the man's cause was hopeless, yet he would not let him venture on alone. He felt the duty to his people as an unyielding force, hanging over him every second of every day. Still how could he make a fitting leader, if at each turn of his life he shied away from friendship and danger, in the name of responsibility?

The King still lived, and was a robust man. If he, the Crowned Prince did not return, the King would grieve and the people mourn but then a new Prince could be conceived. All would be well. The Prince accepted the logic of his heart. Turning to face the worry worn Smith he said, "You will not go alone my friend. I am to be your shield and you are to be mine. Let us hasten, before my meddlesome companion returns to argue against this."

The Smith looked up from his self absorption, a protest on his lips. He saw the set line of the Prince's jaw and the determined look in the man's eyes. A smile welled up from his heart and he knew that he would not now be alone in his hopeless quest.

CHAPTER TWENTY-SEVEN

The scene with Rosita was painted in still life and was not the one that the Smith would have chosen. The Smith and the Prince had gone seeking Rosita, to inform her of their decision. When at last they found her collapsed over the skins of her bed, the Smith could barely keep from pulling her into his arms to lend her his strength.

She had awakened at their entrance and managed to pull herself up enough to smile a weak greeting at them. "So my gallant warriors, you've come at last to join me in the victory dance. Well you would forgive me, I'm sure if I did not rise to join you!"

Quietly she whispered, "I have lost almost two-thirds of my people. We have no home now and no way to defend ourselves. If ever there were a curse to lay upon the feet of a misbegotten, loathsome slime crawler, then I now send it to Gerlock. May he awake with these deaths screaming through his mind and may he never again rest!"

She turned her face into the light and the Smith could see that she was crying. "My love." She said to the Smith. "Some of those who could remember the scenes of their final camp when Gerlock sent them on to their final doom, report that my uncle is prisoner to that madman. They say that those metal monsters had strapped Farhunter to one of their torture machines. They did not let him die but torment him continuously as the fiend watches."

"I can feel him. He screams in my mind. I cannot sleep I cannot close my eyes. All that I hear, all that I see is his face ripped with pain, his voice crying out for death." She turned to him the plea in her eyes plain to read.

"My love," the Smith softly said. "We have come to take our leave of you. The Prince and I shall be away this very afternoon. We will free our friend and brother, Farhunter and we shall reap vengeance for the destruction of your people. This we swear to you, my Lady."

The Prince handed a parchment scroll to Rosita as she looked dazedly up at the two warriors. "Give this, my Lady, to Sir Swiftfoot upon his arrival. It will instruct him to aid your people fully. They are to be treated as brothers and sisters of the Horsepeople. It will also inform him of my decision to Quest with your Lord."

"My Lady we will not fail you!" The Prince glanced at the Smith and turned on his heal, leaving the tent to finish packing for the trek.

Rosita looked only at the Smith. "I would journey with you, but my people sorely need a leader. I must give them my strength. There will not be a second in which I will not think of you, my love."

The Smith went down to his knees and held his Lady tightly to his chest. His lips kissed her hair and his voice cracked with emotion. "My dearest Dawn Star. I love you more than life itself. You must not think of me, for you will need your strength to hold these poor wretches together."

"I fear for you. If you return with your people, to the Den. My heart of hearts tells me that the land will no longer be safe. I Love you, my Dawn Star and I will return. I promise!"

With a last gentle kiss, he parted from his love. The tent flap closing behind him. He was leaving more than a little of his soul inside.

Here ends the first book of the Mirantha Saga. Look for the next book in 2018.

Made in the USA
Middletown, DE
16 November 2022

15062549R00126